DRAGON RIDER

THE DRAGONWALKER BOOK 6

D.K. HOLMBERG

ASH
PUBLISHING

CHAPTER ONE

The skies over the northern mountains were clear, bright blue, and devoid of clouds. Fes stared up at the sky, watching for signs of the dragon, but so far there had been nothing. The massive creature should be here, but considering what it had been through the last time it lived, maybe it was a little more cautious now.

His horse whinnied and stopped to eat a few times, almost as if making her annoyance known. Fes patted the mare's neck, but he doubted that he calmed her at all. There wasn't much that he could do that would calm the horse, at least here.

The landscape was barren but not as bleak as some parts of the northern mountains were. The dragon plains were to the south, and there the earth was cracked and dry, a reminder of the damage that had taken place centuries ago. Steam still rose into the air and from their position here, Fes could practically feel that steam pushing on him, a hot wind that gusted, meeting the cool northerly breeze that blew down from the upper mountains.

Tall grasses grew all around them, and the horses trampled through the grasses. A few copses of trees dotted the landscape. Some of them had fragrant flowers, something that had surprised Fes the first time he'd seen them. He hadn't expected to find flowers on trees, especially not at this time of the year. It was almost peaceful. Strangely, he thought that he should recognize these flowers, though he knew he'd never seen them before.

"Can you detect where he is?" Jayell asked.

She rode next to him on a slightly smaller and sleeker horse. She was dressed in a deep green jacket and pants, and she looked nothing like the priest he had met when they had first encountered each other while traveling. Her deep blue eyes reflected the sky's light, and she stared at it, awaiting the dragon's return, much like him.

"The connection isn't quite like that," Fes said.

"You keep telling me that, but you don't explain what it *is* like," she said.

Fes closed his eyes, trying to imagine the connection to the dragon, but it didn't come to him very easily. He could sense the dragon, and as he tried, he knew that the creature was out there—somewhere. He also knew that the dragon wouldn't make his presence known unless he chose to. There was no reason to do that. Regardless of how large he was, he was able to hide, keeping himself concealed among the craggy rock and sparse tree cover, even as was found here.

"Sometimes I can feel him," he started. "It's there, like an itch at the back of my mind. There is a sort of connection, but I don't know how to explain it."

He wished that there was something more he could explain. He also wished there was an easier way to detect the dragon, but as there wasn't, he had to come searching for him like this. In the weeks since the dragon had emerged, and following the Toulen attack on Anuhr, he had been trying to maintain a consistent connection to the creature, but had found it increasingly difficult to do so. The dragon preferred to circle and fly but continued to make his way farther into the north, to the point where he had abandoned returning to the capital. If Fes was going to help rescue the other two dragons that he knew existed, he needed this dragon to help.

"If we can't find him..." Jayell said.

"If we can't find him, then all of this may be impossible," he said. And they would have to prepare to defend the empire in another way.

"We can't think like that," she said.

"Why not?"

"If we lose faith, we have nothing."

"There's the priestess side of you."

"Did you think that it was gone?"

Fes laughed and shook his head. "Not gone, but it's been a while since I've seen it."

"After we find him, do you still intend to make your way to Javoor?"

"Without the dragon, visiting Javoor wouldn't be sensible. We don't have enough strength to attack."

"There's an alternative," she said.

Fes nodded. There was an alternative, but it was one that he hadn't given that much thought to, knowing that it was risky. It involved somehow recruiting the Asharn, and he'd had some difficult experiences with them. They had been dangerous enough that he wasn't sure he would be able to count on them if it came down to it. They had attacked the palace in Anuhr, but then, they had also helped when it came to protecting the dragons. The more that Fes learned about the Asharn, the more he realized that he was tied to them, descended from the same stock, and though they might not believe it, he was more like them than he was like the Deshazl of the empire.

And the Asharn were the allies he thought they might need.

"I don't know how safe it is to go to them now. Until we have the dragon with us, I don't know that we can risk heading across the sea toward Javoor."

Even once they had the dragon, he wasn't sure what

they might encounter. It had now been long enough that the other two dragons would have been trained, Controlled long enough that they would be used against not only the Asharn, but the empire.

It was his failing that had allowed their capture. Had he only been stronger, had he only been faster, maybe he would have been able to protect the dragons. Perhaps he would have been able to defend them from the Damhur attack, but he had not been. The Damhur had used their Calling, drawing the dragons away and forcing them to serve, something that the dragons had feared and something that Fes had promised they would not need to fear.

In the distance, he felt the sense of the dragon. For the first time in a while, it seemed to be closer.

Was that only his imagination?

Fes kicked his horse into motion, holding lightly onto the reins. He would never be able to catch the dragon by ground, and the most he could hope for was keeping up, but it didn't seem as if the dragon intended to outrun him, at least not yet. The dragon could fly much faster than the horse could run, and when it came to the mountains, the dragon could navigate much better than the horse.

"What is it?" Jayell asked, keeping up with him.

Fes looked over. He wasn't quite sure what it was. It was only that he felt something. It was that strange itch that the dragon gave him, the sense that was there at the back of his mind. It could only be his imagination, though he didn't think so. This was real.

"He's here, somewhere. I can feel him."

"Where? There's nowhere for him to hide here." Her gaze swept around the landscape before settling on him.

She was right. With the steady rise toward the mountain ahead of them, there really wasn't any place for the dragon to hide, especially as he was simply too large to obscure himself. None of the clumps of trees were enough to completely hide within, either. Could there be some other way that he hid? Considering the way the dragon had hid beneath the city, maybe there was someplace similar here. The longer that the dragons were out of the city, the more likely Fes thought it was that the dragon remained nearby... but where?

"What is it?" Jayell asked.

"What if the dragon isn't out in the open, not like I keep thinking it might be?"

"You think he's underground?"

"It's possible for him to be underground. I found him there once."

If he could find the dragon, then others could as well. He didn't want to lose another dragon to the Damhur, and if there was anything that he could do to prevent it, he wanted to ensure that he did.

"That was more by chance than anything else," Fes said.

"Now I think you're selling your connection short."

Fes focused on the sense of the dragon. He was there but seemed to be somewhat distant. Why should that be? It seemed as if he should be able to reach the dragon, but if he was beneath the ground, all Fes would need to do was find an opening, and he should be able to reach him.

The connection to the dragon was weak enough that he wasn't sure whether he was even picking it up accurately. Maybe there was no real connection to the dragon. Maybe this was all his imagination. Or maybe this was merely a connection to Deshazl magic. Regardless, as he strained, he continued to feel as if there were something he hadn't quite mastered.

"I don't know where he is," Fes said.

"We can keep looking," Jayell said.

"We've been looking for the last week."

It had taken them a week to reach the northern mountains, and then they had spent the last week searching. During this time, Azithan and the emperor were waiting for Fes to return with the dragon, to return and provide defense against the Damhur. The moment the Damhur decided to bring the dragons back and attack was the moment everything changed in the empire. War unlike any seen in a thousand years would return. Dragons would attack—and destroy.

Turning back to Jayell, he met her gaze. "Maybe we need to change the focus of our search. It's possible that rather than looking for the dragons, we need to be looking for the dragon sculptures." That had been his backup plan, though he had hoped he would not need to use it.

"Azithan is searching for those. If anyone will find them..."

"If they all contain the essence of the dragon, we need to find them before the Damhur do."

"What if they don't all contain the essence of the dragon?" she asked.

He was more concerned about what would happen if they did. If each of those sculptures represented the essence of the dragon, and each of those was somehow restored, it would potentially turn the tide of any war in favor of whoever managed to control them. If it was the empire, then Fes believed that they would be able to succeed, but if somehow the Damhur managed to gain control over the dragons, and managed to acquire more of the dragon sculptures, then there might not be anything that they could do to stop them.

"Regardless of whether or not they do, we still need to find them. The dragon sculptures are valuable in their own right."

"I think you should focus on one task at a time," she said.

Fes sighed, but it was a frustrated sound more than anything. As much as he wanted to stay on task, it seemed as if his mind was in a dozen different places at once. There were times when he could think only of rescuing the dragons, but in order to do so, he needed to find this dragon, and if that failed, then he needed to somehow find the dragon sculptures that had gone missing, and if he managed to do that, then he could figure out if they contained the essence of the dragon, and figure out a way to restore them, and...

His mind spun. It was a constant struggle to come up with what he should be doing, and even if he did come up with the answer, it seemed as if something new popped up, some challenge that he hadn't expected. Maybe it would always be that way, but he hoped that wouldn't be the case.

"I'm trying to stay focused."

It was just that doing so was difficult, almost impossibly so.

He pulled the reins of the horse and looked around, listening for sounds of anything that might let him know that the dragon would be near. If he could just find this dragon, then everything would be easier. It would have to be.

The fact that they had been here for a week and still hadn't found anything left him troubled. There was only so long that he thought they could be gone. Eventually, he would have to return to Anuhr, and he would have to work with the Dragon Guards to determine what more could be done. The empire had to be defended. It was the only way to protect those who were descended from the Deshazl.

And it might already be too late.

"Do you think we should turn back?"

"I don't think we've given this enough time," Jayell said.

"We've been looking for evidence of the dragon for the last week. We haven't gotten any closer to him."

"You've continued to guide us through the mountains."

"That doesn't mean that I am any more certain of what we will find. Less, if anything."

"Fes—"

He could only shake his head. There wasn't anything that she could do or say that would convince him that sticking around made any sense. It was dangerous, and the longer they were gone, the less time he would have to prepare. The Damhur *were* going to attack. That might be the only thing that he knew.

"It's okay. Whatever it is between me and the dragon, it might take time to develop." At least with this dragon, he didn't doubt that there was some sort of connection between them, and the fact that he couldn't find the dragon only meant that they hadn't had enough time together to secure that bond. He was hopeful that with a little more time together, he might be better able to do so.

"When do you want to return?"

"We can give it the rest of the day, and if we don't find anything more..."

Jayell nodded, but she continued to look around, almost as if she expected to find something where Fes had failed. He couldn't tell, but he suspected she was using her connection to the dragon relics, thinking to use her fire mage magic to uncover the key to the dragons, but that didn't seem to be the best way to find them. Using relics that had come from the dragons to hunt them had a dangerous sort of irony to it.

They continued to wander, zigzagging up the ever-increasing slope of the mountain, and as they went, Fes felt nothing more. There was always that distant sense of the dragon, a remote knowledge of the presence of the creature, but it stayed far enough away that he didn't know if he were imagining it or not. If it were real, then he hadn't managed to get any closer to the dragon. If it worked, then what was it that he detected?

When they paused for the night, setting up camp, Jayell lit a fire using a small dragon claw. They didn't worry about masking the flame or their smoke. They were far enough to the north that they were beyond any onlookers seeing them, and anyone who would find them would likely be from the empire. A part of Fes hoped that they could draw the dragon out, but doing so would involve coaxing the creature away from the safety of wherever he hid.

Fes leaned back on his elbows, staring up at the sky. Stars twinkled as the night grew darker and the half-moon shone down, giving a silver glowing light.

"You're smiling," Jayell said.

Fes glanced over. "I am?"

She nodded. "Since we stopped. You've been smiling. What is it?"

"Maybe it's just that I realize that if we can't find the dragon, it means that others can't, either. If nothing else, doesn't that mean the dragon is safe?"

Jayell smiled. "I hope so."

"That's the thing of it, though I don't really know what to make of it. I feel as if the dragon is out there. It's almost as if I can feel him, but nothing about that sensation changes. If I do feel him, then it's a vague sense. Why does it not change?"

"Probably because you aren't able to control it that well yet. Maybe in time, you will be able to do so, but for now..."

Fes sighed. For now, he had no control. And he realized that maybe that was fine. He didn't necessarily need to have exquisite control over the dragon. Knowing only that the dragon was safe was enough. It had to be enough.

They shared the jerky they had brought with them and sat quietly. He was thankful for her presence, much as he'd been thankful for having her along in the days since they'd left the capital. There had been a time when he wouldn't have minded traveling alone, and he supposed that he still didn't, but it was nice having someone like Jayell with him. She was someone who cared about him, a feeling that he shared. In the time since leaving Anuhr, they had only grown closer.

As darkness began to fall, Fes felt a strange fluttering deep within him.

"Did you feel that?" he asked.

Jayell glanced over. "What was I supposed to feel?"

"I don't know. It's... It's almost as if there is something there."

"That's really not very specific," she said with a laugh.

"I feel a stirring. Almost a fluttering. It comes from deep within me, and..."

It came again, cutting Fes off.

He closed his eyes, trying to focus on the strange sensation deep within himself. It wasn't imagined. That much he was sure of, but what did it come from?

When it came again, this time there was a directionality to it.

His eyes snapped open, and he sat up, looking to the northwest. He squinted against the night, and as he did, he saw a faint shadow flying. When he pointed, Jayell followed the direction and frowned.

"Is that him?"

"It's too large to be a bat. And there is the fact that I could feel it."

"Since you can feel it, can you use that? Can you call to the dragon?"

Fes focused on the fluttering within him. It matched the movement of the dragon, and it seemed to come from all over. He strained, turning his Deshazl connection inward, thinking about what it felt like when he used that connection and tried to reach across the distance between himself and the dragon.

Nothing changed.

Fes latched onto the fluttering sensation deep within him. Maybe that was the key. If he could somehow connect to that fluttering, and if he could somehow figure out a way to reach the dragon, perhaps he would be able to call to it.

Was that a response?

Fes wondered if it was real or imagined.

He continued to focus on his Deshazl connection, using that to strain for the distant dragon. As he did, he hoped that he would be able to reach for something. Anything.

The shape grew increasingly distant.

It wasn't working.

Fes leaned back on his elbows, breathing out in frustration. "Why won't you answer me?" he whispered.

"What was that?" Jayell asked.

He rolled his head over to look at her, taking her hand. When he squeezed, she leaned in and kissed him. In the dancing firelight, shadows seemed to swirl around her face. She was lovely, and the darkness somehow seemed to accent that. "Nothing. It's nothing," he said, breathing out a sigh.

"You said *something*."

"Not to you. To him." He nodded at the dragon and knew that it didn't make a difference. Even when he felt the dragon, even when he had finally managed to connect to him, it still didn't matter. There was still nothing more.

It didn't mean that he would stop trying. He *couldn't* stop trying. It just meant that he was unlikely to be successful.

He rested his head back, letting his eyes drift closed. All he wanted now was to fall asleep. He had seen the dragon, but there hadn't been anything else. There had been no connection to him, not as he thought that there should have been.

Night continued to stretch on, and there came the occasional cool breeze that gusted against the warmth out of the south. Fes tossed and turned, lying close to Jayell as they tried to get some sleep, but what he managed to get was fitful. In his sleep, he had visions of dragons streaking through the sky, and in all of them, he failed to reach out to them.

Worse, not only did he fail to reach out to them, but

in failing to connect to them, he wasn't able to save them. He knew there was something more taking place, and he could feel that if he weren't successful, the dragons would suffer.

When he woke up screaming, Jayell was there. She patted his hand, trying to soothe him, but her soothing did nothing to take away the memories of the Calling, the way the dragons had been dragged from the empire, forced to serve the Damhur. And if they were able to force the dragons, how much longer would it be until they figured out some way of forcing him to serve?

"Fes," she said, whispering.

"It's fine. I'll be fine."

"Fes," she said, more urgency in her voice.

He shook his head, looking away. Tears welled up in his eyes. It was the memory of what had happened that seemed to be the hardest. Would he always struggle with that? Would he always fear that he had let down the dragons by not figuring out a way to save them?

And as much as he had wanted to save them, there just hadn't been anything that he was able to do. He wasn't strong enough to protect them.

Which was why he needed this dragon.

Once he was able to reach this dragon, then together they might be able to do more. They might be able to get to the Asharn and find real allies.

"Fes!"

This time, Jayell hollered his name, and it echoed out in the night.

"What is it?" he asked, rolling over toward her.

When he did, he realized why she had such urgency in her voice.

The dragon sat outlined against the night.

Fes dragged himself to his feet, keeping his gaze locked on the dragon, afraid that if he took his eyes off it, something would change and the dragon would somehow not be real. He approached slowly and carefully, holding his hands upward, almost as if trying to calm a wild horse. He knew the dragon deserved more respect than that, but he seemed just as skittish as any sort of wild horse might.

"You're here," Fes said.

"I saw your dream," the dragon said.

"You saw what dream?"

"Your dream of suffering."

Fes glanced over at Jayell. He didn't want her to know about that dream. It wasn't the first time that he'd had a dream like that, and given everything that he'd gone through, he doubted that it would be the last. More likely than not, he would continue to suffer from images like that, and until he managed to save the dragon, there might not be anything that he could do.

"I'm sorry that you had to see that," he said.

"You blame yourself," the dragon said.

"There's no one else to blame."

"You can blame those who attempt to control the dragons. You can blame those who attempt to control the Deshazl."

"I blame them," Fes said.

"You are a fighter."

Fes smiled to himself. "Sometimes. Only when I have to be."

"You would not fight?"

"It's not that I wouldn't fight, it's just that there are times when I'd prefer not to. Too often, I'm dragged into battles when I'd rather find a peaceful solution." Could he really be having a conversation like this with the dragon? It had been weeks since he had an opportunity to speak to the dragon, and in that time, he had thought about what he would say the next time he came across him, and never had it been a conversation like this. Most of the time, it had been him asking the dragon for help, and maybe he still could, but this was something different.

"Peace sometimes requires fighting."

"Is that what the dragons believed back in the time before they disappeared?"

"The dragons realized that there was a need to fight, even if there was never a desire to do so. The dragons never wanted to destroy men, but there were plenty of men who saw the dragons as a means to power."

Fes let out a heavy sigh. It was the same thing that he

had believed for the entirety of his life. For as long as he could remember, he had thought that the empire had used the dragons, having stolen from their power to defeat them, but that hadn't been it at all. The dragons had given of themselves willingly, allowing the empire to draw strength from them. It was the only way that they had of saving the Deshazl and protecting the remnants of the dragons from those who would take advantage of that power.

"Most men have forgotten what we owe the dragons. Most don't know how much the dragon sacrificed to provide safety."

"Even during my time, men preferred not to recognize the sacrifices made around them. That is not so different."

"Fes? What are the two of you talking about?" Jayell asked, scooting next to him.

He glanced over at her before turning his attention to the dragon. "Is there any way that you can allow her to understand us?" He didn't know how much of it was tied to the connection the Deshazl and the dragon shared, and how much was something that the dragon allowed him to access. If it was all about the Deshazl, then there might not be anything that the dragon could do to grant Jayell the ability to listen. If it were tied to some inherent magical quality of the dragon, then perhaps there would be something that could be done.

"It is done," the dragon said.

Fes glanced over at Jayell. "Why have you been so difficult to find?"

"I have been sleeping for a thousand years. In all that time, I have dreamt."

"I heard that!" Jayell said.

Fes touched her lightly on the elbow. "He granted you the ability to listen." Turning to the dragon, he asked, "You had dreams while you were in the dragon sculpture?"

"In that form, we have known darkness. All I had were the dreams."

"What sort of dreams did you have?"

"The same sort of dreams that you had just now. That's the reason that I came to you. I recognized those dreams as the same as what I have had."

"I've had other dreams."

"What other dreams have you had?" the dragon asked.

"Most of my dreams involved dragons flying. Most of them involve dragons that I've seen."

"They are projections. They are the essence of the dragon choosing for you to host them. It's possible that others would make a similar choice."

Could others be like that? He had seen other dragons in his visions, though the ones that came most commonly were all dragons that he had seen before. There had been the deep blue-scaled dragon, the maroon dragon, and then this one. Then again, he had also seen dragons of green and red and golden-colored scales, all of them with a subtle shade against the darker blackness of their scales. In all of those dreams, he had seen the dragons flying, soaring overhead, and in all of those dreams, they had been free, not subjected to the torture and torment of the Damhur.

Were those actually dreams? Or was it something else? Were they memories of a time before the dragons had to fear the Damhur?

"I need your help," Fes said.

The dragon shook his massive head. He leaned his face close to Fes, his deep glowing eyes catching Fes and holding him for a long moment. "Why do you need my help?"

"I want to save the two dragons that have been captured."

"There is no saving. They are lost."

"Even back in your time, there wasn't anything that could be done?"

"Once they have been captured and Controlled, there is nothing that can be done. They are lost. Their minds have been turned, and there is nothing that can be done to protect them or to save them."

"I have to be able to do something. I've been able to protect myself."

"Not entirely," the dragon said. Fes felt a rifling sense

through him and realized that the dragon was able to read his mind, to pick through his experiences, and seemed to be able to know exactly what he had experienced. If the dragon was that powerful, what did it mean for Fes' ability to withstand the creature's knowing everything that he thought?

Did he even care? It wasn't as if he wanted to hide anything from the dragon, and on the contrary, maybe letting the dragon know just what he was intending might convince the dragon to help him.

He turned to face the dragon and opened himself. He let the dragon reach in his mind and let him begin to sort through his experiences. It felt as if he were laying himself bare, and at first the dragon seemed to hesitate, but he tore through Fes's experiences, ripping through his mind, clearing out experience after experience before finally falling silent.

"It would not be enough," the dragon said.

"Even if it's not enough, there are others who might know more. We need to reach them, and if we can get their help, we can prevent the Damhur from harming the dragons ever again."

The dragon snorted. Steam puffed out from his nose. "It won't be enough."

The dragon started to stand. He perched for a moment on his hind legs, spreading his wings. Fes glanced over at Jayell before launching himself forward, racing toward the dragon. He threw himself at the creature, capturing one of the massive wings. "Please. Have some faith. I will do everything that I can to help, but I need your help, too."

"I have just re-awoken, and I don't intend to slumber again so soon."

"I don't intend for that to happen to you either. But help me. Together, I know that we can do more. I know that we can save those other dragons. With your help, we can rescue them, but I don't think I can do it alone." Fes released his grip on the dragon's wing, realizing that he could have made a grave mistake. The dragon might have shaken him free, and what would he have done then? He might have gone flying, and even his Deshazl magic might not have been enough to protect him.

"Please," he said again.

When the dragon answered, it echoed softly in the night.

CHAPTER TWO

The return to Anuhr took less time than the ride out. They moved swiftly, heading directly south, angling toward the city. Neither Fes nor Jayell paused to rest for very long, and somehow the horses both seemed to recognize their urgency and either agreed or decided that it wasn't worth fighting. No longer did Fes get the stomping of feet from the horse as he had in the first few days out of the city. Now she merely galloped at his urging, seemingly eager to please.

Every so often, when Fes would glance up at the sky, he would see a shadowed shape in the distance. It was high enough that he wasn't sure whether he really saw it or not, but when he did, he felt the same fluttering deep within himself that he had before, and he knew that it was real. The dragon followed.

As the city began to loom into view, Fes finally allowed himself a moment to relax. If this worked, they would have the necessary support to go after the Asharn. They would find allies, and he had dreams of them hunting, working toward a common goal of destroying the Damhur together. No longer would any of them be Called, not as they had been before.

"You don't have to keep looking up at him," Jayell said.

"I can't help it. I'm still not certain that he's following us," he said.

"I can see on your face that he is."

"He's still up there, but he's distant. Distant enough that he won't be easily seen, but close enough that I can feel him."

"You can feel him better than you did before?"

"This is different." Surprisingly, ever since the night when they had spoken to the dragon, the connection that they shared had been stronger. What he now shared with the dragon was powerful. It was deep within him, and he had only to focus on the strange stirring to know exactly where to find the dragon. It left him hopeful.

It also left him nervous and scared. What would he do if that feeling went away? What would happen if one of the Damhur managed to Call *this* dragon? Would he have enough of a connection to save him?

Fes hoped that he did and that he would, but if one of the Trivent came after the dragon, he didn't know whether he would be strong enough to withstand that Calling. He had witnessed it firsthand, and he recognized just how powerful something like that would be.

They continued riding, heading into the outskirts of the city. Not much had changed in the time since he had been here, though there were more dragon sculptures set out than had been here when only the emperor was referred to as the dragon. Some houses had paintings of dragons depicted upon them, often seemingly hastily made, as if the inhabitants believed that painting a picture of a dragon would protect them. And maybe that had been a superstition before. As they headed toward the palace and the emperor, he continued to see evidence of dragons throughout the city. Most were like what he had seen already, paintings, reminders of the dragon, as most within the city had seen the dragon as he had soared overhead.

The city was flush with activity. Crowds filled the streets, giving an almost festival feel to it. There was something of an odor to the air, and he didn't know what to make of it. It wasn't distinctively from the city, but it seemed to have a hint of char mixed with spice, almost as if something had been burned.

On one street, Fes paused, looking down it. If he were to go in this direction, he could reach his friend Tracen's shop. It had been a while since he'd visited him, and it seemed as if there was so much that he needed to share with Tracen, almost as if there was too much to believe. He hesitated, only partly because Tracen had unwittingly helped the attack on Anuhr.

"You keep looking back there," Jayell said.

"I just wonder if perhaps I should stop and visit with him."

"I'm sure Azithan and the emperor would understand if you needed to take a detour first."

"This is the same Azithan that I know?"

"Taking a moment to visit with a friend isn't going to delay the preparations. Besides, how long has it been since you've seen him?"

"It was before the city was attacked."

In the days since then, Fes had been focused on the dragon and his release and what it meant. He hadn't taken the time to go and visit Tracen, though he knew that he probably should have. Partly it was because he feared how connected to Toulen Tracen might be. Partly it was because he didn't want the empire to know how much a part of the attack he had been.

"Go. I will meet you back at the palace."

"Only if you're sure."

She squeezed his hand, and Fes veered off, heading along the side street until he got to a more familiar section of the city. From here, he knew the area quite well. He had spent many days visiting, and though he had never called it home, Tracen had always welcomed him as if it were his home. The shop was no different than it had ever been, though the sign hanging over the door was freshly made. Fes noted a dragon emblem alongside it.

He pushed on the door and glanced inside. Heat pushed back on him. Fes took a deep breath and stepped into the blacksmith shop and looked around. The shop was as completely organized as it had ever been. Tracen was nothing if not completely organized in everything that he did. One table held a selection of knives while another held swords and still another held other types of metal goods that people often came to Tracen for.

He found his friend bent over an anvil, hammering with sharp staccato blows. Fes shuffled closer and waited to interrupt until Tracen took a break.

"Fes?" Tracen asked, setting the hammer down. He glanced at the door, almost as if he expected others to have come with Fes. "Where have you been?" There was more than a hint of accusation in his voice.

How much of the attack did Tracen know about? "I've been busy."

"Busy." Tracen stood and wiped his hands on his leather apron. His gaze drifted to the door again, and Fes wondered who he might be waiting for. There were plenty of people within the city that Fes didn't really want to see, and now that he had a different role within the empire, he thought that he didn't have to see them. "You know what's been taking place?"

"Maybe more than you do," Fes said.

"There was a dragon. A dragon!"

Fes nodded. He debated whether or not to share with Tracen that he had been the one responsible for bringing the dragon back into the world, but decided against it. His friend might not even believe him. "I've seen it," Fes said.

"Most people have seen it. The damned thing is enormous. I've lived my entire life knowing about dragons and believing that they had once existed, but I would never have expected to *see* one. Does Azithan know what happened?"

"Azithan knows," Fes said. It did no good lying about that. Tracen deserved to know, just as he deserved to have as much of the truth shared with him as Fes thought was safe. The problem was, Fes didn't know exactly how much of the truth would be safe to share. Maybe it wasn't *entirely* safe.

Tracen watched him for a long moment. "You were there, weren't you?"

"I was there." Fes sighed. "You remember me telling you about my connection to the Deshazl?"

Tracen nodded.

"Apparently that connection allowed me the ability to help the dragons when it came to it."

Tracen's breath caught, and he looked at Fes with a strange expression. "You... You were responsible for releasing the dragon?"

"I'm not sure that I knew what I was doing at the time. All I knew was that there was a power hidden and it needed to be released."

"People keep waiting for the dragon to attack the city."

"It's not going to happen."

"You don't know that, Fes. We all know what happened during the last war. The dragons were only defeated because the emperor had fire mages. What happens if the fire mages aren't strong enough this time? What happens if the dragon is too powerful and decides to attack the city? How many people will lose their lives because you did something?"

Fes sighed again. "The dragon doesn't want to attack the city. Besides, the empire didn't destroy the dragons a thousand years ago. The empire and the dragons were on the same side."

"You know that's not true," Tracen said.

"That's the thing, Tracen. I know what I had believed, and I know what I've learned to be true. The more that I've learned about the dragons and the empire, the more that I have come to be impressed by both. The dragons made a choice, and they laid down their lives so that the empire could continue to grow. The dragons believed that the empire would one day be able to bring them back."

"Are you telling me that now is that time?"

"I'm not sure that the empire had much choice in it," Fes said.

"But you just said that the dragons—"

"And I also said that I don't think the empire would have made this same choice. I think there is a recognition of the fact that the dragons willingly sacrificed themselves, something that the empire has refused to acknowledge for many years, but if it were up to the emperor, he would prefer the dragons not return."

Tracen watched him for a long moment. "Why tell me this?"

"Because you asked."

Tracen glanced down at the metal work resting on the anvil. Fes couldn't tell what his friend had been working on, but it still glowed a soft orange. "That's it? That's the only reason?"

"I don't know that I would have survived nearly as long as I did without your help, Tracen. I didn't come here intending to share all of this with you, but when you asked…" Fes shrugged and looked around the blacksmith shop. The air held the hot scent of heated metal, and he noticed a shelf with a dozen different totems resting on it, most of them distinctively in the shape of creatures that Tracen preferred.

A question had troubled him, and he hated asking, but he had to know.

"Were you a part of it?" he asked.

"A part of what?"

"The attack. Were you a part of what took place here?"

Tracen turned and followed the direction of Fes's gaze. He stared at the shelf for a long while before turning his attention back to Fes. "I..."

"It's okay if you were. I understand."

"I didn't know what was happening. I'm still not sure that I understand. All I know is that I was hired to make totems, and the ones that I've made out of metal have sold the best."

"Toulen used those totems in the attack."

Tracen stared back at him, his eyes unreadable.

"Did you know?"

"As long as I got paid, it didn't really matter," Tracen said. "It's the same as when I make swords or knives."

Fes could only shake his head, though the comparison was accurate. The totems had been weapons, the same as any other weapon he'd made. "I just wanted to see how you were. I'm going to be gone for a while."

"Where are you going?" Tracen asked.

Fes let out a heavy breath. "With this attack, it changed things for the empire. I need to go and see if there's anything that I can do to help prevent another."

"Since when did you start caring about the empire?"

"It's not about caring about the empire, it's about caring about the people and creatures that live within it. And it's about recognizing that there is something out there worse than the empire. I've experienced it."

Tracen laughed darkly. "I remember. I was here when we experienced the same thing."

"Surprisingly, I think that the Asharn—that's who attacked your shop—might actually be the allies we need."

"You've got to be kidding. You're going to try to trust the people who attempted to kill you? The same people who very nearly killed me?"

"I'm not sure what options we have. The others that we're facing are incredibly powerful, and now that they have two dragons—"

"Wait. I thought there was one dragon."

"There were two, and then they were captured by these others."

Tracen began to shake his head. "Fes, I'm not even sure that I can keep up with your world anymore."

Fes made his way to the shelving with the totems. He remembered just how difficult it had been to deal with the metal totems, and how he had very nearly been destroyed by them. What would Tracen have said had he known that he was responsible for something like that?

It was best that he didn't know. Fes didn't need to bring him into all of this. It was bad enough that he had been brought into part of it, forced to fight for his life under an attack by the Asharn. And now Fes was telling him that he was going to go to the Asharn for help?

He should have known better than that.

"Like I said, I just wanted to let you know that I was still alive, but it might be a while before I make it back. And I wanted to thank you. All these years, you've been the person who's helped me when times were the hardest. You've been a real friend, Tracen, and I haven't had that many of them."

Fes had reached the door when Tracen raced up behind him. "Where is this fight?"

"In a dangerous place."

"Dangerous? By that, you mean somewhere within the empire?"

Fes shook his head. "We can't let the Damhur continue to attack us here. It's time to take the fight outside the empire."

"You're letting the emperor command you now?"

Fes turned to Tracen. "This isn't the emperor commanding me. I'm the one who suggested the strategy."

Tracen stared at Fes, and after a moment, he started shaking his head. "I can't believe you, Fes. I can't believe that *you* have begun to serve the empire."

"I've always served the empire."

"No. You were hired by the empire, but that's

different than serving it. When you worked for Azithan, it was different, and this... this is directly serving the empire and the emperor."

"It's for the right reasons," he said.

"I hope so," Tracen said.

"Stay out of trouble. And maybe don't make too many totems," he said.

"They pay well," Tracen said.

"I'm not so sure that they'll pay all that well after what happened recently."

"That's just it. After what happened, even more people want them. They think that having the totems around will allow them to overthrow the emperor."

Fes groaned. They didn't know just how difficult it had been to defeat those totems, and just how close the people of Toulen had come to overthrowing the empire simply by the nature of the sculptures.

"At least don't pour yourself into them quite so much."

"I'm not sure I know of any other way," Tracen said.

Fes sighed and shook his head before pulling open the door and stepping out into the street. As he started away from the shop, he hazarded a glance back. He found Tracen standing in the doorway, looking out, watching as Fes made his way through the streets and back toward the palace.

There was nothing to say. Maybe he should have gone to Tracen sooner, and certainly after the last attack it would've made sense to have done so, but with everything that he had gone through, he was nothing if not a little preoccupied.

Fes turned away and continued to make his way through the streets. This section of the city was more familiar. The buildings were taller, most of them two or three stories, and wealthier. The shops were owned by some of the more established families within Anuhr, and the gleaming stone of the buildings was often well-kept. Fes hurried along the streets, thinking of times that he had been sent into one building or another, tasked by Horus when he had first come to the city and then subsequently by Azithan later on to complete tasks, many of them demanding that he serve as a thief. Fes had some skill, but he had never been any sort of master thief. It was luck more than anything that had saved him from getting caught.

The palace loomed closer in the distance, and he hurried toward it, ready to make his way onto the next step in this plan. It involved arranging transport by ship, crossing the sea, and somehow finding a way to head into the Asharn stronghold. He wasn't even sure where to find it, only that somehow he would need to do so. Somehow, he would need the dragon to come with him.

When he reached the palace gates, the guards waved him past. Fes glanced up, feeling the slight fluttering within him that told him the dragon still circled, but he was high enough in the sky that he couldn't see him. Hopefully, he didn't attempt to cross the sea without Fes, but if he did, Fes would have to move quickly.

There was activity inside the palace. Fes glanced around, noticing that the Dragon Guard was keeping a steady patrol and servants scurried along the halls— almost all of them newly hired—with everyone in a state of activity. Fes headed toward the emperor's quarters, figuring that would be where he would find Azithan, or at least Jaken and the emperor. Once he did, then he could determine how they intended to approach the crossing. In the time that he'd been gone, he hoped that Jaken had given some thought to it.

The emperor's quarters were empty.

Fes weaved back through the palace until he reached Azithan's rooms. He pushed the door open. There was the familiar scent of spice in the air, and a hearth along one wall crackled softly, but there was no sign of the fire mage. The desk at the back of the room had books stacked along it, and three dragon relics laid on the desk, wealth that was merely set there as if unmindful of the fact that the relics were incredibly valuable.

He turned back and looked around. Where else would they have gone?

Up. That was where he would go.

Fes found his way to the central tower of the palace and climbed the stairs that brought him out of the palace and into the air outside. From here, the view of the empire stretched for leagues. The city spread out around him, and beyond the border of the city was the rolling landscape of the rest of the empire. It was a vantage that he had never seen until recently, and he marveled at it still.

He wasn't the only one out here.

Azithan leaned on the stone railing, looking out into the distance.

"Fezarn. You have been gone for quite some time."

"Didn't Jayell tell you that we were back? I had to make a stop on my way back into the city."

"Your friend?"

"Yes. My friend. I hadn't seen him since the attack."

"Did you ask if he had anything to do with the totems used against us?"

"You knew?"

"I knew that a source of metalsmithed totems were distributed throughout the city before the attack."

"I'm not sure that *distributed* would be the right way to phrase it," Fes said.

"No? How would you describe it? The totems were given to many people throughout the city. It was almost as if they were intentionally set. If that's not a distribution, then what would it be?"

"He might've been responsible for making the totems, but I'm pretty certain that he had no interest in distributing them. I don't think he even knew what they were able to do."

"And if he did? What do you think you would've done then?"

"There's no love between him and the empire, if that's what you are asking. Then again, I felt much the same way."

Azithan turned to him. He had a long face and deep-set eyes. Intensity radiated from him, and Fes could feel him pulling on fire magic. It was a throbbing sort of sense, and though he couldn't see any dragon relic on the mage, there was likely at least a dragon pearl in his pocket, though it could be something even more potent than that. "Were you successful?" Azithan asked.

Fes flicked his gaze up, and somewhere up there, he felt the faint fluttering within him, that stirring sensation that he knew indicated that the dragon was the air. "He returned."

"Good. I fear that we won't have much time."

"Why?" Fes asked.

"Can't you feel it?"

"Feel what?"

"The city has been under attack for the last week."

Fes looked outward, peering all around them, but didn't make out any sort of attack. Even within the city, there hadn't been a sense of an attack. Instead, there was normalcy so soon after Toulen had nearly overthrown the emperor. "I haven't seen anything. We came into the city safely, and there wasn't anything here that would indicate any sort of attack."

"It's not a physical attack. It's a magical attack. If you focus, you will feel it."

Fes closed his eyes, but he didn't pick up on anything. That troubled him somewhat. He was accustomed to being aware of when magic was used around him. It was something that he had begun to take for granted, perhaps too much. When he opened his eyes, he shook his head. "I don't feel anything."

"I suspect it's the Damhur, but it's subtle."

"What is it?"

"Fire magic, or a form of it. It's why I'm pushing out, forcing myself to hold a connection to protect the city."

"I can feel that."

Azithan studied him for a moment. "Perhaps it's the fact that I am using so much energy that you aren't aware of what they are doing. I wonder if I were to release my hold whether you would pick up on anything."

"But you won't."

Azithan shook his head. "I'm not sure that I can."

"What's the intent behind their attack?"

"I don't know. It's possible they don't realize that the Toulen attack was unsuccessful. It's possible that they are aware that it failed and this is some sort of secondary attack." He turned his attention back to the scenery around the outer edge of the tower. "I don't know how long I will be able to resist this attack," Azithan said softly.

"Why does it have to fall on you?"

"The other fire mages are talented, Fezarn, but there are limits to their powers. I have always been able to draw more strongly upon the dragon relics than most of the other fire mages." Fes smiled to himself. He'd been around other fire mages of nearly equal power. "If I weren't holding this, the spell would continue to push on us, and it wouldn't take long before this attack succeeded."

Fes joined him at the stone barrier, looking out over the city. "It's not from the north," Fes said. "I think that we would have detected it traveling from there if that were the case."

"No. I doubt that it would come from the north. And from what Jaken has shared, the western border with Toulen has been fortified. After the last attack, the emperor was not willing to allow another one to slip in. That leaves the south and the east."

"The coasts."

Azithan nodded.

"Jayell returned with me. She can help you."

"Fezarn, she is not ready for such responsibility."

"You're the one who told me that she is incredibly powerful."

"And she is. Yet there are limits to what she can be taught quickly. She must gain that strength naturally."

"Where are the emperor and Jaken?"

"They have traveled south."

"I thought you worried that the attack was coming from the south."

"And I am," Azithan said.

"Why aren't you with them?"

"Because if they fail, then I might be the only one who can prevent the Damhur from reaching us here. Other fire mages assist me, but…"

Azithan turned his attention back to looking out. His eyes were heavy and deep creases formed at the corners of them. Every so often, he would clench his jaw and power would pull from him.

Fes knew how much it fatigued him to pull upon his Deshazl connection, so what must it take from Azithan to continue to hold on to his fire mage connection? And with enough strength that Fes could feel it but enough control that he wasn't aware of it until he was up here?

An enormous amount of energy.

It was something that he wouldn't be able to maintain indefinitely.

Regardless of what he intended, Jayell might have to remain behind to help Azithan. The fire mage might not believe that Jayell was ready, but he suspected that she would be much more useful than he let on. She was an

incredibly powerful fire mage and had grown signifi-
cantly in the time they had been together. Azithan
himself had marveled at her strength and her control,
and that had to mean something.

"Why did they go south? What did they think to find
there?" Fes asked.

"There was evidence of an attack," Azithan said.
Fatigue was evident in his voice.

"An attack involving a dragon?"

"We don't know. A coastal city—Vorandt—was laid to
ruins. The attack was fast, and it's possible that they used
fire mages and not the dragons."

"But you don't know that you believe that."

"Destroying an entire city with fire mages takes
incredible control. Even the empire fire mages might not
be powerful enough for something like that. Not
quickly."

"I've told you that the Damhur fire mages are incredibly skilled."

"Perhaps that's all it is."

"But you don't think so."

Azithan shook his head. "Unfortunately, I think the
Damhur have already readied their attacks on the empire.
I think they have already involved the dragons in them.
And I think war, like we haven't known in a thousand
years, has returned to our shores."

CHAPTER THREE

The dragon flew overhead, and Fes tried to call to him, trying to summon him to land, but he didn't seem to respond. Fes needed to get the dragon to come down to him if only to try and coax him into helping much sooner than either of them had expected.

He remained on top of the tower, wind swirling around him, carrying the scent of the city. It was a mixture of odors, and Fes had been a part of the city long enough that he recognized most of them, but not all. Some seemed foreign and were smells that he couldn't quite place. After a while, he realized why that was—they were the scents of fire mage magic, the scents he had always associated with Azithan.

Azithan remained along the wall, gripping the stone as he stared out into the distance. He had returned to silence and had begun to ignore Fes as if whatever he was doing was much more important than Fes' presence.

And maybe it was.

The emperor had already departed. Jaken was gone. The protections within the empire, those who would defend it from attack, were now missing.

And the Damhur had already begun whatever their plan was.

If it involved the dragons attacking, there might not be anything they would be able to do. Even if the dragon soaring high in the sky offered to help—and Fes still didn't know whether the dragon would be a part of what they needed—having one dragon might not be enough. When it came to facing the Damhur, people who were far more capable than them, a single dragon might be over-powered far too easily.

"I need to see if there's anything I can do," Fes said, breaking the silence.

Azithan breathed out heavily, turning back toward him. "There might not be anything you can do, Fezarn. We—*I*—should have taken the threat more seriously before now."

"You didn't take it seriously enough?"

"Not as I should. When word came of the first attack, I should have known there was something about the Damhur that we needed to fear—and prepare for. You might be the only one in the empire who recognized the threat for what it was."

Fes doubted that was true, but it didn't matter any longer. What mattered was rescuing the dragons. That was how they would change the tide of the war. If they didn't—if *he* didn't—he had little doubt that the empire would attempt to destroy them, the same way they had been destroyed in the past.

"Take this," Azithan said, reaching into his pocket.

Taking the strangely heavy chunk of stone, Fes stared at it. "What is it?"

"The totems gave me the idea. If they could infuse some of themselves into it, then it's possible that I could do the same."

"What did you put into it?" Fes asked, eyeing it strangely.

"I tried to use a piece of dragon bone and turn it into a totem, or, as similar to a totem as I could. This was my attempt."

"Why?"

"If we need to face power like the Damhur, we will need more might than the fire mages. Others could take something like this, use it, and we could have another aspect of power."

"It connects to fire mage magic?"

"Hopefully. It stores the power of the dragons, but it needs to be triggered. I *think* that I have prepared it in such a way that it can be triggered. There is not the time to create many, so hold onto it carefully and use it only if the need is great."

"Thank you, Azithan."

The fire mage sighed. "I wish thanks weren't necessary. Do what you can to stop the attack, Fezarn. Save the dragons if you can. If you cannot..."

Fes knew what Azithan would have to do if he couldn't.

Turning away from the tower, he hurried down the stairs, searching for Jayell. Azithan might not think that she would be of much help, but Fes didn't believe that. He knew what Jayell was capable of, even if Azithan still questioned.

As he hurried through the halls, retracing the steps of the places where she might go, he practically collided with her. "Jayell."

"Fes? You're back already?"

"It was a short visit. And then I came in and spoke to Azithan."

"You found him? I haven't been able to find anyone. The palace is strangely empty."

He explained what he'd learned about how the emperor and Jaken had gone south, though he didn't fully understand the nature of the attack. Her eyes widened when he described what had happened.

"What do you think they're doing?"

"I don't know. Azithan believes there's an attack, and..."

"That's just it," Jayell said. "There *is* an attack taking place. I've been trying to figure out why I feel what I do. The more that I'm here, the more I feel it pressing upon me. It's building, almost as if coming up from within the earth."

"Azithan is on top of the tower, trying to oppose it."

"Just Azithan?"

"There are other fire mages in the city, but he believes that he's the only one strong enough to do this."

"That arrogant bastard."

"Jayell—"

She shook her head. "No, Fes. He has always believed that he's the only one capable of handling specific threats. If it's something like this that is requiring that much of his power, he needs to cooperate with other fire mages."

"I did suggest that he work with you."

"I'm not sure that I'm the next most qualified," she said.

"You're more qualified than most."

"That might be, but if what I detect is right, this attack is powerful and subtle and..."

"You could go and help Azithan."

"I'm not sure that the right strategy," she said.

"Why not?"

"There's something to the attack that is strange." She

closed her eyes and a fire spell built from her, pressing upon Fes. It was steady, and because of the strength she used, it was incredibly powerful. It washed away from her, and when it was done, she opened her eyes and met his. "I'm still not sure what it is. There's something here, but..."

"I can get the dragon to help me."

"What would you do?"

"I need to see what's taking place in the south. If there's an attack, we need to defend the empire."

"Just you and the dragon?"

"I would join the emperor and Jaken and see what help I could offer them."

"What if they are already gone?"

Could the few weeks they'd been gone have made such a difference? He thought they still had time, but maybe it *was* already too late.

Jayell fixed him with a look he couldn't argue with. "If you're heading south, then I'm going to go with you."

Rather than arguing, he motioned for her to follow. They reached the entrance to the palace, and Fes hurried out to the courtyard. The palace created a backdrop here, and there once had been a well-manicured lawn stretching out within the confines of the city, but that lawn had been nearly destroyed by the Toulen attack. The beauty within it had been devastated. He looked around and saw signs of that destruction everywhere.

Turning his attention to the sky, he focused on the fluttering within him. "I need your help," he said softly.

Jayell looked over and watched him, saying nothing for a moment.

Fes continued to stare up at the sky, looking for movement from the dragon. It had to be there, but what was it doing?

He pushed on his Deshazl connection, trying to reach for the dragon through that. When he did, he felt an increase in the stirring, a subtle change to that connection, and for a moment he thought that it would work, but then it faded, leaving him once more with nothing.

He let out a frustrated sigh. "It's not working."

"What do you expect? This is a dragon, and you think that just because you freed the creature, it would certainly be able to do what you want?"

"It's not so much doing what I wanted; it's more about working with me. I thought the dragons and the Deshazl were partners, but it doesn't seem like any sort of partnership, not with what I've seen."

"What if whatever cooperation had existed is different?" Jayell looked at him. "Think about it, Fes. The dragons have been gone for a long time, and in the time before they disappeared, they had a relationship with the Deshazl, but since they've been gone, everything has changed. You say the dragons were sleeping, but how much of that did they remember?"

Fes looked away. It was a good question. How much would the dragons have remembered? The dragon that he had awoken made it seem like there had been only dreams of flight and nothing more. If that were the case, then perhaps there wasn't anything for the dragons to have remembered. If all they remembered was flying, then maybe it had been too much.

"He agreed to help," Fes said.

"Then give him a chance," she said.

Would it come in time?

He stared up at the sky. As he did, he once more thought that he felt the stirring within him. This time, he focused on it. If he could use that faint stirring, and if he could somehow connect to it, maybe he would be able to reach the dragon as he intended.

It had to work.

Rather than trying to talk to the dragon, he pushed through an emotion, trying to send a sense of urgency through. It might not work, and Fes was all too aware that if it didn't, he might find himself heading south on horseback without the dragon, but that didn't mean he wouldn't be going without help. Jayell would be there. Since meeting her, she had always been there for him.

The fluttering came again. Fes held on to it, using that faint connection to the dragon, and continued to push.

It came to him more strongly.

He pushed again, sending his urgency, sending his

emotion, wanting nothing more than to find some way to connect to the dragon. Could it work?

The stirring swirled high overhead.

It was there. There was no question in his mind that he saw it.

He pushed again.

This time, a burst of his Deshazl magic surged from him and toward the distant dragon. It was filled with a sense of urgency and desire and every bit of Deshazl magic that he could summon.

The dragon screeched high overhead.

"What did you do?" Jayell asked.

Fes glanced over. "I'm not completely sure."

Then the dragon started swooping.

At first, he was only aware of it through the faint connection they shared, but then it became clearer, and he started to see the dragon sweeping toward him. It happened quickly, little more than a black shadow on the sky that resolved into the shape of the massive creature. He dove toward the ground, streaking faster and faster until he came crashing next to Fes, landing in the court-yard with a flutter of wings that sent Fes staggering backward.

"There has been an attack," Fes said.

"I haven't decided."

"I know that you haven't, but I don't know that we have time for you to come to terms with what you need to do. The Damhur have used the dragons, and they have attacked."

"I can feel it."

"Is that why you've been up there?" Fes glanced up at the sky for a moment before looking back at the dragon.

"I can feel it," the dragon said again.

"Help us. Help us find a way to stop them from using the dragons."

The dragon breathed out heavily, resting his enormous head next to Fes. His golden eyes glowed, and he seemed to stare through Fes. "Before we slept, we vowed not to attack our kind again."

"I'm not asking you to attack the dragons."

"That is what it will come to."

"It doesn't have to," Fes said. "All I want to do is stop those responsible, not the dragons."

He focused on what he would do, holding that within his mind. Would it work?

After what seemed an eternity, the dragon spoke again. "Climb on."

Fes blinked. "What was that?"

"Climb on before I decide to eat you."

Fes glanced over at Jayell. "Did you hear?"

She laughed softly. "I think he intends for me to hear everything these days. Do you think that he intends to allow me to ride?"

"She must come," the dragon said.

Fes glanced at Jayell again. "Well, I guess that answers that."

He approached the dragon slowly. They had ridden him once, but that was out of necessity and because they had needed to escape from a place hidden within the earth. He hadn't expected the dragon to allow them to ride him again, certainly not without begging. It was almost demeaning to the dragon to have them riding.

He touched the dragon's side, running his hand along the scales, feeling the heat radiating from the creature. It was an enormous presence, and his heart hammered as he approached, moving carefully. When he reached the dragon, he settled his hand, letting it rest on the dragon's side.

He carefully climbed onto the dragon's back. When he was situated, he looked over at Jayell. "You need to come too."

The dragon snorted.

Jayell jerked back a step before catching herself. She glanced from the dragon to Fes before letting out a deep breath and climbing atop the dragon. She situated herself behind Fes, wrapping her arms around him. As she did, she leaned forward. "I'm not sure—"

The dragon launched with a lurch.

They were in the air with a speed that was jarring in its suddenness. Jayell could say nothing more, and even if she was speaking, Fes wasn't going to be able to hear her easily. The dragon moved quickly, reaching a point high above the palace and then climbing even higher. With each slap of his massive wings, they soared again until the city itself was little more than a smear of darkness across the ground.

"We need to go south," Fes said.

"I can feel it," the dragon rumbled.

They veered toward the south, the dragon streaking away. Fes marveled at the speed with which they traveled, knowing that it would have taken him days to have reached the south traveling by horse, and it might have been too late. This way, he wondered if they might reach it in time.

Fes leaned over the side of the dragon, looking down at the ground as it sped past him. Much of this landscape he had not seen before, and certainly not from this vantage. The dragon seemed unmindful of the fact that they were precariously situated on his back and Fes squeezed his scales tightly, not knowing where else to grip. If he slipped, if he lost his handhold, he would fall, and there was no way to survive a fall that far.

Wind whipped around him, the only thing that he heard.

In the distance, he caught sight of glittering blue. It undulated, sweeping away from them, and stretched as far as he could see.

The ocean.

Where would the dragons be?

"Can you see where the attack is taking place?" Fes asked.

"I don't need to see it. I can feel it."

Fes closed his eyes, focusing on the dragon and whether he could feel the same thing. He was searching for a sensation, anything that might push against his magical senses, and he strained, listening.

Then he had it. It was there, a weak sense that left him with an irritation.

Mixed within it came a Calling.

That was unmistakable.

Fes worried about this dragon. Would he be able to protect him?

Fes started focusing, using what he'd learned about the Calling to protect his mind. He focused on himself and pulled on his Deshazl magic, wrapping that within him. When he was done, he pushed that connection through the strange bond he shared with the dragon, stretching from himself to the dragon, trying to ensure that the dragon was safe.

Would it work?

The effect of the Calling eased.

Fire magic slammed around them, and Fes could feel the effect of dozens of fire mages attacking. The power they threw around was enormous, and he couldn't tell if these were empire fire mages or whether these came from the Damhur.

"Can you tell what spell they're using?" he asked Jayell.

"Not from here," she said.

"I think we're going to need to land," Fes said.

The dragon snorted but started diving. They sped toward the ground, and it shot up toward them, faster and faster, to the point where Fes wanted to shield his eyes. He knew the dragon had control, but how fast they were moving still left him uncomfortable. When he started to see the ground in front of him, his body tensed. The dragon wasn't slowing.

For a moment, Fes worried that the Calling had overwhelmed the dragon, but then, with a great flap of wings, the dragon dropped to the ground.

Fes looked around.

They were at the edge of a forest. The trees had been scorched, leaving husks. Steam and smoke rose up around them, reminding him of the dragon plains. In the distance, Fes heard voices but saw no one moving.

"Are you sure this is where they are?"

"Your people are nearby."

"Will you stay?" Fes asked.

The dragon grunted, a sound that came out like a deep throaty rumble. Fes decided to take that as agreement. He jumped from the dragon's back and searched for signs of anyone nearby. He didn't have to search for long. A familiar face appeared in the distance, coming out from within the smoke, leading a grouping of a hundred soldiers.

"Jaken," Fes said.

Jaken breathed a sigh of relief and motioned for the soldiers to head back to the trees. When he reached Fes, he clasped his arm. "Fes. We were worried that—"

Fes nodded, glancing back at the dragon. "You were worried that this was one of the other dragons?"

"They've been attacking. We have tried to hold them back, but..."

"We have to stop the Calling. That's the only way we're going to be able to succeed."

"My father thinks there is another way with the fire mages."

"Not destroying the dragons," Fes said.

"We can't let them destroy the empire," Jaken said. "If nothing else, we have to protect it."

"If we destroy the dragons now, they will never return."

Jaken made a point of looking at Fes and not at the dragon. "What if they shouldn't have returned?"

Fes glanced back to see the dragon watching him. He was several dozen paces away, but given what he knew of the dragons, Fes suspected his hearing was exquisite. How much of this had he already heard?

"The dragons are our allies. We need to find a way to defend them, and we need to find some way of stopping the Damhur, nothing else."

"We're trying." Jaken breathed out a heavy sigh and motioned for Fes to follow him. "Come on. We could use your help here."

Fes and Jayell followed Jaken. He guided them through the trees and toward a camp where the empire soldiers were stationed. Fes hesitated as he approached, taking everything in. There were thousands of soldiers, enough to provide some protection, but many of them were injured.

"What happened here?" Fes asked.

Jaken paused, and Fes realized that he rested one hand on the hilt of his sword as he turned to face him. "What happened? We were attacked."

"We weren't gone that long," Fes said, glancing over at Jayell.

"It didn't take long. Azithan detected the presence of the attack, and we moved to stop them, but there was only so much that we could do."

Fes breathed out in a heavy sigh. "What have the attacks been like?"

He shook his head, a haunted expression in his eyes. "Terrible. In my years, I've seen fire mages attack, and I've seen the destructive way that they can use their magic, but this is something else. We've been forced back from the shore, and even though we continue to try to oppose them, the fire mages can only do so much."

He cocked his head to the side and Fes could tell that there was something he wasn't telling him. "What is it?"

"They are using Deshazl."

Fes looked around the encampment. It seemed hastily made, rows of tents and food getting distributed, but everything about it had a look of impermanence. They appeared ready to march at a moment's notice, which meant that they would have to throw tents onto the backs of horses or into wagons rapidly enough that they could march off quickly.

"You mean the Damhur Deshazl?"

He shook his head. "Not from what I can tell. It seems as if they are using the empire Deshazl."

"There shouldn't be many Deshazl remaining. Arudis was going to—"

Jaken breathed out a sigh. "I know what she was going to do, but either she failed or there are some who don't have as profound a connection that she overlooked." He stared at Fes for a moment. "We're doing everything we can to avoid harming them, but there are limitations to just how willing my father is to avoid hurting someone who is actively attacking us."

Fes stared beyond the border of the camp. He knew just how difficult it was to ignore a Calling. Yet he didn't want the Deshazl to be destroyed. With everything else that he had done, he had attempted to rescue them, to save them, and wanted nothing more than to protect as many of them as he could. Would it turn out that he could do nothing?

If they lost everything, would it even matter?

"The dragon can help," Fes said.

Jaken shook his head. "I don't know how the dragon will help. All it does is introduce another layer of danger. It might be better if you return to Anuhr."

"Better? How is that any better?"

"What would happen if they managed to Call that dragon? It's already hard enough facing two dragons. The fire mages have managed to hold them back, but they are growing weaker. At some point, we might not be able to withstand the pressure from these dragon attacks. If you add a third dragon, I just don't know how it would be possible to withstand it."

"I can protect it. I can prevent them from Calling—"

Jaken shook his head. "You couldn't even protect yourself from the Calling."

Fes looked along the line of soldiers. Everyone had a grim look upon their face, the kind of expression that he had never seen among the empire soldiers. They were already defeated. He could see it in their eyes as he walked through the camp with Jaken. He didn't need to speak to anyone to know that they believed that they couldn't stop the dragons. Pressure from fire mage spells continued to build, and he turned away, not wanting to do anything to disrupt them. It might not even be possible to do anything against it anyway, but if there was, he didn't want to throw off what the fire mages were doing.

"Let me speak to the emperor."

"Fes," Jaken said, turning to him. "Don't push on this. You were right. We made a mistake not recognizing the danger of the Damhur. We should have protected the dragons better, and in that, we made another mistake, but please, don't allow us to make yet another one. Let this end."

"What would you have me do with the dragon?"

"Have him return to the north. It was hard enough for you to find him, it seems, so bring him back and let him hide from the Damhur until this is over."

"And what happens if the Damhur manage to break through the lines here?"

"If they do, then we might need something else, but the fire mages are holding. You know the history as well as I do. There's only one way that we were able to defeat the dragons."

"The dragons were our allies."

"Not all of them, Fes. Don't pretend that the Damhur didn't control the dragons a thousand years ago. Fire mages were the only way we were able to defeat them.

We have that power now, and we need to use it." Jaken turned and continued into the camp.

Fes watched him go, debating whether or not to follow. What was the point? Jaken was right. If he pushed, if he attempted to go against the wishes of the empire, he did run the risk of the dragon getting Called and controlled by the Damhur.

Jayell rested her hand on his back. He turned to her. "What are you going to do?" she asked in a whisper.

Fes looked to the south and could feel the pressure of the fire mage spells pulsing against him. Somewhere out there, the Damhur continued to attack. But beyond the sea, there was the hope of something else. Could he reach it in time to get help? Would the Asharn even be willing to help?

"I need to see what happened."

Fes followed Jaken as he wound beyond the main part of the camp. As Fes walked, his gaze continued to drift to the injured Dragon Guards, so many of them with significant wounds and so many seemingly lost to the war already. The empire had a conscription army, but even that might not be enough to fight a foe like the Damhur and their Called Deshazl.

"When did they first start to attack?"

"Shortly after you left," Jaken said softly, his gaze sweeping over the wounded. "It was fire mages first—at least, what the Damhur consider their fire mages. They

Called Deshazl along the shore, far more than I ever would have expected."

"The Deshazl have blended within the empire for centuries," Jayell said.

Jaken looked over at her and nodded slowly. "I'm beginning to wonder how many of our people don't have some semblance of Deshazl blood within them."

They made their way beyond the line of fallen soldiers, beyond the haphazard camp, and from there, the stench of charred grass and ground drifted to him with an increasing potency. With every step, dread began to fill Fes, and he knew exactly what it was that he would see when he crested the small rise.

Jaken held up his hand, slowing their approach.

"Is this safe?" Jayell asked.

"None of this is safe anymore," he said.

They took another few steps and reached a small rise. From there, Jaken crouched and motioned for Fes and Jayell to do the same. Getting low to the ground, he peered outward.

Even without looking down at the ground below him, he could feel the effect of the attack. Fire mage magic exploded around him, filling him with the same thrill that he felt every time it occurred. Dozens of attacks happened at the same time, an unrelenting torrent of power. Were it for another reason, he might want to sit back and marvel at it. He'd never experienced power quite like this, not even when the Damhur attacked the temple.

"You can feel it, can't you?" Jaken asked.

Fes nodded. "There's so much power used."

"And it's been like this for days," Jaken said.

"How long can they hold out?" Fes asked.

"Azithan thinks we have enough Dragon relics for a few weeks of constant attack, but after that..."

A few weeks? That was it? With all of the relics the empire had on hand, all of the power that they had accumulated over the years, it would be wasted in a few weeks?

He turned to Jayell, but she shook her head. "There are too many using them at one time," she said.

"There isn't a choice." Jaken pointed to the sky, and Fes looked out to see two small shapes circling, never getting too close, but they were a constant threat. As he focused on them, he opened himself to the sense of a Calling, listening to see if there was anything that he could detect and curious if he could intervene in some way. If the dragons were Called, trained by the Damhur, it would be unlikely that he would be able to do anything at all. Somehow, he would need to connect to them, but how could he do that when he still had not yet fully connected to the dragon he had raised?

"They do all that they can to hold those two at bay. Occasionally, the hold slips and they are unable to keep them back, but for the most part, they have been success-ful." Jaken scanned the ground, his gaze drifting back toward the fire mages down on the distant plain. "We didn't know that they would attack with the dragons at first."

"You knew they had Called the dragons," Fes said.

"We knew they had Called them, but we didn't know that they would bring them to attack so soon. We were unprepared for this."

Fes bit back the comment that he wanted to make. Jaken had seen and experienced too much loss for him to take out his frustration, but he couldn't shake the irrita-tion he felt. They could have—and should have—prepared for the use of the dragons against the empire. Of anyone, Jaken understood just what the Damhur might do and understood how powerful they were when it came to using that magic.

Instead, Fes looked down at the ground, his gaze taking in the destruction. Far below him, a line of dark-robed figures stood toward the back. The fire mages. Many of them stood, others knelt, while others were lying on the ground, likely fire mages who had expended significant energy already. Occasionally, Fes caught a flash of glowing light from their relics, which wasn't surprising considering how much power the fire mages were slinging around. An enormous section of bone rested near the middle of the fire mages, and he wondered how hard that had been to carry here. There had to be hundreds more like that, all collected from the Dragon Plains, but how many had been saved from the temple, and how many had the Damhur stolen?

In front of the fire mages, hundreds upon hundreds of soldiers waited. A line of archers near the back row fired volleys, but Fes doubted those arrows did much against the power of the Damhur.

An expanse of charred and blackened lands stretched in the middle. No life existed on that emptiness. Fire mage magic—or flames from the dragons—had obliterated everything through there. On the other side were the rows of Damhur—and their Deshazl.

There had to be several thousand. If they were already this many, and if they had secured their strip of land, holding their own against the might the empire could bring to bear, it wouldn't be long before the rest of the empire troops were overwhelmed.

Through it all came the steady effect of the Calling.

He could ignore it, but if he didn't, he would have felt compelled to go down to the shoreline, perhaps to join in the fighting, but not for the empire—against the empire. That call was clear, a distinct signal that thrummed within him.

"Have you seen enough?" Jaken asked.

Fes nodded, backing away.

"And you understand why we can't have your dragon here?"

Fes turned back toward the distant empire campground. The fire mages had managed to hold off the two dragons, but they were able to focus their efforts in a single direction. If they had to attack from behind them, if for some reason the Damhur managed to Call the dragon Fes had raised, then the other two dragons would be able to press closer to shore.

As he watched, the dragons crashed into some invisible barrier, slamming into it, spinning back, but not before there came a pulse of power from the fire mages.

How much effort did it take to only hold that barrier in place? How much more power to take to fortify it?

Fes glanced over at Jayell. He would be of no use here. The dragon would be of no use here. Worse, if something happened and he was Called, it was possible that he would cause more difficulty through his presence. It would be better for him to return to Anuhr, help Azithan make whatever preparations he needed to make, and... do what? Hope that the empire somehow succeeded?

There was no way they could withstand this attack indefinitely.

They needed others, even more than he had believed before.

That meant going to beg and plead with the Asharn. They needed someone who had experience defeating the

Damhur. The experience the empire had was over a thousand years old, and in that time, the Damhur had continued to prepare while the empire had thought themselves safe.

The dragons slammed into the invisible barrier again before circling back out. As they did, fire mage magic surged once again, but even that wasn't going to last.

"Come on," he said to Jayell.

"Where are we going to go?"

"It's time for Arudis to return to her homeland. It's time for her to help us find the allies we will need to survive."

CHAPTER FOUR

R iding atop the dragon didn't feel any less strange than it had the last time Fes had done it. The wind whistling around them made it difficult to talk, and while Fes didn't mind the pressure from Jayell pushing up behind him, he focused his thoughts on what they were doing and whether there was anything that he would even be able to accomplish. He hated that they had abandoned Jaken so quickly after finding him, but Jaken was right that keeping the dragon there put them at risk, especially with the Calling Fes had detected the moment they had arrived.

Finding Arudis would take more effort. He didn't have the same way of tracking her, and even once he found her, he wasn't sure that she would be willing to accompany him back across the sea and to the Asharn.

She had escaped from Javoor long enough ago that he suspected she had no interest in returning. Yet she was the only one who might be able to help. Without her, he didn't know whether they would be able to find—and stop—the Damhur.

When the forest loomed into view, the dragon began to descend. Fes was better prepared this time, and when they landed with a hard thud, he jumped from the dragon's back, helped Jayell off, and they raced toward the village. Situated at the edge of the forest, the village had once been a dragon base, a place that the empire had used to defend itself during the last war, and in that time had become little more than a relic itself.

Fes was relieved to see that the village was filled with people. All of them were Deshazl, and many of them were people that he knew, people he had helped save, and thankfully they remained here and had not been Called back by the Damhur. They had suffered enough under their influence already.

He ran into Sarah, a woman with mousy brown hair and a seemingly permanent frown etched on her face. She blinked when she saw him, and then she looked past him, apparently noticing the dragon out beyond the edge of the village.

"I'm looking for Arudis."

"She's there," Sarah said. "But Fes—"

Before she had a chance to finish, he turned away and

raced toward the building. It was a two-story structure, a place that seemed almost like a tavern or town hall, and he threw open the door, coming to a stop inside.

He surveyed the room and saw three people surrounding a bed. None of the three were Arudis, which meant... Fes raced forward and saw Arudis lying with a thin sheet pulled up to her chest. Her eyes were sunken, and her skin was yellowed.

"What happened to her?"

A tall, slender woman looked over at Fes. "She's been sick for the last week or so. We don't really know what happened. We tried helping, but nothing that we've done has made a difference."

He glanced at the table near the bed and realized that it was covered with various bottles and jars, concoctions that had been intended to heal and restore her. Some of them had a pungent aroma while others were sweet, almost sickly so. He didn't recognize a single one of them.

Fes was thankful that there were healers who could try to help her but wished that there was more that could be done. He glanced over at Jayell, who had stayed a step behind him. "Is there anything that you can do with your magic?"

She took a step forward and pulled a dragon pearl from her pocket, resting it on her hand. "We need to conserve these somewhat," she said softly.

"This is Arudis," Fes said.

"I understand who she is and what she means. I'm just saying that we need to conserve our stores. They aren't limitless. And with the war—"

A short woman standing on the opposite side of the bed looked up. "War?" Mariah asked.

Fes nodded. "The Damhur have resumed their attack. Now that they have control over the dragons, they have begun to push toward the empire."

"If they're using the dragons..." Jennifer started.

Fes considered her. She was a stout woman, with black hair and streaks of gray. She was older than the other two women, and he knew her to have a sharp mind but an equally sharp tongue. "The fire mages have managed to hold them at bay so far, but I'm not sure how long they will be able to withstand the attack."

"Is that why you wanted Arudis?" Mariah asked.

"I need Arudis so that I can ask her expertise about the Asharn."

"But she is not from Asharn."

"No. She was once one of the Damhur Deshazl, but she knows more about the Asharn then she's shared so far, and we need her. The empire needs her." Fes stared at her. Her breathing seemed erratic and irregular, and her skin was moist. "The dragons need her."

Jayell raised her hands, cupping a dragon pearl between them. Her fire magic built and green began to swirl from her hands, forming something like strands of color that arched out from her. She set the pearl on Arudis's chest and then spread her hands out and down, bringing them on either side of Arudis. The bands of color pressed into the sick woman, slowly drifting through her.

Arudis let out a quiet gasp.

Jayell held her hands in place, and as she did, Fes had to hope that what she was doing would be enough. Could it be effective against whatever illness had taken her?

"I'm not sure what this is, but it's nothing that I've ever seen before," Jayell whispered.

"Keep trying," Fes said.

"I wasn't saying that I wasn't going to try. I'm just warning you that I haven't seen anything like this before," she said.

Her fire mage spell built and power flowed from her, washing over Arudis. Colors streaked from her hands, forming a spiderweb that she wound around the older woman. This time, she used the spell differently than she had the first time, pulling it from the top of the bed, focused on Arudis's head and dragging it along the entire length of the bed until it reached her toes. When she was done, she let out a shaky breath.

"I think that's all I can do," Jayell said in a breathy whisper.

"It should be enough," Fes said.

"I'm not sure if it is. I... I haven't seen anything like this before, and it's difficult for me to know whether or not my attempt was even successful."

He turned his attention to Arudis, resting his hands on her. He could still feel the tingling energy flowing through the older woman from the spell that Jayell had used on her. It practically shook within her, a building pressure that washed over her and left her vibrating with energy.

"What did you do?"

"I tried something different than I've tried before. I thought that I would see if I could leave a lingering bit of the dragon pearl energy within her. If it works, then maybe it can continue to restore her, but if it doesn't, then..." She shook her head. "Again, I haven't seen anything like this, and I don't know if what I've done is enough."

The spell she'd used was far more complex than what he had seen from her before. Maybe Azithan had really underestimated her. She had increased in her ability over the last year.

"Arudis?" Fes asked. He kept his gaze fixed on her but couldn't shake the sense that the others all looked at him, wondering whether they had made her situation worse. They wouldn't have been able to feel the effect of what Jayell had done, but they certainly would've been able to see it.

Looking at how sick she was, he didn't really expect her to answer, but surprisingly she stirred, rolling her head toward the sound of his voice. She blinked and looked at him, and a hint of a smile came to her face. "Fezarn. You've returned."

"What happened?"

She coughed and covered her mouth with her arm, looking around to see the three Deshazl women standing around her bed. She offered a tight smile, but it had none of the strength that she was known for. "You don't need to be worrying about me," she said to them.

"I don't know that you can convince them otherwise," Fes said.

"I can try," she coughed.

"Do you know what happened?"

"I got sick. There's not much more to know than that," she said.

"Jayell was able to heal you, but she wasn't able to identify what happened."

"No. I suppose that she wouldn't." She closed her eyes and rolled her head back, almost as if she wanted to stare up at the ceiling. "This is an illness that she can't heal with her fire magic."

"What is it?"

"It's tied to the Calling."

"But you can ignore the Calling."

"I can ignore the Calling, but there's only so much

that I can do to ignore the effect of it. I fight, but I'm not able to overpower it, not indefinitely."

"How?"

"I was tormented by them for too long. All those years where I lived in Javoor, and all those years when they were holding me, using the Calling to train me, it... it changed me. There are some who are lucky enough to get away when they are younger, but even then, they still struggle. We have learned ways of dealing with it, and when I was younger, I was able to counter it with my own Deshazl connection, but as I grow older and weaker and suffer from the effects of the Calling more often, I no longer can fight it quite as I had."

"Why was Jayell able to help you?"

"Jayell was able to temporize the effects, but they are with me permanently."

"Will the same happen to the rest of us?"

She shook her head. "The rest weren't subjected to it from birth. It's only those of the Damhur Deshazl, those like myself—"

"And me," Fes said.

"You might have been subjected to it when you were first born, but your parents managed to escape before the full effects of the Calling were able to overtake you. It's why you have been able to ignore them for so long. Without what your parents did, I'm not sure that it would have been possible for you at this point."

Fes couldn't ask what he needed of Arudis, not in the condition that she was in.

"Ask it," she said, looking up at him. "There is something that you think you need to know."

"The Damhur have started their attack," he said.

"So soon?"

He nodded. "It started along the coast. They attacked a city there, and they have destroyed most of it, forcing the Dragon Guard back. The emperor is there, doing what he can—"

"The emperor shouldn't be there. Not with what he is."

"There are dozens of fire mages, and all of them are trying to oppose the attack, but I don't know that they're strong enough."

"Why are you here?"

"Because I need help rescuing the dragons."

"There is no help. With the attack on these lands, I am needed here to protect as many as I can."

"There are others who can help now. They've been trained." Hopefully, well enough to avoid a Calling. If not, then they would need to keep moving, staying ahead of the Damhur so they didn't attack the empire. "What we need are others who know how to fight the Damhur, like the Asharn. They helped us once—"

"The Asharn have no interest in helping anyone other than themselves. They have fought the Damhur for centuries, and in all that time, there is much that they would have been able to do had they only been willing to do it. No," she said, trying to sit up before giving up and lying back down. "The Asharn aren't the ally you're looking for."

"We don't have any other options," Fes said.

"Then we need to find some. You may not think that there are other options, but there has to be something."

"Not to protect the remaining dragon."

"It's true," she said, breathing out.

Fes nodded. "Come with me. I need to show you this."

He glanced at the Deshazl women, and they all stepped back. He scooped up Arudis, feeling how light she was and wishing that she was heavier and that he wouldn't have to feel her bones practically crunching beneath him as he hoisted her. He carried her out of the building and through the village, then paused. He cradled her, angling her so that she could look out and see the distant form of the massive dragon.

"Oh," Arudis said with a breathy sigh.

"I found the key to the dragon's essence."

"The essence?"

"They have been sleeping, held within statues that were designed to contain their essence over the years until such a time that they could be reawakened. There are others, but..."

"But what?"

"But many of them have been lost. We need to find them, and if we can, we can not only help reawaken the dragons, but we can use those sculptures to defeat the Damhur."

"Or make them stronger," she said.

"They're already stronger than us. What we need is something different, a way of overpowering them. We need to take a risk, and if we don't..."

"If we don't, then all is lost. I understand," she said.

"I want to protect the dragons, but I can't do it without the Asharn. We can't protect the others without the Asharn. And I can't reach the Asharn without your help."

"Fes, what you're asking is not something that I can do. I haven't seen any evidence that the Asharn are willing to work with us," she said.

"They don't have to be willing to work with us. They only need to be willing to work with the dragons."

Arudis struggled in his arms and motioned for him to lower her to the ground. He did so carefully and kept his arm around her waist, ensuring that she was still standing and stable. When he was comfortable that she wasn't going to fall down, he guided her toward the dragon.

"This one is so much larger than the other two," she said with a whisper.

"I have a sense that he was one of the elder dragons, once upon a time."

"To have an elder reborn would be an enormous gift, especially with what we've been trying to face," she said.

"It would be, but he remains hesitant. He's almost as reluctant as you."

She glanced over at him.

"It's taken quite a bit of convincing on my part to coax him into working with us. Even then, I'm not sure that he is completely willing to help. It is sort of the same as with you. I need both of you to help."

"Reaching Asharn is an incredible journey. Even going across the sea to Javoor would take us weeks, and that's with a fast ship and not needing to worry about the possibility of the Damhur attacking us, or the dragons they have Called. I'm not sure that we can make it."

"What if we travel by dragon?"

"What?"

Fes nodded toward the dragon. "He has carried us."

"A dragon rider? I don't know that I've ever heard of such a thing, even when the Deshazl were still connected to the dragons."

"I get the sense that he doesn't do so very eagerly, but he understands the need, and because of that, he has been willing to work with us."

Fes reached the dragon. He motioned to the massive

creature, pointing to Arudis. "She is Deshazl," he said to the dragon.

The dragon rumbled and let out a breath of steam. "I can tell."

"I can't understand him," Arudis said.

"Somehow, he gets to choose who understands him," Fes said.

"And her?" Arudis kept her gaze on Jayell and Fes nodded.

"He has granted her the ability to understand what he's saying."

"Something else that's rare. Not only has he allowed you to ride him, but he has granted someone not of the Deshazl the ability to understand him. That is an incredibly rare gift."

"The world has changed," the dragon said.

"Is that why you have been willing to let me ride you?" Fes asked.

"I can't change the world, not without changing alongside it. And you have need of a faster means of transportation. If you had your own wings, I would not have any need."

Fes laughed.

"What is it?" Arudis asked.

"I think the dragon just made a joke."

"Dragons don't jest," Arudis said.

"This one did."

"If you can teach me how to sprout wings," Fes said to the dragon, "then I will avoid riding you."

"Your connection to the dragons isn't so great that you would have the ability to sprout wings," the dragon said.

"Or maybe your connection to the Deshazl isn't so great that you can help me sprout wings," Fes said.

The dragon rumbled again and stirred himself from the ground and started to make a steady circle. Fes glanced over his shoulder and realized that dozens of people from the village had all come to look. They all stared, watching the dragon. Fes couldn't blame them; the dragon was an enormous creature and incredibly massive, much larger than the other two dragons that had been in the forest. Those had been impressive at the time, but they were nothing quite like this blue-scaled dragon.

"We can't delay for too much longer," Fes said to Arudis. "I don't know how long we have to deflect the attack, and the sense I get from Jaken is that they can't hold out for too much longer, and if they fail..."

"If they fail, then the empire falls. I understand what happens. I'm just saying that I don't know that going to the Asharn is the best solution."

"No. But it might be the only solution." Fes reached the dragon, Jayell behind him. He started climbing up the dragon's back, pulling Jayell up behind him. He looked down at Arudis and held his hand out, waiting to see if she would agree to join him.

After a moment, she looked back at the village before turning and climbing toward the dragon. "I'm still not certain this is the right thing to do," she said.

"I don't know that you need to be certain. I'm not certain that much of what we've been doing is right," Fes said.

She situated herself behind him on the dragon, positioned near Jayell. Without the wind whistling around him, he could hear her breathing heavily and could practically feel the tension in her.

"We need to travel south. We're looking for Asharn. They are people like the Deshazl, but—"

The dragon rumbled and stood. "I know where you want us to go."

With a massive jump, the dragon lifted into the air. Arudis screamed, and he hoped that Jayell would help hold her, not wanting to have her fall, but he had to believe that Arudis would figure out just exactly what she needed to do to maintain her balance.

The dragon streaked out to the east, looping out over the water. It took Fes a moment to realize what exactly the dragon was doing, and when he did, he marveled at how intelligent the dragon was. It was his way of ensuring that they avoided the Damhur. If they were attacking along the southern coast, then the dragon would avoid them altogether by sweeping out around to the east.

Water flowed below them, massive waves flowing in the depths of the sea. They caught glimpses of small islands as they flew, but nothing that would provide much of a place for them to do more than take a break. He didn't want to pause until they reached the Asharn.

The wind continued to whistle around him, but it seemed less than before. The dragon wasn't flying with the same intensity, and Fes decided that it was partly because the dragon didn't want to fatigue himself and so had chosen to take a more cautious pace. At times, he would set his wings out and practically glide, something that surprised Fes.

He twisted so that he could look at Jayell and Arudis. Neither of them was speaking, and Arudis looked shocked. "What's the best way to get beyond Javoor?" he asked.

"Javoor is enormous. It stretches all across the entirety of the continent. There is a forest that the Asharn are believed to hide within, but—"

Fes blinked. "Wait. You don't even know where the Asharn can be found?"

"I thought that I told you that."

"I'm pretty sure that you didn't. How have the Asharn hidden from the Damhur?"

"The Asharn aren't a nation. They are a people, sort of

like the Deshazl, and they fight as a resistance. They hide. If the Damhur were to find them, they would destroy them as quickly as they could. They know the threat the Asharn pose, especially as the Asharn are one of the few people who are capable of resisting them."

How were they going to find the Asharn if there wasn't a place to go?

He had believed that they had to travel through Javoor, and finding the dragon had left him hopeful that they could just fly over the Damhur lands and could avoid an attack altogether, but if the Asharn couldn't be found so simply, traveling this way wasn't going to get him there any sooner. They would be delayed in trying to find where the Asharn were hiding, and even when they did find them, there might not be enough time to make a difference when it came to the Damhur attack on the empire.

"There is a place that we can look first," she said.

"Where?"

"Well, it was going to be difficult had you not had the dragon, but seeing as how you have a unique way of traveling, I think that you might be able to reach it when others cannot."

"What is it?"

"It's deep within a forest. Javoor is a rocky land for much of it. It transitions into something of a rolling plain, and then a line of forest, a massive canopy of trees, grows in one section. It's long been rumored to be dangerous, and the people of Javoor fear it, thinking that the forest itself is somehow haunted, as if some great power lived within it."

"Is it possible that some great power *does* live within it?"

"We never knew. Even when I was still with the Damhur, there was a belief that the Asharn might be hiding within the forest, but that was never proven. The Damhur had often swept through the forest, taking teams of people through, searching for evidence of the Asharn, but they never came away with anything that was convincing."

"How are we going to reach the forest?"

"Like I said, we can fly there."

"No. What you said is that the forest is in the middle of Javoor. How do you expect us to reach it without the Damhur noticing?"

"We can travel at night," Jayell suggested.

"What happens if there is a Calling?" Fes asked.

He wouldn't put it past the Damhur to be prepared for the possibility of an attack like this and to keep a Calling radiating out. If that were the case, there might not be any way for the dragon to safely pass through the Damhur lands.

"They don't waste their effort on the Calling, not like that, and not in their lands," Arudis said.

"I've felt the effect of the Damhur when they were simply marching. There was no difficulty holding onto a Calling."

"That was when they were trying to summon the Deshazl."

"They don't do the same in Javoor?"

"Why would they need to? They know who is descended from the Deshazl."

"How?"

"Because they keep a tight rein on all of those who are born from a Deshazl union. They don't allow them to mingle. Can you imagine being born into a society when you were part Deshazl and part something else? It's not only forbidden, but it's also dangerous."

"What is the best way for us to approach so that we don't get caught?"

"We come in out of the west," she said. "The harbor will provide a natural distraction, and from there, it's the shortest distance to the forest."

Fes stared at her. A part of him worried that she might not be telling him everything that he needed to know, but what other choice did he have? He needed to trust that she was sharing what she could and that what she knew was accurate, because if it weren't, then they would get caught, and if they failed... The Damhur would have three dragons.

CHAPTER FIVE

They reached the outer edge of Javoor near midnight. The dragon had begun to circle, taking his time as he approached, and Fes rested against its massive side. He was thankful that they hadn't seen any evidence of the Damhur, and had worried a little bit that they might encounter one of the other dragons, but that hadn't been the case.

As they neared the coastline, he began to feel it.

A Calling.

It began softly, a subtle irritation at the back of his mind, and it began to build more and more the farther they flew. Maybe it was mostly for the people of Javoor, but as they approached, he started to wonder if that were true or not. Perhaps this was a mistake.

"What is it?" Jayell asked, leaning toward him.

He twisted so that he could look at her. Her eyes were drawn tight, and he realized that she had been using a fire spell and wondered at its intent. Was she doing it merely to have a warning? Or was she trying to protect them in some way?

"I feel a Calling," he said.

"You were worried about that," she said.

"Worried, and it seems as if for good reason."

"There isn't anything that we can do about it."

"I don't know that approaching in this direction is the right strategy," he said. He glanced over at Arudis. She was sleeping soundly, slumped forward, her arms wrapped around the dragon. Something still wasn't quite right with her, and he worried that it was all tied to the residual effects of the Calling, and the illness that she claimed came from it, but it bothered him that she had fallen ill so quickly. "We still don't really know what happened to her. What if the Calling forces her to betray us?"

"She's been fighting against the Damhur all along."

"I know, but..."

"If anyone can resist the Calling, it will be her. She's been responsible for protecting the Deshazl for years."

As he looked over the side of the dragon at the edge of Javoor in view, he frowned. "Why would she have us come through the harbor?"

"She said it was the closest distance to the forest."

An idea came to him. "How good is your eyesight?" he asked the dragon.

"Much better than yours."

"Go higher," he said.

The dragon began straining, flying higher. As he did, the effect of the Calling began to recede. As it began to disappear, he felt more relaxed. Tension began to leave him.

"We're looking for a forest. It should be in the middle of the continent," he said to the dragon.

"I see it," the dragon rumbled.

"Do you think that you can come down directly toward it, and maybe look for a clearing in the middle, much like at the heart of the forest and the empire?"

"There is no such place."

Fes frowned. "Is there anything there that you would say would look inhabited?"

"Not in the forest."

"Is it too dense for you to see through?"

"Are you too dense to understand what I'm telling you?"

Fes chuckled. "Maybe I am. We are looking for something. There are people who are trying to hide, though it's not a separate nation, at least not according to Arudis."

"There is a place beyond," the dragon said.

"What you mean?"

"Beyond."

"Beyond what?"

"I cannot explain."

"Can you try?"

"There is the forest. There are mountains, though not nearly as large as what is in the north and my homeland. And there is a valley. Beyond the valley, there is something."

Fes twisted and looked back at Arudis. Could this be the place where the Asharn had gone? Could they have found a place of their own?

Maybe they had always had it and had just never revealed it. That would make sense, especially as there would be no reason for someone like Arudis to have known about it. They would have wanted to keep it secretive, and revealing its presence would have drawn the attention of the Damhur, practically inviting an attack.

"That's where we need to go," Fes said.

"I'm already heading there," the dragon said.

"Do you need to rest?"

"Soon. Rest, and I'll need to eat."

"I didn't think that you ever got tired, but maybe I was wrong."

"I've been carrying too much weight."

"I'll let the women know that you said that."

"They aren't even large enough to consider a snack," he said.

"Are you implying that I'm too heavy for you?" Fes asked, smiling to himself.

"You would be far too much gristle," the dragon said and made a strange sound that Fes realized was his laughter.

He shook his head. "I'm glad that I can amuse you."

"After centuries of sleep, it's good that anything can amuse me."

There was something much more serious about that comment. He could hear the pain within the dragon and knew that he still suffered from the decades of sleep. It wasn't anything that Fes could ever understand. Men just couldn't sleep like the dragons had. All he could do was support the dragon and continue to try to help ensure that they weren't enslaved by the Damhur.

He watched the ground as they flew, noticing the change from the forest to the mountains as little more than streaks of color along the ground. There was a long, jagged gash that he suspected indicated the valley, and from there, the landscape changed again.

Fes couldn't see what it was, not clearly, and he strained, trying to stare down at the ground, wanting to know where the dragon was bringing them. He didn't feel any effect of the Calling anymore. The air had changed, taking on a little less of the bitter chill than he'd felt during the journey across the ocean. His ears popped as they began to descend. He held onto the side of the dragon, every so often looking over and seeing if there was anything else that he could pick up on.

Arudis stirred and asked, "Are we there? Are we in Javoor?"

"Not exactly," he said.

"Then where are we?"

"Beyond."

She gasped. "Oh, no. We can't go beyond. There is nothing safe there. Only danger and death live beyond."

"That's not what it seems like to the dragon," he said.

"We need to turn back," she said. She grabbed his shoulder and pulled him so that he could see her. "When I was here, the Damhur feared anything that was beyond. They knew it was dangerous to risk coming this way."

"Only because they made it dangerous."

"No, you don't understand. Beyond the lands of Javoor is a bleak and deadly landscape."

Fes leaned over the side of the dragon and looked down. From what he could tell, there was no bleakness there. It was life. Tall grasses stretched in the distance. Trees dotted the ground. Hills undulated, rolling outward, with wildflowers growing along the hilt. Everything carried a sweet fragrance.

"Look," he said, pointing down.

Arudis leaned over the side of the dragon and her breath caught. "That shouldn't be here."

"I don't know what should or shouldn't be here, but this is what's here."

"Is it real?"

"What?"

"Is it real?"

Fes frowned. "I didn't realize it would be possible to fake life like this."

Arudis glanced over at Jayell. "Look at your friend. She has much power with the dragon relics. Using something like that, it would be possible to forge life."

Fes focused on the sense of a fire mage spell. As he did, he detected nothing. Everything felt as if it should, as if it were real, as if the life that he saw and smelled down below them was real.

And maybe it was only because he wanted to believe that it was real.

"Is it possible?" he asked the dragon.

"Anything is possible, but this smells real. And I can feel the heat within it."

"What does that have to do with anything?"

"The heat tells me whether it's alive or not. I can feel the variations of heat within this land. Those variations are too complex for someone to have faked."

Fes hoped that was true. "We're looking for someplace with people."

"It's near," the dragon said.

Fes looked over the side of the dragon and continued to watch the ground as they streaked north. They were close to the ground now, close enough that he thought he could jump and survive the landing, yet doing so at this speed would still be painful and likely shatter most of the bones in his body. Everything blurred by him and he marveled at the speed with which they traveled, speed which the dragon still managed despite flying for as long as he had been. And if something went wrong, they might need the dragon to travel at higher speed again.

"We should take a break before we reveal ourselves," Fes said.

"We are almost there," the dragon said.

"I still think we need to be more careful." If they could take a few hours to recover, then the dragon wouldn't end up too weak for whatever they might encounter.

"What would you have me do?" the dragon asked with a deep rumble.

Fes nodded to the ground. "We should land, if only for a little while."

The dragon started down, descending quickly, and landed with a thud. With a flap of his wings, he settled to the ground. Fes climbed off the dragon, looking up at the others with him. They got off the dragon slowly. Arudis looked uncomfortable.

"I don't like this. The Asharn—"

"You don't have to like it. We're looking for help, and we can't necessarily choose who we go to for help. The Asharn *have* fought the Damhur. We need to do this to save the dragons."

Arudis watched him for a long moment before turning away.

Fes made his way from the dragon, looking around the landscape. It was lush, everything filled with dense greenery and life, and there was something about it that felt comforting.

"None of this should be here," Arudis said, approaching slowly and looking all around her.

"What should be here?"

She shook her head. "When I was in Javoor, we always knew that there was nothing beyond the valley. Nothing could live. It was a barren wasteland."

Fes looked around. "Does this look like a barren wasteland?"

"It doesn't, but why would they have made that claim?"

"Maybe they were afraid of what's here."

Arudis turned toward him, shaking her head. "The Damhur do not fear the Asharn. They view them as servants who have escaped, and if it were up to the Damhur, they would capture the remaining Asharn and force them back into servitude."

"They're slaves," Fes said. "Whatever else you want to

call them, that is what they are, at least to the Damhur. They are forced to serve, forced to do whatever the Damhur ask of them."

"I know much better than you do, Fezarn," she said.

"Then don't forget what they did to you," Fes said. "Remember how much of it was lies told to control you. Even in this."

He made his way toward the distant line of trees, scanning for signs of movement. When he'd been riding on the dragon, it had been too difficult to see if there were any signs of movement, but from here, he thought that maybe he could see it more clearly. There was nothing.

Maybe he should take back to the air, riding with the dragon and using him as a way to look for someone —anyone.

"Fes?"

He turned to Jayell. A spell built from her, the power of it pushing out, sweeping in a circle away from her. It was similar to what Azithan had once done, and he felt how it went deep into the ground, pushing out as she searched for evidence of anyone nearby. With a spell like that, she would be able to determine whether they were alone or whether they needed to worry about others nearby.

"Do you detect anything?"

"It's strange," she said.

"Strange how?"

"My magic. There's something that's not quite right about it."

"You can't use it?" He could feel the spell she was using, so that couldn't be it, but was there something different than what she was able to explain?

"It's not so much that I can't use it. I can certainly feel the way that magic swells up within me, and I know that it's there, but..." She shook her head. "It's almost as if my connection to it has changed, as if I can't quite reach what I'm supposed to with it."

"Do you think something is working against you?"

"I can't tell," she said.

The frustration in her voice was clear, and she pushed harder with her magic, the effect of the fire spell radiating out from her, sweeping over the land. With that spell, she could detect anyone approaching.

At least, she *should* be able to do so.

Somehow, that magic failed.

When she let go of the spell, Fes could see the slump in her shoulders. Had the Damhur figured out a way to override a fire mage? The Deshazl could remove fire mage magic, but what Jayell described sounded different.

Unless this was the Asharn.

When he'd fought them before, he had seen just how powerful they were, and he had observed the way that they were able to use their magic, controlling that of the fire mages. They had power, the same sort of power Fes possessed. Deshazl power.

Was there any way for him to detect whether they were using Deshazl magic?

And if there was, was there anything that he could do against it?

It was unlikely that there was. Deshazl magic was different than that of the fire mages. He wasn't aware of others using any around him, not the same way as he was with fire mages, and when he tried to connect to others, there wasn't anything that would help him identify what they were doing.

Fes turned back to the dragon. "Can you detect anything?"

The dragon huffed at him, and a deep rumble rolled from his throat.

"If this is Deshazl magic, you are connected to it," Fes said.

"As are you."

"Not the same way. The dragons and the Deshazl were connected, but I don't know how to pick up on individual Deshazl magic," he said.

"Only because you choose not to try."

"Even if I could try, I doubt that my magic connects to me the same way as it does to the fire mages." He looked up at the dragon, meeting his golden eyes. "Can you try?"

The dragon sat up, using his wings to help prop him

up, and a strange sense rolled off him. It was a mixture of heat and a tingling that washed over Fes, a sense of power that he could feel but wasn't certain what it meant.

Hopefully, it meant that the dragon was using his connection to his magic and trying to reach for the Deshazl, but even if he did, was there anything that the dragon would be able to do once it managed to connect to them?

Was there anything that he could accomplish in doing so?

"We are not alone," the dragon said.

"There are others?" Fes asked.

The dragon launched himself into the air and flew, staying high enough that arrows or other similar weapons would not be able to reach him.

"What happened?" Jayell asked.

"I don't know. He said we weren't alone and then he took to the air. I..."

As he said it, he began to see movement coming from near the trees.

A dozen or more people approached. They were all on foot, and from what he could tell, they were dressed in dark leathers. As they neared, Fes realized that they wore strange colors, almost as if the leathers were shaped into costumes. It took him a moment to realize that they were shaped like dragons.

"Fes?" Jayell said.

"Stay close," he said.

"I can't even reach my magic," she whispered.

She managed to keep the fear out of her voice, but Fes knew just how scared she would be at such an inability. Especially when confronted with strange people approaching. It made him nervous, and he still was able to reach for his Deshazl connection.

"Arudis?"

She could only stare.

"Arudis!"

Fes grabbed her arm, pulling her so that she looked over at him.

"I've never seen anything like it," she said.

"Are they the Asharn?" Fes asked.

He only had a limited experience with the Asharn, and certainly not in numbers like this. When they had attacked the palace, they had done so dressed more in clothing befitting the empire, which made sense, as they would have wanted to blend in.

These people would never have blended in. This was designed to stand out.

"I can feel them," Arudis said.

"What you mean that you can *feel* them?" Fes asked.

"Can you not?" she said.

"I don't feel anything. What is this?"

They were one hundred yards away, and they were approaching steadily. As they neared, Fes realized that the leathers they wore appeared to shimmer, almost as if made of scales.

He flicked his gaze up to the sky where the dragon was flying. Not just an appearance of scales. These had to have been real scales. Dragon scales.

Skies of Fire. Could these people have attacked the dragons? Could he have led them to someone who might try to harm the dragons?

"What is this?" Jayell asked.

Fes could only stare. He had no idea what was coming, and there was no place for them to go. He wanted to run, but could he? As he looked around, he knew that running would not get him anywhere, not before these people reached him.

Which meant they were at the mercy of whatever they intended.

Three of them split off and started toward Fes and the others. As they did, their shimmering scales drew his attention, and he couldn't help but stare. Would they know about the dragon that they came with? And if they did, would they want to harm it?

Fes nodded to them as they approached. "I'm Fes. We're looking for—"

He didn't have a chance to finish.

Power slammed into him, throwing him to the ground, and he couldn't move. He tried, but his body didn't seem to respond, and he lay there, looking over to see Arudis lying next to him.

Where was Jayell?

He tried to turn and look, but his head was ringing.

By the time it cleared, and he managed to finally sit up, he realized that they had taken Jayell.

And they had left him and Arudis.

Fes tried to stand up, but his body hurt. Whatever they had used on him had been fast and explosive and filled with power, and it was enough that he could barely move.

Arudis moaned though she said nothing else.

"You have to get up," Fes said.

"Everything hurts," she said.

"It's the same for me, but we need to get up before they return."

"I doubt that they will return," she said.

Fes reached her and helped her to her feet. As they stood and looked around, he realized that the attackers had already reached the edge of the trees and disappeared. Jayell was gone, carried away with them.

"They took her?"

Fes stared at the departing attackers. Their timing couldn't have been chance. Jayell had been using her fire mage spells and had been pushing out with power, and that seemed to have drawn their attention.

Could they have thought that she was with the Damhur?

Another thought came to him, one that was equally chilling. What if they believed she was one of those who could Call?

He glanced up and saw the dragon still circling high overhead. If they believed that the dragon was with the Damhur—and knowing that the dragons had been captured, it was possible that these attackers had seen a dragon before—they might believe that they were with the Damhur.

If that was the case, then he somehow had to convince them otherwise.

"We have to go after her," Fes said.

"What do you think you can do against power like that? They knocked us back without saying a word. What makes you think that you can go after her?"

"I have to try," Fes said.

"Fezarn, if they come after you the same way, there's no way that you can do anything."

Maybe not, he realized, but there was something else that came to mind.

"If they were able to attack us so easily, these could be exactly the kind of allies that we need."

CHAPTER SIX

When Fes reached the edge of the tree line, he glanced up at the dragon. He had asked the dragon to circle, to keep watch, and to head back toward the empire if they didn't return in a reasonable amount of time. Fes wasn't sure what that would be and hoped that, considering the dragon had been asleep for centuries, he would have some level of patience, but he didn't want to demand that the dragon simply stay circling. Doing so risked exposing him to the Damhur.

The trees were different than what he was accustomed to. There was a shininess to their bark, and streaks of color ran through it, making them shimmer. As he stared at the line of trees, it took him a moment to realize what it was about them that seemed so different.

It was almost as if they were scaled, much the

same as the attackers had been wearing scales. The surface of the bark was moist, and he traced his hand along it, looking for something—anything—that would help him feel more at home. Everything about this land had a similarity to it, but it also felt so strangely alien.

"We could just ask the dragon to keep an eye on us," Arudis said.

"I'm not sure how much he can see through the canopy," Fes said. When they were flying, there were sections of the landscape that had been difficult to see through. Even though the dragon claimed his eyesight was excellent, Fes suspected that he still had limitations. The dragon would never admit it, but as Fes attempted to peer through the forest, he had a hard time thinking that the dragon would be successful in looking through the canopy.

And it would be different than what they experienced in the forest within the empire. The dragons could move through the trees, but the trees here grew a little closer together, and many had vines that wrapped from one to the next, almost as if designed to prevent easy movement. There was no way the dragon would be able to navigate through here quite the same way as it had in the other forest.

They were on their own.

"I'm not leaving her, and while it is dangerous for us

to go into the forest, they could've killed us, but they didn't." That had to matter.

The only thing that he could come up with was the possibility that they viewed him and Arudis as Deshazl serving the Damhur. The fact that they hadn't harmed either himself or Arudis any more than throwing them back in the way that they had made him hopeful that perhaps they could be reasoned with.

Then again, reasoning with them meant they had to first get to them, and with as thick as the forest was, and with these strange trees growing within it, finding their attackers—and Jayell—would be incredibly difficult.

As they stepped into the forest, the air seemed to change. Everything around him took on a strange quality, the shimmering of the tree trunks seeming to catch the light, making the trees themselves appear to move and shift. Fes knew it was only his imagination, but he couldn't shake the impression.

He took another step and was entirely engulfed by the trees.

He glanced back to see Arudis following him, her eyes wide. She looked around, jerking her head from side to side as she trailed after him. "There's something unnatural about this," she said in a soft whisper.

"It's almost as if the forest itself is trying to hide these people."

With the strange flickering of lights, he could almost

imagine that the scales they wore, the clothing they were dressed in, would be difficult to see. The contours of the trees would hide them, but the way they were dressed would hide them just as much.

"We need to stay close together," Fes said.

"This is dangerous," she said to him.

He took Arudis's arm and guided her through the trees, moving carefully. Many of the trees grew quite close together. As he had thought, the vines that wrapped from one tree to the other made it so that he had to duck and twist, contorting himself as he attempted to meander along.

The forest floor was soft and spongy, and it seemed almost as if it wanted to suck at his boots, trying to slow him, forcing each step to be deliberate. After a while, Fes took to grabbing for the vines, using those to keep from stepping completely into the soggy muck of the forest floor. Arudis copied him, moving with more confidence the longer they went, and after a while, she started to suggest different ways that they could take to travel through there.

He paused after they'd been walking for a while. It didn't seem as if they had gone very far. There was no way to walk nearly as fast as they could over open ground. It might be that there was no way to move with any sort of speed. They were forced by the landscape, limited in how quickly they could even move, and though he tried to keep a steady pace, he doubted that they would be able to keep up with their attackers.

"I don't know how you intend to find her in here," Arudis said. "It's too dense. There's no way to see anything."

"We have to keep trying," Fes said.

"And when you continue to be unable to find anything?"

Fes paused and looked around. At what point would they even be able to get back out of the forest? It was possible that they had already traveled too deeply inside to be able to easily navigate back out. Every direction looked the same.

With that realization, he understood that he'd made a mistake. He should have marked their passing better, but he hadn't, and now they would have no way of knowing how to get back out. The only way to figure out where to go from here was to keep pushing, heading through the forest.

Fes grabbed onto a vine and found himself dropped to the ground, a snake slithering across him. He jumped to his feet, kicking the snake out of the way and grunting.

"What was that?" Arudis asked.

"Apparently, the vines and the snakes are no different here," he said.

She started laughing.

"I'm not sure that's funny," he said.

"It's kind of funny," she said.

He glared at her. "Maybe you want to be the one grabbing at the vines from here out."

She continued laughing. "Oh, no. I think you are doing a much better job."

Because of how spongy the ground was, there was no way for him to even determine where they had come from. As trapped as they were, he couldn't tell the passing of time. As far as he knew, it could have been moments or it could have been hours.

Every so often, Fes would glance up at the sky, but the canopy was far too dense to see anything well. The trees blocked the light, and because of that, they prevented any sign of the dragon. He could still feel him, so there was that reassurance, but if they needed help, there might not be anything the dragon could do.

"This was a mistake," he said.

"You're only now realizing that?" Arudis said.

"I think the forest is trying to obfuscate things."

"The forest isn't doing anything. We simply can't tell anything here."

"Because of the forest," he said.

She shook her head. "We could have those people directly in front of us, and we wouldn't know it."

Fes hesitated. That was something he hadn't thought of. They *could* have the attackers right in front of them, and it was possible that they were only staying ahead of them, watching as they struggled to make their way through the forest. They probably were amused by how much difficulty they were having.

"Maybe we need to stop looking for them and wait for them to come to us."

"What makes you think that they even will come to us?"

"They're not going to want us in their forest."

"They're not going to care if they think we can't find our way around here."

"I think they will care. Either they will, or we'll have to make certain that they do."

Fes grabbed onto one of the vines, hanging on it for a moment, swinging in place. He looked around at the trees, thinking that maybe there would be some way to stay here, but if they stayed in place, they would be stuck in the spongy ground.

Whatever else they did, they needed to keep to higher ground, out of the muck.

Could they climb the tree?

He started up the vine, grabbing on it as he pulled himself higher. He grappled, holding along the edge of the trunk, but the moisture of the strange bark seemed to force him back down, and he slipped, sliding back to the ground.

Fes swore under his breath. That wasn't the way to get up the tree, but he wasn't entirely sure what it was going to take. Maybe the vine was the key. He grabbed the vine, pulling himself, trying to use that to leverage himself to reach the top of the tree. As he climbed, he tried to get higher but continued to slip.

Was there no way to reach the top of the trees?

"Be careful, Fezarn," Arudis hollered up at him.

He looked down. It seemed as if he should be much higher than he was, but as he had continued to slip, he was no more than ten feet in the air.

Fes dropped back down to the ground, looking around as he did. His feet squished into the muck, and he pulled his boots free, hating the way that the forest pulled at him.

He glanced up again. If they reached the top of the trees, it was possible that they could climb their way out, but he wasn't that optimistic that it would work. They would need to get the attention of the dragon, and the dragon would need to be willing to fly down to pluck them from the treetops, and if the dragon did that, Fes still didn't know whether they would be able to get free. He might be able to climb to the top of the tree, but would Arudis? They had to get to Jayell. He wasn't going to leave her.

He looked back at the older woman. She wasn't going to be able to make it that way. It meant that he would have to find some other solution, though what would it be?

It meant waiting, as he had intended before.

Fes hung on the vine, swinging from it for a moment as he looked around. There was no sign of anyone else who had moved through the forest, and he worried that even doing this would be a mistake. If there was no way to get the attention of their attackers, how would they find a way free?

"She's lost," Arudis said.

"I refuse to believe that. And if she's lost, then we have lost. The empire has lost."

"We haven't lost."

"They are our help," Fes said.

"Why do you think they will be even willing to help?"

"Someone has to help us oppose the Damhur," he said softly.

He hated the fact that after everything they'd been through, after all that he'd survived, it would come down to the Damhur winning.

Regardless of what he wanted, he wasn't strong enough to stop the Damhur. Certainly not alone. The Damhur had the dragons, and though he had one, the dragon that he had with him wasn't going to be enough, either.

Arudis climbed up into the tree, pulling herself by the vine until she could situate herself next to him. She looked over at Fes and smiled at him sadly. "I know that you want to do more than what has been done, but we have failed. There is no harm in admitting that."

"We can't return without having help."

"I can try to infiltrate Javoor. I know enough about the nation and the people from my time there that I might be able to help free others."

"And even if you free others, what will that accomplish? How much do you think we'll be able to do if we free even a few of the Deshazl?"

"I was just thinking…"

Fes shook his head. "You were right. I made a mistake in coming here, and I should have known better. We didn't know enough. And now the Damhur—"

"What do you know of the Damhur?"

The voice came out of the forest, and it had a strange accent.

Fes looked around, searching for whoever had said it, but couldn't find them.

Could the attackers have returned, or had they been there all along?

He reached for his sword but decided not to unsheathe. Even if he did, in the confines of the forest, a sword wouldn't be of much use. His daggers, on the other hand, would have been incredibly valuable.

"The Damhur invaded my homeland," Fes said. "They are attacking my people, and we came looking for help."

"There is no help when it comes to the Damhur."

"If you fight them, then you know that there is some way of resisting. Please..." Fes started.

He stared into the trees, looking for evidence of whoever had been speaking, and for long moments, nothing changed. Then, slowly, he noticed a shimmering as a person separated from two nearby trees. For a moment, he thought that he had imagined it, but a figure covered in scales from head to toe with only their face showing stepped forward.

"Why are you here?" the person asked.

With the scales covering them, Fes couldn't even tell if it was a man or a woman. They carried two daggers, and it struck him how similar the daggers were to the ones that he had once carried.

Could his parents have been from here?

From what Arudis had told him, his parents had been from Javoor, and they had once been Damhur Deshazl, but the similarity to his own now lost daggers gave him pause.

"I told you why we are here."

"Are you the one who brought the Damhur?"

"I didn't bring any Damhur. The person you took from me is from the empire, not from Damhur."

"What empire?"

"The empire. Across the ocean."

"There is nothing across the ocean."

"There is. There's an entire continent of people, and

it's filled with lives, men and women who want to resist the effect of the Damhur. We've been attacked, and some of us are susceptible to their attack, and as much as we try to resist, we can't all fight the effect of their Calling."

The person stepped closer. Fes watched, waiting for any signs of an attack, but none came. Whoever this person was, and whatever they wanted, they didn't appear afraid.

Then again, what was there for them to be afraid of? It was possible that they had been listening to the conversation between himself and Arudis for some time. Maybe they had heard that they were lost, trapped by the forest itself, and without any way of escaping.

"Are you with the Asharn? We came looking for help from the Asharn, and if that's who you are with—"

"The Asharn will not help you."

"Why?" Fes asked, jumping down to the ground to stand in front of the other person. They were shorter than him, barely coming up to the top of his neck, and had the sweet fragrance of the forest, something they wore almost like a perfume. "The Asharn also attacked my homeland, but I think they did so because they believed that we were helping the Damhur."

"*Have* you been helping the Damhur?"

Fes shook his head. "I've told you that we haven't. I've told you that the Damhur have attacked my people, people that we call the Deshazl, and—"

The person took a step back. "Where did you learn that name?"

"Deshazl?" Fes frowned and glanced over at Arudis. She had been silent, but she was studying this person, her face screwed up into a tight frown as she did. "The Deshazl is their name. Our name. I am Deshazl."

"Where did you hear this?"

"I heard it from those who were once known as Deshazl."

The person pushed back the hood of their dragon-scaled cloak—for that was what it had to be. Long, black hair hung down to the middle of her back.

"Who are you?" she asked.

"I'm Fes. Fezarn."

Her eyes widened.

Could it be that she recognized that name? It had significance to the Deshazl, but why would it be recognized here?

"Please. Help me. We didn't come to attack. And we're not with the Damhur. My friend isn't with the Damhur, either. She is what's known as a fire mage."

"She was wasting the power."

"She wasn't wasting anything. She was using power gifted to our homeland, given by the dragons."

"Wasted."

"I know that some believe that, but I have seen that the dragons willingly sacrificed themselves. They gave themselves up so that the Damhur wouldn't win. There was a war fought over a thousand years ago, and had the dragons not done so, the Damhur would have won."

"The Damhur have won."

"Maybe here, but not in my land. In my land, the Damhur never won. Where I'm from, there are no Damhur." But then, in the empire, there hadn't been any dragons, either.

Fes hadn't put much thought to it, but it seemed as if everyone had lost during the old war. The people of the empire and the Deshazl had lost the wonder of the dragons, and the Damhur had seemingly lost the war.

What had these people lost?

"Who are you?" Fes asked. "Why are you so afraid of the Damhur?"

"The Damhur destroy and control."

"That has been my brief experience with them, too."

"They take. They steal our children. They force them to fight against us. And they destroy everything that we care for. The Damhur are a great terror, a nightmare, and they are the reason that we are here."

"Yes, but where is here?" Fes asked.

"You have come but you don't know where?"

"I came by dragon."

The woman's breath caught, and she made a strange motion across her heart before glancing up at the sky.

"The dragon is up there. You can't see him through the canopy, but he's with me. He won't attack."

"Nothing can attack us here. We are safe."

"Why?"

"This land has been designed to keep us safe."

"Designed?" Fes asked.

Arudis gasped. "That's why," she said.

"That's why what?" Fes asked.

"That's why this all feels strange."

"What is it?" Fes asked.

"All of this. There's something different, but I wasn't able to completely tell what it was. It feels unnatural because it is."

"What you mean?"

"The trees. Look at them. They shimmer, but not for the same reason as I was thinking. I thought that maybe they were alive and that they were simply a different species than what we know, but they remind me of something else, something that took me too long to realize what it was."

"What?" Fes asked.

"Compare it to your sword or your dagger."

The other woman simply stared, watching them.

Fes glanced down at his sheathed weapons, and as he did, he frowned. Could that be the key? Could they be dragonglass? If that's what this was, if the trees were dragonglass of some sort, how? They felt wet, slick, but because they were moist and not because they were like dragonglass.

And the vines had felt alive, enough so that when the snake had appeared, he had believed that they were alive.

Even the ground was soft and spongy, the effect of leaves falling and rotting.

"I don't think that's it," he said to Arudis.

"I can feel it. It's similar."

"Similar, but not the same."

"What are you talking about?" the woman asked.

"Your trees."

"The trees have been placed here to protect us. They defend us against the Damhur. They hide us from others within Javoor. The trees give life."

"What do you mean that they give life?"

"The trees protect us," she said again.

Fes glanced over at Arudis before turning his attention back to the woman. "Where are we?"

"Don't you know?"

Fes shook his head. "Apparently not."

"You are in the Dragonlands. You are in my home."

CHAPTER SEVEN

The woman headed back into the forest and Fes motioned for Arudis to follow after her before she had a chance to fully disappear. Arudis did so, but he could tell that there was a certain reluctance to her, and it was one that he shared. He was a little nervous about going after this woman, especially as it meant going deeper into the forest and considering they didn't entirely know where they were, other than the fact that they were in a place she called the Dragonlands. If they didn't go with her, they would learn nothing, and she was the first living thing that he had found within the forest, other than the snake. If there was anything that they could discover here, any way to find where the rest of the people had gone, he needed to go with her. If he didn't go, then Jayell was truly lost.

The woman glanced back, almost as if she expected them to follow. He kept pace but didn't make nearly as good time. She somehow floated above the detritus, her feet not getting stuck in the muck the same way his did. Every so often, she grabbed onto a vine, swinging from one place to another, and after losing his footing more than once, Fes took to copying her movements. When he did, he found that it was easier to navigate, and while he didn't keep up nearly as well, he was able to walk much faster than he had been. Fes had the sense that she was slowing for his benefit.

He glanced over at Arudis. She struggled to follow him as they climbed over the sections of ground, and as she pulled on the vines to lift herself, she began to grunt more loudly. Fes was reminded that she had been sick when he'd come for her.

"How are you doing?" he asked.

"As well as I can," Arudis said.

"Are you sure?"

She glared at him. "I am not so weak as to need to delay."

"It's understandable if you need us to slow."

"If we slow, then we lose her, Fezarn."

The woman leading them glanced back at the use of his name.

"You recognize it, don't you?" he asked. The woman

hesitated but didn't look back at him. He smiled to himself. "How is it that you recognize my name?"

"How is it that you're named after him?" she finally asked, swinging on a vine for a moment.

"Named after who?"

"Named after him. How is it that you're named after him?"

Fes shook his head. "If you mean how I'm named after a dragon, I don't know. My parents were the ones who gave me my name, as I imagine most people even in your lands are."

She glanced over at him. "That's not what I mean."

"Then what is it that you do mean?"

"You don't know?"

"Apparently not."

"How is it that you don't know? Everyone knows of Fezarn."

Fes glanced over at Arudis. Would she know something about this other Fezarn?

She shook her head.

"Who is this person that I'm supposedly named after?"

"You'll see," the woman said.

They continued to follow, weaving through the forest. Every so often, she would grab the vines, swinging above the ground. Fes continued to do this, and once when he did, he realized that the earth seemed designed to attempt to swallow him, and by swinging, he barely managed to avoid landing in a pool of murky water. The water seemed to shimmer and ripple, almost as if there was something in it, and he was thankful that he had avoided it, uncertain what might be in it—if anything— but was happy to just avoid it.

She was taking a fairly direct route, and though Fes couldn't tell the direction they were heading, he hoped that wherever it was meant that he would find Jayell.

"Is this where you brought her?" he asked after they had traveled for a while.

"We brought who?"

"The woman you think is Damhur."

Her face clouded and she stared for a moment. "The Damhur should not have been here."

"She's not Damhur. I said she's my—"

The woman raised her hand, and Fes cut off. He frowned, waiting for her to say something—*anything*— but she didn't. She stood, motionless, and it took a moment to realize that there was movement around them.

"What is this?" Arudis asked.

Fes shook his head. "I don't know."

"Can you feel it?"

He could, and it seemed to come from everywhere all at once. The sense of movement swirled around him, and at first, Fes thought that maybe he only imagined it, but the movement continued to persist and move faster and faster, swirling around him to the point where he felt himself growing dizzy. He forced himself to look through the sense of movement, to see beyond whatever strangeness was there, and as he did, he realized that they were no longer alone. There had to be five or six others all around them.

Fes stared at them, trying to figure out how many there were, but the scales of their clothing made it difficult to count them.

"I see three," Arudis said.

"I see at least five," he said.

"There are eleven of us," a voice said from his left.

Fes jerked his head around and saw the faint outline of a person standing near one of the trees. It was a deep voice, and the man behind it was tall and solid, and he was dressed much like the others had been, in the strange, scaled clothing.

He stepped forward. His head was clean shaven, including his eyebrows. He had streaks of paint on his face that seemed to blend in with the shimmering colors of his scales. Everything about him was designed to intimidate. Fes noticed that he had a pair of daggers sheathed at his waist, and they again reminded him of what he once had carried.

"Who are you?" Fes asked.

"You've come to the Dragonlands, and you question us?"

"We came looking for help. You were the ones who attacked us."

"We attacked one of the Damhur."

"As I've been telling your friend here, she is not one of the Damhur."

"We know the magic the Damhur wield."

Fes dropped down to the ground, swinging off the vine he'd been holding. He landed in front of the man. Fes was tall and muscular from his days fighting in the streets, but this man had him at a disadvantage. He was at least two inches taller and probably had several stones of weight on him. He was enormous, and the way that he had moved from the trees implied that he had a certain stealthiness.

"I know the magic the Damhur wield, too. Did you feel the effect of the Calling?"

The man frowned. "What is a Calling?"

"If you're familiar with the Damhur, then you would be familiar with a Calling. It's the magic they use to influence those born with specific power."

He was taking a gamble. It was possible that they didn't know about the Calling, and he wouldn't have known had he not been Deshazl. Others who weren't

Deshazl didn't know or feel the effect of the Damhur quite as easily.

"We call it something different, but she is there."

"What did you do to her?"

"We haven't done anything to her, but we have prevented her from influencing us."

Fes laughed bitterly, looking around the trees. He still could only make out six—maybe seven—and not easily. He couldn't tell how the others were hiding, but that was part of the point.

More than ever, he felt confident that he needed to get these people on his side. If he could somehow figure out a way to turn them into his allies, it was possible they might have enough strength to defeat the Damhur.

"You don't have to worry about her influencing you. She cannot Call, or whatever it is you call it."

"She was using the dragon gift," he said.

"So?"

"Only those of the Damhur would use that."

"Many in the empire use it. None of them are Damhur. All of them are fighting the Damhur as they attack on our shores."

"What is this empire?"

"It's what I've been trying to share with your friend. We came here looking for help with the Damhur. They attacked my people, and we need help."

"If they have attacked your people, there is no hope. The Damhur attack and destroy, and then they rule."

"It doesn't have to be that way. If you would help, even if it's just a little, then maybe we could—"

The man started to turn, and Fes grabbed for him.

A strange sound, something like a chirp or a squeal, echoed softly in the forest, and the man spun, his daggers both out.

Fes was forced to take a step back, barely able to react in time. He held his hands up. "I'm not trying to do anything. I'm trying to see if you could help us."

"There is no help when it comes to the Damhur. We must destroy them if they come to us, but we don't chase them."

"Because you're afraid?"

"Fear would be not knowing a reason to worry. We recognize the danger that they pose, and we fear it. It is better that way, better that we don't run the risk of endangering our people."

They continued to depart, and Fes wanted to reach for the man again, but given how quickly he had reacted and how slow Fes felt near him, he wasn't sure that was a good idea.

"What about the dragons?" Fes asked as the man reached one of the trees. He began to blend in, and Fes already could no longer keep track of two of the people that he had seen around them. They were there—he knew that they had to be—but he couldn't see them easily.

"Dragons?"

Fes pointed up to the sky. "You know. Giant creatures that can fly? Filled with power? Dragons." He nodded toward their scaled clothing.

The man turned back toward him and took a step forward. "Where have you seen these creatures?"

"I came on one of these creatures."

"And you are not with the Damhur?"

Fes shook his head.

"How is that possible? There have been stories of the Damhur having controlled two sky beasts."

"Sky beasts? I'm not sure that the dragons would care for you calling them that."

"What would it matter if the sky beasts cared?"

"Because the dragons are our allies. The dragons are meant to work with people like me. Like us." He didn't know whether it was true, but it seemed as if it fit. It seemed as if this man had to be Deshazl, and that that was part of the reason for his movement and speed and the power that he had in the ability to hide in the forest. One of the Deshazl would have that ability, and Fes had hoped that he would be willing to share with Fes how to control it. He had some understanding of his Deshazl ability, but it was not a great understanding, and it was all self-taught. If there were other Deshazl that he could learn from and who could teach him how to master his ability, maybe he would be able to be much more effective with it.

"Is it your pet?" the man asked.

"The dragon chooses whether to help. I had to beg him to bring us here."

"Why?"

"Because the Damhur control two like it. I need the help of others who can resist, and who can help the dragons resist. If you have some way of fighting the Calling, or whatever your name is for it, then we need to know. The dragons need to know."

The man stared up at the treetops. His gaze lingered there for a moment, and Fes began to feel a strange stirring, a slight chill that washed over him. Was that the effect of Deshazl magic that he felt, or was it something else? It was possible that this man—and the others with him—had some other kind of magic.

"You rode this?" the man asked.

Fes stared up at the sky. He couldn't see the dragon, but if everything had gone as planned, the dragon was still there, still circling, and maybe it was enough to help turn the tide in their favor. Perhaps the man would be motivated by the fact that they had a dragon with them to convince him to work with Fes and the others.

"We came with him. He's our friend."

"Friend. So not a pet."

"I've already told you that he is not a pet."

"And I've told you how I find it difficult to believe that a creature like that would allow you to simply travel with him, at least not without a way for you to control him."

"Others might try to control, but I'm not like the Damhur. The Deshazl don't control dragons."

Fes had almost forgotten the way the other woman had reacted when he had used the term *Deshazl*. Much like her, the man froze. He stared at Fes for a long moment before turning and looking at the other woman. She was silent and seemed frozen in place, as if she should have said something to this other man first, but now that he had heard it from Fes, it appeared as if he didn't quite know how to react.

"I know that you recognize that term," Fes said. "I'm not sure how or what it means to you, but I know that it is somehow significant. I am Deshazl. Arudis is Deshazl. We came here looking for help."

Fes was growing exasperated. He knew that he shouldn't be and that letting his frustration get the best of him would not serve any purpose, but he couldn't help himself. These people were willing to attack him, but they didn't seem as if they were willing to help, and right now, all he needed was someone able—and willing —to help.

More than that, he needed to get to Jayell.

"Please. Where is she? Where is my friend?"

The man studied him for a moment. "Come with me."

"Chornan—"

Chornan raised his hand, silencing whoever had thought to question him. Fes couldn't tell, and with the trees around, he now could only see two others. The rest had retreated, hiding, and had disappeared into the forest entirely.

"You will come with me."

Chornan guided them through the forest. Fes looked around, searching for the woman who had led them this far, but she was gone.

Where had she disappeared to?

"They are very distrusting," Arudis said.

"Can you blame them?" Fes asked.

"This is not the Asharn," she said.

"It's not the Asharn, but I wonder if this is something better."

"I don't know. They are strange and seem very... different."

"Different or not, they are all we have."

Fes hurried and caught up to Chornan, and as they made their way through the trees, he glanced over at him. "We came here looking for the Asharn."

"We are not the Asharn."

"But you know of them."

Chornan glanced over. The corners of his eyes twitched. "We are not the Asharn."

"Why do you dislike them?"

"Come with us. That is all."

The ground became more accessible to walk through, and it seemed as if the trees tugged at them less and less, and the vines were fewer, not pulling at him quite as frequently as they had been before, and Fes had an easier time keeping up with Chornan. He saw occasional glimpses of others in the trees, but not so often that he was able to tell where they were.

How far had they brought Jayell into the forest?

And what would she have done?

He imagined that she was continuing to try to fight, but even when they were out on the plains outside the forest, she had said that her magic hadn't worked as it should have. Somehow they were able to suppress that magic. Fes had a similar effect on fire mages, but it required that he focus, and he didn't think that he would be able to shut Jayell down entirely, not all by himself.

Whatever they were doing to her was much more impressive than what he could do. Would they be able to teach him to do the same? And if they could, was there any way that they could use that magic against the Damhur?

"Do you have a way of resisting the Calling?"

"No questions until we reach our destination."

"Where is the destination?"

"You are going to Thoras."

"And who is Thoras?"

"It is a place and not a person."

"Your city? That's where you're bringing me?" If that's where they were bringing him, then at least he had a hope of finding Jayell.

"Fes," Arudis whispered, grabbing his arm. "This has me troubled."

"All of this has me troubled, too."

"It's different. They aren't the Asharn, though they seem to share a similar connection."

"I noticed that."

"And they don't care for the Damhur."

"What's your point?"

"They recognize the term Deshazl, but they haven't shared with us why—or what it means to them." She glanced at Chornan before turning her attention back to Fes. "What if these people fought the Deshazl?"

"The Damhur fought the Deshazl."

"They do now, but at the time, back when the Deshazl lived in the north, they had no known enemies, at least not really. What if that wasn't the case? What if these people were their enemies?"

"I don't know. All I know is that they have considerable power."

"And I know that you want to use that considerable power, but it's dangerous, especially without knowing anything more about them."

"Which is why we're here."

"We are here because you wanted to find the Asharn. We aren't going anywhere near the Asharn."

"Because you didn't know how to find them."

"The Asharn are found throughout Javoor. I told you that."

Fes shot her a stern look. "This is more than your illness. Something else is off for you. What is it?"

"It's here. This place. Everything about it is odd. I don't care for it."

"We don't have to care for it. We just have to find others who have a common enemy, and from what I can tell, we have."

"And I'm not sure that this common enemy is right for us."

"I'm not sure that we have much choice in the matter," Fes said.

"Fes—"

Arudis didn't have a chance to answer. They reached a place where the trees thinned before stopping altogether, forming a clearing. Fes stood at the edge of the trees, frozen. It was a huge opening, and from here, the forest ended, leading into a massive valley that swept down below. Within the entirety of the valley stretched an enormous city. The buildings were all made with the same scaled, shimmering colors that he saw covering the people who had guided him here, and most of the buildings shimmered when he turned his head from one side to another. A sense of heat radiated from everything.

"Oh," Arudis whispered.

"This is Thoras?" Fes asked Chornan.

"This is our home," he said.

Fes glanced over at Arudis. She shook her head. "We didn't know anything like this was here."

"It's on the other side of the impossible-to-cross valley," Fes said. "I'm not sure that even the Damhur would have been able to reach this."

"Before," Arudis said. She flicked her gaze up to the sky. Fes followed the direction of her gaze and saw the dragon still flying, circling ever closer. Did the dragon know that they were here?

As he focused on the dragon, he could practically feel power emanating from him. It seemed to be pressed down toward him, as if the dragon wanted Fes to know that he was there, and that Fes could use his power if needed.

Something was reassuring about that knowledge.

Even more reassuring was the fact that the dragon made clear that he knew where they were. If it came down to it, if there came the need, would the dragon be able to reach them in time?

Fes looked around and saw the eleven others who Chornan claimed were there. They stood at the edge of the forest, still blending in with the trees, making it difficult to easily be seen. They hid with impressive skill, even standing out in the open.

"Are they going to come with us?" Fes asked Chornan.

"They will stay and patrol."

"That's how you found us?"

"We could feel the magic used by the Damhur."

"And I've told you that it's not—"

"I understand what you have told us. And I tell you what we know. That magic that we detected is what we know of from the Damhur."

Fes took a deep breath. He kept his gaze focused on the distant city. Somewhere in there, he would find Jayell, and somewhere in there he would need to get her free. If they didn't guide him to her, there might not be any way to know where she was.

Unless she used her fire mage magic.

Could he pick up on that?

Fes closed his eyes for a moment, focusing. If Jayell knew that he was trying to track her, maybe she would be using it. Then again, maybe these people had told her not to, and given the fact that they knew how to detect what she was doing, they might be well aware of her using magic and instructing her to stop.

There was no sense of fire mage magic.

Wherever Jayell was, it was not someplace where he could detect her.

"Where is my friend?" he asked Chornan.

"She is where we bring all of the Damhur."

"And where is that?"

"To the Dragon's Eye."

Fes glanced at Arudis. Somehow, he didn't like the sound of that.

CHAPTER EIGHT

F es followed Chornan, making his way quickly along the outskirts of the city. It was almost as if Chornan didn't want to lead him into the city itself, as if to keep Fes and Arudis away from the inhabitants of Thoras. They skirted around the city itself, moving slowly, carefully, but making certain to avoid anyone who might be out. They came close enough to the buildings that Fes had a chance to see some of the structures, and he marveled at the strange design. The way that the buildings were made, the scaled structures seemed to grow out of the ground, but he couldn't see how that would be possible. As he walked past, colors shimmered, and some of the buildings appeared even more impressive than they had at first blush.

"How do you think they make these?" he asked Arudis.

Arudis every so often would look over at the buildings, and she stared at them, watching them, almost as if trying to answer that question as well. "I'm not certain," she said.

"Have you seen anything like it before?"

"Even in Javoor, there is nothing like this."

Chornan glanced back at her. "You know Javoor?"

Fes wasn't sure if she was going to answer, but she nodded. "I know Javoor. I was born and raised there."

"But you are not Damhur."

"I'm not Damhur, but I was raised by the Damhur. They used their Calling, and controlled me and others like me."

"You were a slave?"

"Not anymore," Arudis said.

It was the most agitation that Fes had seen from Arudis since coming to this place, and she practically spat it, angry at the mere assumption that she might be still a slave. He needed that Arudis. He needed the woman who would stand firm and who would object to the idea of becoming a slave. He needed the strong woman who would help them escape, and would help them reach Jayell to do so. When still in the empire, he had seen that side of her, but since coming back for her, that woman had been missing.

She wasn't sharing something with him, and maybe it was only her sickness, the weakness that had claimed her that made it so that she wasn't able to be nearly as strong as she usually was, but he didn't think that was entirely it.

They continued to make their way along the outside of the city. Every so often, Fes would glance back and see the forest shimmering in the distance. He remained curious about the forest, curious about the nature of the trees within it, and doubted that he would even be able to make his way back through it were it necessary. As a barrier, as a means of protecting the people of this land, it would be incredibly effective.

A shadow drifted across the ground, and Fes glanced up to see the dragon still circling. The dragon stayed high overhead but close enough that Fes could make him out.

"He still follows us," he said to Arudis.

"I see that, but what happens when they begin to notice?" she asked, nodding to Chornan.

"I don't know how they couldn't notice."

Chornan glanced over at him, studying him for a moment. As he did, he tapped on his chest with a steady rhythm for a few moments before halting. "We have seen this creature since you first came to the lands."

"And?"

Chornan turned his gaze to the sky. Fes was taken aback by the heat within his gaze. "And we know enough to fear it."

"You know enough to fear it, but you still didn't try to hurt us."

Chornan frowned at him.

"If you'd wanted to hurt us, you could have done so. You simply knocked us back so that you could grab my friend."

"We have no reason to hurt the slaves of the Damhur."

"Is it because you know they are Deshazl?"

He used the word intentionally this time, wanting to try to draw out Chornan, to see if there was anything that he could do that might get answers, but Chornan didn't take the bait. Instead he merely watched Fes, staring at him with his heated gaze.

Fes smiled to himself when Chornan turned away.

"I'm not sure that you should be doing that," Arudis said.

"Doing what?"

"What you're doing. I'm not sure that you should be attempting to anger them."

"I'm not trying to anger them at all. All I'm trying to do is see if there is anything more they know—and will tell us."

"Why?"

"You've seen the reaction they have when we mention the Deshazl. Whatever it is matters to them. For some reason, they know the Deshazl, but they hesitate when it comes to explaining what it is that they know."

"What if they don't care for the Deshazl?"

"If that's the answer, then we have to deal with it."

"Deal with it. After you've already told them that we are Deshazl?"

"If they wanted to hurt us, they would've done so when they first had the chance. They knocked us out, nothing more than that, and they have brought us here. Whatever else they might be doing, it's not coming from a desire to harm us."

He hoped that he was right, but he wasn't entirely sure that he was. What if they did want to harm them? What if bringing them to this Dragon's Eye was their way of somehow trying to torment them?

They needed to be careful, but Fes wasn't entirely sure about what.

The city was enormous, and as they made their way around it, passing similar buildings, all of them built with a nearly identical design, the same scaled features that shimmered as they walked, he marveled at the sheer size of this place. How many people lived here?

"Fezarn," Arudis said.

Fes glanced over. "What is it?"

"Have you noticed anything?"

"Such as the strangeness of this city?"

"No. Such as the *emptiness* of the city."

Fes frowned and, as he did, he looked around, staring at the buildings before realizing that what she said was true. There was a certain emptiness to this place that didn't fit with the size and scope of it. Could all of the people who lived here be gone? Could something have happened?

Or maybe there was a more straightforward answer. Perhaps they hid.

"Where are your people, Chornan?"

"You have seen my people," Chornan said.

"How many live here?"

Chornan glanced over his shoulder at him. "Here?"

"Yes. How many people live here?"

"It was once the home to a great number of people, but much has changed over the years. Our experience with the Damhur has changed us."

"How has it changed you?"

"The Damhur tried to destroy us. They continue to try."

"What do you mean that they continue to try? I thought they couldn't reach you here?"

"They can't reach us here, but that doesn't mean that they don't want to try. We have done everything that we can to separate ourselves from them and have as many barriers as possible, but the ability that we have to do so has begun to wane."

"Why?" Fes asked.

"There are only so many things that can be done, and now that the Damhur have gained the power of the sky beasts, they have become even more unstoppable. We will continue to fight, but if they can travel to our lands..."

As they swept around the outer edge of the city, they reached a trail that led deeper into the valley. Chornan took this trail, guiding them along it. As they went, they saw no sign of anyone else. It was possible that there were hundreds upon hundreds of people within the city, and possible that they all blended into the buildings, the same way that the people had blended into the forest, but Fes began to wonder if that were the case at all. Maybe there was no one here.

If not, where had they gone? There had to have been an enormous population once. If Chornan spoke the truth, and if there were no people still here, at least not in the numbers that the size of the city would suggest, Thoras once had held a massive population. Could the battle with the Damhur have decimated this place?

If it had, it was even more reason to fear what they might do to the empire.

"Is Javoor like this?" he asked Arudis.

"Javoor is a very regimented land," she said. "The Trivent leads in Javoor, and the Damhur require service from the Deshazl they Call, forcing them to become soldiers. They use them to ensure compliance of all citizens within Javoor."

"Compliance?"

"There is no questioning the Trivent. Any attempt to do so would lead to punishment."

"What kind of punishment?"

"Most of the time, pushing the Trivent leads to death."

Fes frowned. "Even the empire isn't nearly so strict."

"No. The emperor has shown a different sort of rule. He is not necessarily benevolent, but he certainly does not lead angrily, not the same way as in Javoor."

The path led them away from the city. Every so often, Fes would glance back, and the homes would grow more distant. They walked deeper into a valley formed by two massive hills that came to a lower point. They wound along the road, and Chornan didn't speak. Grasses grew on either side, though they had wide and broad leaves, nothing like the grasses in the empire. Occasional flowers dotted the ground, lending a fragrance to the air. There were no trees.

The road curved around, and as it did, Fes' breath caught. A mountain loomed in the distance, but it was what sat in front of it that caught his attention.

There was a massive lake. It seemed to glow, almost as if it were filled with molten lava, but no steam rose off it. A row of simple buildings sat in front of it, all constructed in a more traditional manner, and nothing like those of the city they had left behind. They were homes that would have fit within the empire, but there were not that many.

It was a village, and no different than what he would find in the empire. Given the size of the village, there couldn't be more than several hundred people who lived here.

"This is it?" he asked Chornan.

"This is our place," he said.

"And the Dragon's Eye?"

Chornan pointed to the pond in the distance. "That is the Dragon's Eye."

They reached the edge of the water, still set apart from the rest of the village. Fes looked down and realized that the glowing seemed to come from deep within the water. It was almost as if there was something there. He could imagine how it would look like a Dragon's Eye from above, as if the water burned with the fire of the dragons.

Fes glanced up at the dragon soaring overhead. What must it look like from his vantage?

He wished there was some way to signal the dragon that he could land, but Fes still wasn't certain that it was safe to do so. He wasn't sure what Chornan and his people would do, other than to know that they seemed to have no interest in harming him.

That had to matter. It certainly mattered to Fes, especially as he felt so out of place, but if Chornan were going to harm him, he would have done so before now. The fact that he had guided him here made Fes think that perhaps they wanted something from him.

"Why did you bring us here?"

"You came to us," Chornan said.

Fes glanced over at Arudis. "We came to you, but there's something that you are after. Why?"

"You wanted to know about your friend?"

"I did."

Fes searched for any sensation of fire magic being used, and now that they were here, at the edge of the water, away from the city, he thought that maybe they would be able to pick up on something, but there still wasn't anything. Then again, he still didn't think that Jayell would attempt to use her magic, not when surrounded by people who were so capable.

"Is this your home?"

"I've shown you our home."

"You showed me an empty city."

"It's not entirely empty. This place is where we bring the Damhur."

"You bring the Damhur out here?"

He couldn't shake the confusion he felt. He had assumed that they would destroy the Damhur, but if they brought them here, why?

"We bring them where they can do no harm. We bring them where the land holds them. There is nothing that they will be able to do to hurt our people."

"You don't kill them?"

"If we wanted to kill them, we would have done so, but we prefer a different path for them."

"And that path is here? Why this place? What's so significant about the Dragon's Eye?"

"The significance is that there is power within this place that controls them. It prevents them from reaching whatever it is they would reach."

Fes glanced at Arudis before turning his attention to the water. For the first time, he wished that he had fire mage magic and that he would be able to know what it was that Jayell might feel, but there was nothing. There had to be some way for him to understand what they were talking about, but he could pick up on nothing at all. There was no sense of fire magic being used around him, but he attributed that more to the people somehow restricting that usage, not from the place itself.

What if it was this place? What if there was some way to prevent fire magic from getting used? If there was, the Damhur might be restricted—but so too would the empire and their fire mages.

"Does this place keep the Damhur from using their Calling?" Fes asked.

"This place, the Dragon's Eye, does not allow the Damhur to control us. We will not be slaves."

"How?" Arudis asked.

"How what?"

"How does it work?"

"There is power here. We have been blessed by the Great One," he said. He glanced up, and Fes followed the direction of his gaze but saw nothing. Somewhere up there, the dragon still circled, but he was high enough that Fes couldn't see him well. The only thing he saw was the sun shining, but even that was obscured by banks of clouds.

Could these people worship the sun?

It seemed odd, but no stranger than some of the people of the empire worshiping the dragons.

"The Great One?"

Chornan nodded.

Arudis stepped toward the water, staring down in it. "I can see why they call it the Dragon's Eye," she whispered. "There is something here. I can feel it. It seems to be calling to me."

"Arudis?"

"I've struggled for so long, Fezarn." She didn't look up. She clasped her hands in front of her, standing at the edge of the water. Her eyes were wrinkled as she did, and it seemed as if she came to a decision as she stood there, almost as if she had struggled with some great decision for a long time. "I've fought, and have done my best, but when they returned..."

"What are you talking about?"

"The effect of the Calling," she whispered. She glanced

over at him. "I got away from it. For so many years, I managed to escape from it. When the Damhur returned, I started to feel the pulling. I forgot how hard it was, and how painful it was to resist, and though I am strong, I could feel my strength waning. There will come a time when I won't be able to resist, and I refuse to go back to the Damhur."

"You don't have to go back," he said. "We will protect you."

"There is only so much that can be done to protect me. Before you, there were no others who could resist the Calling. It was only me. And I was responsible for protecting as many of the Deshazl as I could, which was part of the reason I had not searched for others. How could I when I could barely protect and defend myself?"

"What are you saying, Arudis?"

"They will continue to come. The Damhur continue to push, and now that they have acquired the dragons, there is nothing that we will be able to do to withstand them. When they push, spreading across the empire, the last place of safety will be gone. And then... And then they will Call again. It may not be Elsanelle; it might be another. But eventually, someone with power will come, and when they do, I have little doubt that I will have the ability to resist for long."

"We will stay safe," Fes said. Was this what had been bothering her? He couldn't believe that she would be so troubled by it. She had always seemed to be the one with strength, and she was the reason that he believed that there was a way to resist the Calling, but if Arudis no longer believed, what did it mean for the rest of the Deshazl? Would everyone begin to suffer and fall?

Without Arudis to protect them, it was possible that they would. She was the reason that they had been safe. And without her, if she fell, there would be no good way of ensuring their safety. Fes was limited in what he could do.

Chornan stepped up next to her and rested a hand on her arm. "You were from Javoor," he said.

She nodded slowly. "I've already told you that I was in Javoor," she said.

"You still struggle with it?" he said.

"How can I not?" she asked.

"There is something that you could do," he said.

She looked up at him. "What?"

With that, he pushed.

Arudis staggered forward and splashed into the water. She stayed there for a long moment, continuing to kick at the water, and Fes raced to the edge, reaching for her, but Chornan grabbed his arm, pulling him back.

"What did you do?" Fes hollered at him, trying to throw the other man off. Chornan was too large and too strong to just shrug off.

"What needed to be done."

"I don't understand." Fes stood at the edge of the water, looking helplessly down at Arudis. She didn't attempt to move and only lay in the water, floating. She floated higher in the water than he would've expected her to, as if the water itself had some strange buoyancy that propelled her upward. She splashed at it, but nothing more than that.

"And you will not. She was given something necessary," he said.

"I don't understand. What did you do to her?" He turned away from Arudis and to Chornan. He felt helpless, but he didn't think that he would be able to overpower Chornan, and if he couldn't reach Arudis, there would be no way to pull her free from the water.

"The water can heal."

"What do you mean?"

"Some of our people have suffered under the Damhur. The water, and the Dragon's Eye, will help cleanse that touch from her."

"What do you mean *cleanse that touch?*"

"Those who have fallen to the effect of the Damhur suffer a residual effect. It prevents them from reaching everything that they could be."

"I've suffered under the Damhur. I managed to escape, but they Called me and—"

Fes barely had a chance to react when Chornan grabbed him and shoved him into the water after Arudis.

He had a moment to realize that he was floundering, flailing as he was thrown, and went splashing into the water before he spun around, looking up at Chornan. The water was warm, almost unpleasantly so, and he flailed, trying to swim to shore, but it felt as if he were stuck in something thicker than water.

"Arudis," he hollered. Arudis ignored him, focused on the water rather than on him. "Arudis. We need to get out of the water."

She turned to look at him. Her eyes were glassy, and she wore a blank expression. What had happened to her? Would the same thing happen to him?

"Chornan. Please. Don't do this," he said.

He looked up, but Chornan had already begun to back away from the shore. He watched Fes and Arudis, and as he did, Fes realized that he was starting to sink, as if the water were starting to suck him down. He stared up at Chornan, waiting for the other man to offer a hand, but it never came.

They would drown.

The water was unpleasantly warm, and he was pulled under, much more rapidly then Arudis was. He looked over at her, trying to figure out some way of getting free. He couldn't kick, not with enough strength to get free. The density to the water was too much, as if he were trying to swim through syrup. And then he sunk to his neck.

That was when panic set in.

Fes could swim and had never feared water before, but this was something else entirely. This wasn't merely attempting to swim, this was trying to fight for his life in a place where it was drawing him down, deeper and deeper, to the point where he didn't think that he would be able to get free.

Why would they have done this to him?

He sunk to his chin.

As it reached his chin, Fes tried harder. He focused on his Deshazl connection, panicking as he tried to reach for that magic, pushing it out from him, thinking that if he could focus it and hold his magic, maybe he would be able to find a way to get free. In his panicked state, the Deshazl magic didn't come to him quite as well as it should.

He tried to focus, settling himself for a moment, long enough that he could allow the Deshazl magic to come to him. He was able to grab onto it, but only for a moment, barely long enough to do anything with.

He pushed out with that Deshazl connection, straining, trying to use it to propel himself upward, but it wasn't enough. *He* wasn't enough.

He glanced over at Arudis. Only his eyes were above the water, leaving his mouth and nose now below it. It had a strange smell to it, and he didn't dare open his mouth, not daring to expose himself to the full effect. It didn't seem fair that he should sink faster than Arudis, but then, he was larger than her.

When he sank entirely below the surface of the water, Fes gave one last look around him, searching for some way to escape, but there was none.

There would be no help.

CHAPTER NINE

F es floated below the surface of the water. He was
drowning and was doing so in water so dense that
he could not even move. He waited for the moment when
he could no longer hold his breath, knowing that there
was nothing that he could do to fight.

This would be the way that he died.

It felt anticlimactic, especially after everything that he
had been through. He had survived so much, and had
managed to escape from threats that were much greater
than this, so to suffer and die in this way left him feeling
hollow, as if he were cheated of something that he was
meant to have.

Thoughts raced through his mind, memories of
everything that he'd been through over the years, starting
with his parents' demise. Fes had struggled with their

loss, and still did, though he had come to terms with the fact that they had escaped from a greater horror, and had done so in a way that they had hoped to find safety for him and his brother. How could they have known that his brother would have fallen, too? Fes had done his best to protect his brother when they first had reached Anuhr, but there was only so much that he was able to do.

The loss of his brother had driven him. Safety had meant gaining skills, mastering himself, reaching a point where he would never suffer again. It had meant that he had taken on increasingly difficult jobs. If he hadn't, there would have been no way to have escaped the poverty that came with being an orphan in a strange city. And if he hadn't, he would never have come to the attention of Azithan, and without Azithan, Fes might never have realized that he was Deshazl.

That power burned within him. It was the same power the dragons had, only the Deshazl had a different attachment to it. And without learning of the Deshazl, and without doing what he had, the dragons would never have been restored.

That had been valuable. Fes felt a certain pride in the fact that had he not been there, the dragons would never have managed to have returned. Because of him, the dragons had been allowed to return, which meant that some good had come.

With his death, would the dragons' last hope fail?

He didn't know and didn't think that his loss would be the reason that the dragons failed, but he might be their last hope.

And now he wasn't.

There would be others. There would have to be others.

It just wouldn't be him.

Everything that he'd gone through had led him to this point, and it seemed a cruel fate. When he had taken the job that had led him out of the city, after the dragon heart, he had no idea of what would befall him, and during that journey, he had hoped that perhaps he might find some connection with Alison once more, only to have been betrayed by her.

Fes couldn't even be angry. He understood why she had done what she had, thinking that it was necessary for the rebellion to have the resources they needed to defeat the empire, but the rebellion had been mistaken, and because of their decisions, the Damhur had gained a foothold.

Why did he think about these things?

How much longer did he have? He was dying, and all he had to do was wait for his last gasp, and then he would die completely.

Maybe in his last moments, time stretched out.

All of these thoughts came to him, filling his mind,

racing through him. He was not ready for death, but did he fear it?

Fes hadn't given it much thought. He had always been skilled, reasonably powerful, and he had been able to use that skill to help him defeat countless enemies. Without it, he would have fallen long ago.

Fes thought about how he had reached the dragon and the strange connection that he shared with it. He was thankful for that.

Perhaps there would have been more time for them to have a more significant connection, and if there had, maybe Fes would have been able to do more, but even the brief connection had been something. Without him, the great dragon, possibly a dragon elder, would never have returned.

It was time. He was ready.

Fes felt the warmth of the water all around him. Something was soothing about it. How had he ever felt that it was unpleasantly warm?

If this was the way they tormented everyone from the Damhur, he thought that there were worse ways to go. Dying in this manner allowed him the opportunity to reflect, and with that time, and that reflection, he felt more at peace than he had in a long time.

Fes opened his mouth. Water filled it. It was a combination of bitter and sweet, reminding him of tears.

It was a strange thought, but then again, every thought he might have would be strange in this place and during this time. For the first time, he wondered what it would be like after he died. Would there be something more? The dragons had talked about sleeping and then awakening once more, but then again, they were dragons. They had poured their essence, the entirety of their magic, into the dragon sculptures, and those sculptures had allowed them to be preserved. He wished that he would've had time to find more of the sculptures, but without them, there was no way for anyone to restore more of them.

If there was no sleep for him, would there only be nothingness? Would it be emptiness, a void, or... Could this be death?

Maybe he already had died, and the fact that he drifted, his mind wandering like this, racing with a hundred different thoughts, was how he managed to find the afterlife.

If this was what it was, Fes wondered if there would be an eternity like this. Would he be stuck with these thoughts, always trying to know what was next, or would he eventually move on to different thoughts? Maybe he would join a greater consciousness, combine with it, allowing him to live with and merge with something more.

He should have taken more time with the priests. Jayell would appreciate that realization.

Jayell.

Her name drifted into his mind, and he felt a sense of unfinished business. There had been something between him and Jayell that should have become something more, but now... Now there would be nothing. And he had failed her. He was the reason that she was captured, believed to be Damhur, by merely using her fire magic.

That bothered him more than anything else.

Fes hated to be the reason that others suffered, and he wished that he could have done more for her, but he had to hope that Chornan wasn't lying when he said that the Damhur were allowed to live here along the shores of the Dragon's Eye. Maybe Jayell would be safe while the others within the empire would suffer. That didn't make him feel any better, but the idea of her safety did. He didn't want any harm to befall Jayell. She deserved more —much more.

The water worked its way down his throat, settling into his stomach.

As it did, he felt a strangeness. The warmth began to spread throughout his body in a way that it hadn't before. Before it had seeped through the pores of his skin, soaking him, and he had felt the warmth, but now he felt it from within, pushing outward.

Fes marveled at the warmth. It was a heat that worked through him. Heat continued to flow through him, working through his stomach and spreading outward from there. For some reason, he focused on that rather than on the fact that he was dying.

As it spread, he noticed something else. His connection to his Deshazl magic changed.

He couldn't describe what it was, only that it seemed almost as if it were unmasked, as if he could reach it, and it exploded within him.

Fes had thought that he had a strong connection to the Deshazl magic before, but this was even more powerful. This washed over him, slamming through him, leaving him gasping. With the gasp, even more of the strange water flowed into his mouth and lungs, filling him.

What was happening?

Fes reached for his Deshazl connection, trying to use it to pull himself out of the water, but his magic didn't work like that. Maybe if he was a fire mage, and perhaps if he had some way of using a spell, he might be able to he might be able to free himself, but that wasn't the nature of his magic.

He wrapped himself in it.

Fes had learned that there was a way to create a barrier using his magic, and with that barrier, he had to hope and believe that maybe he could hold himself safe, but how? Would that magic allow him to protect himself? He didn't know if it was strong enough to do so in that way, or if there was anything else that he could use it for.

Wrapping himself in that power, a warmth filled him that seemed to be much like the water. Were they connected?

Fes held onto his Deshazl connection.

Was there any way that he could use this, that he could hold onto it, and that he could pull, drawing this magic through him?

Maybe that wasn't the key. Perhaps it wasn't that he needed to use the Deshazl connection to wrap around him, but that he could use this Deshazl connection to get out of the pool differently.

Fes focused on the dragon.

He was up there, he knew that. Even if he couldn't see the dragon, Fes thought that he could *feel* the dragon flying overhead. Somehow he needed to reach him, and if that meant that he would reach through the connection forged by the Deshazl, he would do so.

Would the Deshazl magic allow him to reach the dragon from here?

He didn't know why it wouldn't.

Fes focused, imagining the dragon and remembering the connection that he had formed with him when he had helped him rise.

Power surged away from him.

Fes was aware of the way the power surged, feeling the way it swept out, shooting out from his body, seeming to come from deep within his core.

When it reached the dragon, a connection formed.

He was aware of the dragon and could practically see the ground through his eyes, as if he could share that connection, as if the two of them were merged into one.

Help me.

Would the dragon even know what he needed?

Fes had to believe that he would. He had to believe that the Deshazl connection, that magic that burned within him, the shared link between himself and the dragon, would allow the dragon to recognize what he needed.

Help me.

He focused, holding onto his Deshazl connection, worried that maybe there would be nothing. Could the dragon recognize what he needed? Could the dragon even do anything?

For the longest moments, nothing happened. Nothing changed.

And then Fes felt pressure around him.

It took a moment to realize that that pressure represented the dragon reaching into the water and grabbing him with massive talons.

The warmth still flowed through him, and as it did, as Fes felt that warmth, he embraced it. He welcomed that warmth, letting it continue to flow through him, letting it fill him, and he could feel the powerful Deshazl connection, and it was that connection that tied him to the dragon. They were bonded, though Fes wasn't entirely certain what that meant. The bond connected them, allowing him to know that the dragon was there, dragging him free from the water, and practically granted him the understanding of what the dragon was thinking, though Fes wasn't sure if that was real or imagined.

It had to be real, didn't it?

He was pulled, moving slowly, dragged out of the water. At first it was only his eyes. And then more came free, and then more, and as it did, Fes was able to see the area around him. Darkness had fallen, and he wondered how that was possible. The sun had been out when he had begun to sink into the water, but now with it dark, hours had to have passed, when in his mind it had felt like moments. How had he survived?

More of him came free, and he looked around, realizing that Arudis was not near him as she had been. Could she have sunk all the way, or had she been freed?

How would she have been freed? The dragon would have needed to pull her out of the water, and he wasn't sure that the dragon would've known, or that Arudis would've had that same connection to the dragon.

His face was entirely freed from the water. He spit out the water from his mouth and coughed, freeing the rest of it. The cough tore through him, and he practically threw up an enormous amount of water until he stopped coughing. It came slowly, leaving him weakened, and then his chest came free.

Fes glanced up at the dragon. He was beating his wings furiously, pounding at the sky, trying to get Fes free, and he could see the effort that it took for the dragon to yank him clean out of the water.

Did the dragon know what had happened to him? Did the dragon know that he had nearly drowned? Or was the connection that he felt to the dragon shared?

His chest came free.

Fes took a gasping breath. He could breathe more easily, and he looked around, overwhelmed by the fact that he had managed to get free.

His waist came free. Then his legs.

Fes was completely out of the water.

The dragon continued to fly, lifting him higher and higher. Fes looked down, and he could see the reflection off the water. Whereas before he thought the water caught the sunlight, glowing with that, now he could see that it seemed to glow with its own internal light. It was a deep orange, almost a red, and it moved, practically shimmering, carrying with it a sense of power.

The Dragon's Eye.

From up above, Fes could see how it looked like a Dragon's Eye. It was almost as if it were looking up at them, staring at them much like this dragon would look at him, and the reflection from the Dragon's Eye caught Fes and the dragon.

"Where are you taking me?" Fes asked.

"Out," the dragon rumbled.

"I need to find the others."

"Are you safe?"

"I... I don't think that I was intended to die there."

"You would not have died. You are protected."

"What is that place?"

"It is a connection to our shared powers."

"How?"

"It is greater than either of us. There is something to it, but it is not anything that I understand," the dragon said.

"Can you take me down toward the buildings?"

The dragon rumbled and shot a streamer of steam out his nostrils, but he circled around, carrying Fes away from the water and over toward the shore. As they descended, Fes felt as if people were watching him, though he couldn't see them.

It was possible that they were camouflaged much as the attackers had been camouflaged in the forest. Maybe they blended in with the buildings, or perhaps they had some other way of concealing themselves. Either way, he had to be prepared for the possibility that there would be more than just Chornan.

And if there was, would it matter? Was there anything that he could even do?

They landed on the ground. The dragon released him before he landed, allowing Fes to stagger away rather than getting crushed, and he hurried toward the buildings. The dragon sat with his wings propped on the ground, heat radiating from his enormous body. His scales glimmered in the fading light, and Fes smiled to himself. A dragon like that would cast an imposing figure, enough that the people who had attacked them might give a moment's pause. Then again, had they really attacked them? They might have forced him into the water, but the water hadn't killed him. He would have died had he truly been underwater, but whatever he had sunk into had been something else, and though it had swallowed him, it had not killed him.

Which meant that there was something else going on.

Fes reached the outskirts of the village, where he was greeted by Chornan and two others. They were wearing their strange scaled armor, and they stared at him before their gaze flickered past him to look at the dragon.

"What was that?" Fes asked.

"That was a test," Chornan said.

"A test? That's the reason that you pushed me into the water?"

"You claimed that the Damhur had controlled you. It was meant as a way to cleanse you."

Fes focused on his Deshazl connection. It was greater than it had been before, but he didn't know whether that was merely because he had been forced to use it, or was it because his time in that strange pool of water, in the Dragon's Eye, had somehow unlocked something within him?

"What did you do?"

"We did nothing. The Dragon's Eye recognizes the taint, and for those who are worthy, they are cleansed of the Damhur touch."

"Worthy?"

"Not all will survive the test."

Fes flicked his gaze over to the Dragon's Eye. From here, the orange continued to glow, giving a burning to the night. Would it be like that throughout the night? Even in the darkness, would the light continue to glow with a steady intensity?

"What happened to Arudis?"

"The woman who came with you survived."

He breathed out heavily. "She survived. Where is she?"

"She is recovering. Most who experience the Dragon's Eye need time to recover from its effects."

"Most? Not all?"

"Not all survive, as I said."

"How do they get out?"

"The Dragon's Eye expels them," Chornan said.

Fes frowned. "The Dragon's Eye didn't expel me. The dragon pulled me free."

"So it appears."

"Why?"

"Why what?"

"Why does it appear that you aren't excited about the fact that I managed to get free?" Fes glanced at the two others with Chornan. Both were nearly as large and had the same square set to their jaw and the same hidden muscles beneath their strange armor. Fes suspected that in a fight, they would be incredibly difficult to defeat. Not that he wanted to fight them. He doubted that he would be able to defeat Chornan one on one, especially not with the power he suspected Chornan possessed.

"When you sunk beneath the water, we believed that you were gone. You had failed the testing."

"That's it? When you sink beneath the water, you fail?"

"None have ever returned after sinking beneath the surface of the water."

"None?"

"That is the test."

"What if your test is flawed?"

"The Dragon's Eye decides. The Dragon's Eye knows all."

Fes laughed. "Apparently not." He glanced back at the dragon who sat perched, watching. If he needed help, would the dragon offer it? "The dragon saved me. The dragon, not the Dragon's Eye. And it's because of the connection we share."

"You have stolen power from the sky beast?"

"I don't steal power from the dragon. We are connected." As he thought about it, Fes realized that the connection was what granted him an easier attachment to his Deshazl magic. It was almost as if the connection now allowed him to reach his Deshazl power much easier than he had been able to before.

Fes glanced back at the dragon. Could that be the key?

If it was, was there any way to help protect the dragon's mind? If he could, would they be safe from the Damhur influence?

He didn't know whether that was even possible or not, but if it was, if there was anything that he could do, he needed to. And if there was, was it possible to help the other two dragons? Could there be some way of forging a connection to them, linking to them so that others could protect them?

Fes didn't know if he was intended to be the one to do so or if it was meant for someone else.

"Where are my friends?"

"As I said, they are—"

Fes stepped toward him, pulling on his Deshazl power. Unseen magic slammed into him, and he pressed out, blocking it, ignoring the effect, using a connection to power that had not been there before. He didn't know whether the Dragon's Eye had cleansed anything for him or whether it was only his need to better connect to the dragon that had changed. Either way, he used that power and drew upon it, pushing out and forcing Chornan back a step.

"I would see my friends," he said.

The other two with Chornan stepped forward, and Fes turned his attention to them. Would this end up being a display of power? He didn't want to get into anything like that, especially as he didn't control his power as well as they probably did.

He raised a hand, trying to halt them, but they took a step forward.

Fes let out a frustrated sigh. When he did, he pushed out with his Deshazl connection. That power swirled around the men, holding them in a barrier. He hadn't used his magic like this before, but he knew that it was possible. He had seen it used similarly before.

Neither of the men were able to reach him, and Fes turned his attention back to Chornan. He took a step toward the other man, still holding onto his Deshazl connection. As Chornan attacked, Fes found that the dragon pushed through him, helping him resist. Fes didn't even need to know what was happening and didn't even need to know how to control it to be able to defend himself.

"My friends," he said, lowering his voice to a low and angry whisper. "I would have my friends released."

"You are Deshazl, aren't you?"

Fes stared at him. "That's what I've been saying."

"The Damhur have claimed to know the Deshazl, but they use it with derision. They don't know the Deshazl, not as they claim."

"Well, I am Deshazl. How do you know the Deshazl?"

Chornan looked around, glancing over at the others with him, before turning his attention back to Fes. "Because we are the true Deshazl."

CHAPTER TEN

When Arudis was brought out to him, she was dressed in a strange robe. It had the same sort of shimmering qualities to it that he had seen from the clothing of these others. Deshazl, if he were to believe them. Fes still didn't know whether or not to believe them but didn't think they would lie about that, and it did fit with what he had seen so far.

"What happened to you?" Fes asked Arudis as she approached.

She smiled widely. "The pain. It's gone."

"What pain?"

"The pain that I've been feeling. I... I didn't even know how bad it was before, but now that it's gone..."

"What was it?" he asked.

"I don't know. It was there, a constant presence, and

now… Now the pain is gone completely. Whatever they did, throwing me in the water, it healed me."

"They claim that it removes the influence of the Damhur."

"I can reach my connection much easier," she said, lowering her voice.

"I can, too."

"You always had a great connection to your Deshazl magic," Arudis said. "I have long suspected it's because you were raised in the empire, away from the influence of the Damhur."

"But I was still Called."

"And that Calling both helped you understand your connection but also held you back."

That was Fes's belief, too. He would never have learned to control his Deshazl magic without having been Called. He had been forced to master it, and because of that, they had given him something of a gift, but he now thought he understood that the Calling had also confined him. Even when he had been freed from it, he had never truly been freed.

Was he now?

Fes didn't even know, but maybe that wasn't the point. Perhaps it didn't matter that he no longer suffered under the effect of the Calling and that all that really mattered was that he was here and had a better connection to the dragon. Because of that connection, Fes believed that he would be able to defend himself. He might even be able to use that power to attack the Deshazl, and if that were the case, then he could get the dragons free.

"They claim that they are Deshazl," Fes said.

Arudis stared at Chornan. He spoke softly with two others, but not the same two who had come to confront Fes. One was a tall and slender woman who had deep brown hair and eyes that were as green as the grasses growing around them. The other was an older man, with silver hair and a bit of a paunch to his belly visible through his scaled robe. Something about both of them told Fes that they were powerful.

It seemed as if since leaving the Dragon's Eye, he was much more aware of power. He could feel the power from those three, in particular. Each of them was strong, gifted in a strange way, and it seemed as if they were connected to the Dragon's Eye.

Was that the key? Could it be that they were attached to the Dragon's Eye? The dragon had made it seem as if the water was somehow tied to some greater power, though Fes wasn't entirely sure if that were true or what it meant if it were.

"I can't tell."

"Were you always able to tell?"

"The Calling was the easiest way. Having the Damhur

Call has been the most consistent way that we've been able to determine who was Deshazl."

"And by then, they will have left their touch upon you."

She nodded. "That is the challenge. The moment that they place their Calling, it is almost too late. Some things can be done to protect oneself, and when I had been around, I used everything that I could to protect those who were with us from the effect of the Calling, but it wasn't always entirely effective."

"So all of the Deshazl that you have helped in the empire—"

Arudis nodded. "They are all still touched by the Damhur."

Fes looked over at the glowing form of the Dragon's Eye. As night stretched on and the moon began to climb in the sky, the Dragon's Eye glowed softly. It gave off the appearance of a smoldering fire. There was something impressive about it, and Fes wanted nothing more than to stand at the shores of the Dragon's Eye, looking down at the water, and to wonder whether there was anything that he could do to feel that warmth and power once again. Then again, even with that question, he knew it was dangerous. Attempting to do so would only place him close to death, and while he had the temptation, he also now felt a different connection, one that brought him close to the dragon.

"Have you seen Jayell?"

Arudis shook her head. "They haven't allowed me to see her, and I'm not sure whether they will."

"They will," Fes said. He was determined to get to Jayell, and if it meant that he would have to fight through Chornan and the others, then he would do it. Now that he had a connection to the dragon, he felt incredibly powerful, almost as if there was nothing they could do to stop him.

A sense of warning suddenly surged within him.

Fes glanced back, recognizing that it came from the dragon.

What was it? Why would the dragon want to warn him?

It was because the dragon didn't want to stir up trouble.

Fes left Arudis and headed over to the dragon. He sat apart from the rest, away from the small village, and remained perched with his wings off to either side, ready for whatever might happen. Heat radiated from him, creating a small field of steam all around him.

"What is it?" Fes asked as he approached.

"They are not your enemy," the dragon said.

"Even if they have Jayell?"

"They are afraid."

"You know this?"

"I can smell their fear," the dragon rumbled. "But fear does not mean that they are your enemy."

"They claim that they are Deshazl."

"They are among the oldest," the dragon said.

"What does that mean?"

"The people known as the Deshazl in your land were not the first. There were others who came before them, others who had a connection to the dragons and a connection to power. Even in my time, that connection was different. Many of us knew of such a connection, but knowing of it and having experienced it are different things."

"Are you saying that you didn't even know that these people existed?"

"I lived in the mountains. I lived in the north. I never traveled this far. Many parts of this world are unexplored by dragons."

"How could the dragons not have explored out here?"

"We were under attack," the dragon said. "And with the attack, we knew better than to risk ourselves. Doing so only placed us in grave danger."

"So you stayed hidden?" Fes asked.

"We worked with the Deshazl. They helped protect us."

"How did the Deshazl get there in the north if they came from here?"

"I don't know. Perhaps they can tell you. Again, they are not your enemy."

Fes looked over at Chornan. He stood with the other two, and they were all watching him, staring at the dragon. If they were Deshazl—and he didn't doubt that they were—what did it mean? They didn't know the dragons the way the people in the north did.

Could they have come from a different place? Could it be that the Deshazl had left the north, looking for safety, and come here? Or was it the other way? Could the people who were the Deshazl in the north have come from this place?

Either way, Fes had questions, and he didn't know that he would get answers by rushing in to attack. He would need to exercise restraint, and that had never been a great strength of his.

The dragon seemed to chuckle.

Fes glanced up. "What is it?"

"I recognize your struggle."

"You can read my thoughts?"

"Not read them, but it is more an impression. I can detect warring emotions within you."

"How?" Fes asked.

"I'm not sure quite how," the dragon said. "Since you were immersed in that water, something changed within you. And when it did, something changed within me."

"It feels as if we are bonded in some way. Linked.

Almost as if I can reach my magic more effectively because of you."

"That has always been there," the dragon said.

"Not for me."

"Only because you failed to look for it," the dragon said. "That connection has always been there, and if you were able to pay attention to it, you would have known that."

"So you want me to work with them?"

"Isn't that why you came here?"

"We came here looking for allies, but I'm not sure what to make of them."

"From what I can tell, they feel much the same way."

Fes stared up at the dragon for another moment before leaving him and heading over to Chornan and the others. They remained near Arudis, who stood with the same uncertain expression on her face that she had worn since Fes first saw her when he had returned. How much had she suffered before she had been immersed in the pool?

It had to have been significant, but how had she managed to hide it?

Fes approached Chornan, leaving Arudis. "I would like to see my friend if it's possible," he said.

"She is Damhur—"

Fes raised his hand, making a point of not reaching for his Deshazl connection. He didn't want Chornan to think that he was attempting to attack, even if an attack would make a difference. "She is not Damhur. And you have seen from Arudis and myself that we are not the type of Deshazl that you are accustomed to. We are not slaves of the Damhur."

"Yet she knows Javoor."

"She knows Javoor because she was born and raised there, but she escaped."

"Those who escape become soldiers," he said, his face twisting in a look of disgust.

Fes stared at him for a moment. Was that it? Did they dislike the Asharn?

"What have the Asharn done?"

"Asharn have chosen a different path," Chornan said.

"And that path is offensive to you. Just because they choose to fight?"

"They choose to fight, but they do not choose to come here for testing."

"You're mad because they don't come here to run the risk of drowning?" Fes laughed at the idea. That seemed ridiculous, especially given the fact that he didn't know whether he would have willingly submerged himself in the Dragon's Eye if he had known exactly what might take place. How could any of the Asharn be willing to do so, especially if they knew what might happen?

"They allow themselves to remain tormented. It makes them angry. It makes them afraid."

"I've seen the Asharn. I've seen the way that they are able to attack. They aren't afraid, not from what I have seen."

"They are afraid. That's why they hide. They refused to return home."

"How many of them even know that this should be their home?"

"They know," Chornan said.

Fes didn't know how much to make of what Chornan said, but maybe it didn't matter. They were here for something else entirely, and now that he had discovered Chornan and the others, he had to hope that they would be able to help him.

"I would like to see my friend," he said.

He stared at Chornan, wondering whether the other man would allow him to finally see Jayell. After everything that he'd been through, it was time to find her again, and then what?

They needed the allies that they had come here for, but now that they were here, and now that he saw the people who this place had to offer, he wasn't sure whether they would be allies. They had come this far thinking to find the Asharn, knowing that they would have a way of countering the threat of the Damhur. More than ever, he realized it was time to keep moving.

"Come with me," Chornan said.

Fes glanced over at Arudis, but she remained near the

shore, staring out at the water. It was late enough that he doubted that she could see very much, if anything, and with the deep glowing within the water, it didn't seem as if there was anything to find. Despite that, she stared out at the water as if she might find some answer hidden within the depths of the lake.

Chornan guided him through the small village, weaving between the buildings. Fes kept pace with him and looked around as they went, feeling more than a little uncertain about where Chornan guided him. He saw no evidence of anyone else here, which left him worried that perhaps the other man might be taking him someplace where Fes would not find Jayell.

"Where is she, Chornan?"

The other man glanced over. Since Fes had returned from the lake, Chornan had regarded him more cautiously than he had before, and now was no different. He eyed Fes with an expression tinged with concern. "She's up here."

"If she's harmed—"

"She's not harmed," he said.

They reached another building, this one smaller and more compact. There were no windows along the face, and there was nothing other than a small door. He pressed his hand upon the door, and Fes felt a stirring within him as Chornan used whatever power he summoned. There was a flash of light, and the door popped open.

Heat built and Chornan pushed his hands forward, extinguishing the sudden appearance of a fire mage spell.

Fes shouldered past him and into the room. It was sparsely decorated, a chair and a table occupying part of the space. A small cot rested along one wall. A basin of water on the floor near it seemed to glow with a soft orange, much like the lake.

Had they taken water from the lake?

"Fes?"

He jerked his head around and found Jayell standing in one corner. She gripped a dragon pearl in one hand, and she held her other in front of her, though no fire mage spell built. Whatever restrictions the people here placed prevented her from using her magic effectively.

"Are you okay?" Fes asked.

"What happened?"

"I'm not entirely sure," Fes said. He glanced over at Chornan. "It seems as if the people here are Deshazl."

"If they're Deshazl, why did they put you through all of this?"

Fes hurried over to Jayell and took her hand, looking to ensure that she wasn't harmed. She seemed well enough, but he didn't know whether they had done anything to her that would impact her ability to use her fire magic. They might feel a particular way about fire mages, and it was admittedly similar to the way that Fes had once felt, but he had plenty of experience with Jayell and others like her to know that she didn't abuse that power. If anything, she used it well—and wisely.

"I'm fine," Jayell whispered.

"What did they do to you?"

"They brought me here. I haven't been able to use my magic, but they didn't do anything else to me."

Fes glanced over at Chornan. "What did you do to her?"

"We did the same to her as we have done to all of the Damhur. We ensured that she couldn't harm us."

"She wouldn't harm you anyway," Fes said.

Chornan stared at him defiantly. "She is Damhur."

"She is of the empire. She is a fire mage. She has fought the Damhur." Fes glanced down at the water in the basin. "Have you been drinking that?"

She nodded slowly. "I didn't have much choice."

"I suspect that has prevented you from reaching your magic," Fes said.

"How?"

"Something is in the lake. Somehow it's connected to the Deshazl magic."

"How do you know?"

Fes glanced over at Chornan. "Because they threw me into it." He turned his attention back to Jayell and met her eyes. "It was a test, and apparently I passed, though I passed in a way that's different than what they expected. Then again, I suspect they didn't anticipate me passing at all. Or Arudis. They didn't believe that either of us was Deshazl."

"Even though you can use Deshazl magic?"

"Many of the people controlled by the Damhur can use their connection," Chornan said. "And just because they can use it doesn't mean that they don't still serve the Damhur."

Fes guided Jayell out of the building. He ignored Chornan, who tried to block him from leaving. He shot him a hard look as he passed, and then he and Jayell stepped out into the night. He took a deep breath, inhaling the cool air and looking up at the sky. There were no clouds and stars twinkled brightly. There was something peaceful about this place, though it felt strange to admit that, especially given what he had already gone through here.

They made their way back out to the space at the edge of the village. The dragon still sat, perched on his wings and on his back legs, heat radiating from him as he stared forward. When Fes appeared, he lowered his head, and his deep golden eyes blinked.

"We can go," he said to the dragon.

"Did you get what you came for?" the dragon asked.

Fes shook his head, glancing back at the others here in the clearing. "They oppose the Damhur, but they fear them, too. I'm not sure that there's anything here that we can find." It pained him, especially after how far they had come and how little there seemed to be to stop the Damhur.

"We can stay. We can continue to search," Jayell said.

"How long should we stay away?" Fes asked. He looked over at Chornan, who had rejoined the others. He stared at Fes, and while there was an expression of uncertainty on his face, there was something else mixed with it. Fes couldn't tell what it was. Anger? Hatred? Maybe it was disappointment. Whatever it was, Fes doubted that they would be willing to leave their land and risk going to face the Damhur. Why would they, when they had to protect this place? "The longer that we're gone, the farther into the empire the Damhur are able to push." He breathed out a heavy sigh. "I think... I think it's time for us to return."

"Are you sure?" Jayell asked.

"I'm not sure about anything, but when it comes to this place and these people, I begin to doubt there is anything that we will be able to do with them."

Jayell squeezed his hand, and he started forward, wanting to reach Arudis to grab her and bring her with them. They would climb back atop the dragon, and they would leave. Maybe they could still find help from the Asharn, or perhaps having been submerged in the lake and the connection it had granted him would protect them so that they didn't have to fear the Calling. There was only one way to know, and while that involved testing themselves against the Damhur, wasn't that worthwhile?

As he reached Chornan and the others, the larger man stood in front of him, glancing from Fes to Jayell. "We have been troubled by how it is that you are Deshazl."

"It doesn't matter," Fes said. "I'm going to take the other woman who came with us, and we are going to leave your lands. My people still need help. The Damhur have attacked, and if we don't return, my people will continue to suffer."

"It does matter," Chornan said.

"From what I understand, my parents escaped from the Damhur. They traveled across the sea, and I was raised in the empire."

"You are not from those lands?"

"I am now. There are others there who are like me, who have a connection to the Deshazl, and I have worked with them, trying to help protect them from the Damhur. So has Arudis," he said, pointing through the line of people to her as she stood along the shore. She still hadn't moved, and he couldn't help but wonder what it was that she saw in the water. Maybe she had experienced something during her testing that had left her troubled. Or maybe there was nothing, and she was trying to understand the power within the lake.

"Why do you oppose the Damhur?" one of the other people with Chornan asked. She was small and petite and had jet black hair that caught the wind, blowing around the base of her neck.

"Why?" Fes glanced over his shoulder at the dragon. "There are those among my people, including the dragons, who can't oppose the Damhur. They don't have the necessary strength or ability, and they need those of us who can fight to do so." That wasn't his entire reason. Part of his reason came from the fact that he had been captured by the Damhur, and he had felt the effect of the Calling, and he had suffered under it and wanted to ensure that others didn't have to suffer in the same way. If there was anything that he could do, he wanted to do so. "Why don't you fight the Damhur?"

"We have opposed the Damhur for many years, but the fight has always led to our suffering. We have established a place here, a place of safety where we are connected and protected."

"And you refuse to leave," Fes said.

"It's not about refusing, it's about remaining where it's safe. In this place, connected as we are to our natural abilities, we have no reason to leave. We are free from the influence of the Damhur. We no longer have to suffer, experiencing the way they use their powers. We are safe."

"You are safe, but others like you are not. You

disparage the Asharn, but they continue to fight, resisting the Damhur."

"You don't understand the dynamics of the Asharn," Chornan said.

"I'm sure that I don't, but I understand well enough to know that they continue to fight. Whether or not they fight for the same reason that you would, the fact that they are willing to fight tells me that they want to change what has taken place. The Asharn would free the ones who are still trapped by the Damhur. What have you done?"

It was a little harsh, and even as he said it, he somewhat regretted the words. He didn't know these people, and he didn't know everything that they had been through, only that they remained hidden, and while they might be connected to the same power that flowed through him, they chose to use it differently.

The short woman stared at Fes. "Before you leave, come with us."

"Where?"

"To understand."

CHAPTER ELEVEN

The small woman led them away from the lake. The Dragon's Eye seemed to occupy an enormous space, but it quickly disappeared behind them as they made their way back toward the city. Arudis walked behind Fes and Jayell, a step or so back, saying nothing. The dragon flew overhead, circling high in the air, and surprisingly, Fes could feel the connection between himself and the dragon, and he was fully aware of the fact that the dragon watched them as he circled.

When the rest of the city came into view, Fes almost stopped. The buildings shimmered, gleaming with an impossible light, the strange scales along the surface of the buildings seeming to move.

He never seen anything like it. In the daylight, the buildings had been impressive, but also completely alien.

At night, with the moonlight streaking across the surfaces, there was something almost magical about it. He could practically feel how the buildings were infused with Deshazl magic, filling them.

"Did you see them when you came through here?" Fes asked.

"They had covered my eyes," Jayell said. She stared at the buildings much the same way that Fes did. "They dragged me through here, and I was aware of others around me, but I didn't know there was a city like this. The cover was taken off when they reached the village."

Fes grunted. If they used the village as a way to hide the Damhur, then it made sense that they wouldn't want the Damhur to know that a city like this even existed. They would want to hide it, preventing any of the Damhur from ever learning that they had more—and might *be* more.

When they reached the outskirts of the city, the woman guided them down a wide street. More of the same buildings rose up on either side, and up close, the scales were even more impressive. Fes couldn't tell how they'd been made, only that they seemed to house incredible power. He could feel it seeping out of the buildings themselves. Lantern light flickered in some of the windows, giving them a warmth, making the entire city seem like some shimmering dragon.

"How long have your people been here?" Fes asked the woman.

She glanced back at him before her gaze drifted to Jayell. "There was a time when we lived side by side with the Damhur."

"How long ago was that?" Fes asked.

"It has been many years since our peoples had peace."

"How long?" Fes asked. The size of the city made more sense if they all had lived here, and seeing it now, seeing how enormous this place was, Fes could practically feel the power that must have been here one time. Now, from what he'd seen, there weren't nearly as many people, certainly not enough to occupy the entirety of the city, despite the fact that light glowed from within many of the buildings.

"Centuries have passed since we worked together."

"Centuries?"

Could the timing be similar? Could the Damhur have headed north, across the sea, wanting to gain power so that they could enslave these people too? Could that be the reason they had turned their attention north? If that were the case, then the fates of both places were far more intertwined than Fes would ever have imagined.

"We have known peace for centuries," she said. "We exiled the Damhur and made it so they could not return."

"How did you make it so that they could not return?"

"The Dragon's Eye provides a way," she said.

Fes glanced back. As he did, he thought that he could feel the power coming from the Dragon's Eye. Maybe they used that Deshazl magic, that deep-seated power that was buried within it, and tied that power into protecting their city. Would the dragon know? The dragon seemed to have some connection to the Dragon's Eye and the water and power within it, but Fes would need to have more time to understand.

"What was it like when you lived with the Damhur?" Jayell asked.

The had been walking for quite some time, passing more and more of the buildings, each of them similar, rounded structures that were covered with the strange shimmery dragon scales.

"It was a time of great prosperity," the woman said. "It was a time where we all were able to work together, understanding our powers and how they worked together."

"How did they work together?" Fes asked. Was there some secret that he could learn? If there was, maybe he would need to return to Toulen and see if there was anything that Indra and her people could do. They might have attacked the empire, but she hadn't wanted them to attack. Indra couldn't be alone in that. There were far too many people within Toulen who had known the empire over the years, and there were far too many people who would want peace.

"We have often wondered. Too many years have passed for us to remember. All that we know is that together, our peoples were much more powerful." She swept her hand around her, motioning to the rest of the city. "All of this was built when our peoples were together."

"This was a time when the Damhur worked *with* the Deshazl?" Fes asked.

The woman nodded. "The key to building these structures has been lost. Most believe that it's tied to something that our people did together, though none have managed to learn what that was. Even the Damhur that we brought here, keeping them concealed from the rest of the city, using the Dragon's Eye to ensure our safety, have not been able to help us understand anything more about the nature of our abilities than what we already know."

They began to slow as they neared a more massive structure. It was likely in the center of the town, and it was completely rounded, much like the others, rising the equivalent of three stories high. Windows ringed it on each level, and light glowed from within. Dozens of different colors shimmered, catching the lantern light that seeped out of the windows.

"It looks like a dragon pearl," Jayell whispered.

Fes blinked. He hadn't made the connection, but now

that Jayell had, he could see what she did. "Not a dragon pearl," he said. "A dragon heart."

Jayell's breath caught.

Fes looked over at the woman as they reached the doorway to the building. "What changed with the Damhur?"

The woman hesitated, her hand resting on the door for a moment. "They began to realize they could use their power in a way that allowed them to control us, to force us, though the strongest among the Deshazl were able to resist. Not all had that ability, and some of the Damhur chose to continue using their abilities, forcing the weakest of our people to serve them. The peace that we had known for a long time fractured, and we were forced to send them away."

She pushed the door open and guided Fes and the others inside. He hesitated on the other side of the doorway, looking around the room. It was an enormous room and completely open inside. The curved ceiling arched overhead, so high that he could barely see the top. Shadows swirled around, the lantern light not stretching far enough into the dark recesses to suppress them.

Within the room were a dozen people, all dressed in the same strange scaled clothing as the people they had encountered within the forest. Out in the open like this, there was no camouflage, nothing that would make it harder for them to be seen.

"What have you done, Jesla?" a man asked, approaching the woman who had guided them here.

Jesla took a step forward, pressure building from her, tugging on Fes's connection to his Deshazl magic. She pulled a considerable amount of power and then she pushed it out away from her, so that it slammed into the man, forcing him back a step. The control she had was impressive.

"I have done what was necessary," she said.

"You bring outsiders into this place?"

Jesla turned to look at Fes. "He survived the Dragon's Eye."

"From what I understand, he failed."

"Did he? And yet now he stands before you."

"He had the help of the sky beast."

"The sky beast?" Fes asked. He ignored a warning glance from Jesla—and Jayell. "That sky beast is a dragon. A dragon," he repeated, staring at the man. The others in the room all were silent, watching. Whoever this man was, it seemed to Fes that he led the others. "And that sky beast is what you honor through the way that you have decorated your city. That sky beast is the same as what you call that lake. That sky beast is the name you give your lands!"

"I am aware of what the sky beast is," the man said.

"I'm not sure that you do. If you were aware, you would recognize that referring to a dragon as a sky beast would end up with you devoured by said sky beast."

Behind him, someone let out a soft chuckle. The man glanced over his shoulder, and the person who had laughed cut off, but not before the tension in the room had eased. The others were all watching Fes, and they seemed to wait to see how Jesla and this other man would get along. Were these the two who ruled?

Somebody stepped forward. "Is it true that you control the dragon?" He was an older man and had graying hair, but like most of the men Fes had seen, there was a particular strength to him.

"I don't control the dragon. I speak to the dragon, and we work together."

"Could we speak to the dragon?" another woman asked. She had chestnut brown hair and freckles along her face. Her deep brown eyes sparkled.

"I don't see why not. You have the necessary connections."

"A dragon," someone said excitedly. "All these years, and now we have a dragon?"

"This is not the only dragon," Fes said, glancing over at Jesla. Hadn't he told them that the Damhur had controlled two others?

"So we have heard," the first man said. He glared at Jesla for a moment before turning away.

"What's that about?" Fes asked.

"He worries that we will be drawn into battle," she said. "He worries that is the reason you came."

"It *is* the reason I came."

"I know."

Jayell took his hand, squeezing it softly. They continued into the room, and Fes looked back to see that Arudis hadn't followed. Where had she gone? He should have paid more attention, but maybe she had gone off with Chornan.

"Where did she go?" Fes whispered.

Jayell shook her head. "I don't know. She was behind us as we were making our way into the city."

"Something is bothering her that she hasn't shared with us," Fes said.

"Whatever it is, we need to support her," she said.

"I think it's returning to these lands, coming here. I think this has been hard on her, probably harder than she has let on," he said.

"Not here," Jayell said. "There's nothing about coming here that troubled her."

Fes wasn't convinced of that. There was something about this place that bothered Arudis, though he wasn't certain what it was. Why would she be so troubled by coming here?

Jesla took a seat at a table in the center of the room and motioned for Fes and Jayell to join her. The others were speaking softly, excitedly, and the murmuring began to die down as they took their seats. Jesla leaned forward, resting her elbows on the solid table. It wasn't any species of wood that Fes had ever seen before. The grain was tight and the surface entirely smooth. It had been stained a deep, rich tone that was nearly black, and much like everything else that he'd seen in the city, it had a strange shimmering quality to it that made it almost appear like a dragon relic.

The forgers within the empire would have been able to learn quite a lot from these people. He could just imagine what they might be able to do had they access to the techniques the people here used. There were plenty of forgeries throughout the empire, and Fes had even used a skilled forger once before, but none of them rivaled what he'd seen here. None of them had anywhere near the skill these people did.

Then again, he had a sense that what was here wasn't forgery at all. They had created their entire city to look something like the dragons and using that, they managed something that Fes doubted was replicated anywhere else.

"We will wait for Chornan," Jesla said.

"We already know how Chornan would vote," the man said.

"Marcus, you don't know how Chornan would vote. How often have you been able to predict exactly what he might say?" Jesla looked around the room at the others seated around the table. "And the rest of you? Do you know what Chornan might decide?"

Fes sat back, glancing from Jesla to the others. It seemed as if these were the leaders of the city, though he didn't know quite why they had been brought here.

"Chornan was down by the Dragon's Eye. We know what he would have said," Marcus said.

The door opened, and Chornan strode in. He was dressed in the same scaled clothing as the others, and he took a seat near the opposite end of the table from Jesla and glanced along it. When his gaze reached Fes, he nodded once.

"Now that we're all here, we can begin," Jesla said.

"Why have you summoned this meeting?" Marcus asked. He looked over at Fes, staring at him. "And why have you brought outsiders into our midst?"

"You have all seen the reason that we have made this decision," Chornan said.

"Not all of us have seen it," Marcus said.

Chornan turned to him, resting his hands on the table. He leaned forward. "The sky beast has been visible for the last day. There is no denying what that creature is, much as there is no denying that it is bound to him," he said, nodding to Fes.

Was that what this was about? Did they give him credit for somehow connecting to the dragon? He didn't know what that meant, if anything.

"They should not have been able to reach this place, not without something having changed, and we have no reason to believe that the Dragon's Eye has failed us. That alone should tell us that there is something, a reason for their presence."

"The reason is that you have allowed a Damhur to sit at our table," Marcus said.

Chornan nodded slowly. "I don't deny the fact that I believed her to be Damhur," he said. "When we went to investigate the sky beast, we came across the Damhur power. We could feel it, and we could feel who was using power, but..."

"But what?" one of the other women at the table asked.

Chornan shook his head. "But I no longer believe that she is Damhur."

"Even though she uses their magic?"

"She uses a part of their magic, but she doesn't use all of it. And he vouches for her." Chornan nodded at Fes again.

Marcus laughed bitterly. "You trust the word of this outsider?"

"I trust the decision of the Dragon's Eye. How can I not, when he should have died, yet he returned to us. The Dragon's Eye allowed him to live."

"How long was he under?" one of the others asked.

"Over half the day," Chornan said.

A soft murmuring began to spread around the table, and several people started to look at Fes with a different interest. Fes shifted in his seat, uncomfortable with the attention. He had never cared for attention, and cared for it even less now, especially with the way that they were looking at him.

But this was what he needed. If he intended to get help, he needed to reach these people, and he had to believe that they had some way of helping him. They might not have been willing to face the Damhur, choosing to hide here, but they had the ability to do so. That ability was going to be crucial if Fes was going to be successful.

"There hasn't been someone who survived half a day for centuries," someone said.

"Listen to him. He can't be one of us."

"The sky beast helped save him," someone said.

"We don't know if he serves the Damhur. He brought one of them with him."

"Chornan believes."

"Chornan is always eager to believe. He would go after the Asharn."

When Fes heard the last, he turned his attention to Chornan. *He would have gone after the Asharn?* He had thought Chornan was opposed to the Asharn, and his comments had made it seem as if he were disgusted by them, but had Fes had misread that?

It was possible that Chornan was the one he needed to try to work with. Maybe he needed to see if there was anything that he could do to convince Chornan of the need to help him deal with the threat from Damhur.

"Enough," Chornan said, raising his hand. "We have come here to decide what we will do."

"There is no decision needed for what we will do," Marcus said. "How could there be?"

"How could there be?" Chornan fixed Marcus with a hard expression. "We have remained here, waiting for a sign that we should intervene. This is that sign."

"You have chosen to view it that way," Marcus said. "Just because the sky beast has come, you would put the rest of our people in danger."

"We have always been in danger," Chornan said. "Staying here, hiding, has done nothing other than—"

"It has done nothing other than keep our people safe," Marcus said. He looked around the table, trying to draw attention from the others.

Fes tried to weigh the mood within the room but had a hard time telling whether the people here sided more with Marcus or whether they sided more with Chornan. There were some who looked on Fes with interest, but there were just as many who regarded him suspiciously. He had the sense that whatever was decided here would determine whether these people would offer any help.

And if they didn't?

Would they even allow him to leave?

He thought that he could get free, and thought that his connection to the dragon would be enough that he shouldn't have any difficulty escaping if it were to come to that, but he hoped that it wouldn't. It wasn't that he wanted to fight his way free from here. And he wasn't sure just how powerful they were. He had seen some glimmer of their abilities and knew that many of them were incredibly gifted, powerfully connected to their Deshazl magic, perhaps more so than Fes. If that were the case, then it might be that there was nothing that he would be able to do to get free if they decided to hold them here.

Jayell reached for his hand under the table, and he glanced over at her.

"What if they—" Jayell started, but she cut off when Fes shook his head.

"We will be fine," he whispered.

He could tell that she wasn't put at ease. And how could she be?

The people around the table were arguing, voices overlapping, making it hard for Fes to follow one line of conversation or another. They were angry over the fact that Chornan had allowed Fes and Arudis to come, mostly angry that they had allowed them to see them and their way into the city. He had a sense that wasn't typically allowed, though some seemed even more angry about the fact that Marcus and those who sided with him were opposed to working with Fes. They viewed the presence of the dragon as a sign, and they wanted to work with Fes, regardless of what he might ask.

The longer that he listened, the more it became clear that was what they were concerned about. It was what he might ask for that bothered them. Those who were here feared that Fes might demand something they couldn't and shouldn't offer.

They were scared.

How much experience must they have with the Damhur to be afraid like this?

He glanced over at Jesla, who had been silent much of the time. She watched the others, and as she did, the frown on her face continued to deepen.

"How often do you encounter the Damhur?" Fes asked her.

"Not often. We have found ways of avoiding them."

"But it must be often enough that you fear them," he said.

She nodded. "We lose some of our people to them each year. It's not many, but it's enough that we fear encountering them."

"But you don't destroy them."

"No."

"Why not?"

"I told you about our experience with the Damhur."

"You told me that you once worked together."

Jesla nodded. "We once worked together, and we once were more united. There are those of us who fear the Damhur and fear that they will continue to attack, thinking to use their abilities to claim our people. Many of the Damhur have grown skilled over the years, powerful. It's with that power that they are able to take others of my people," she said.

She looked around the room, watching the others. There was sadness in her eyes, and Fes wondered what role she had. She served some purpose with the Deshazl here, and it was more than that of a leader. Her silence made it seem as if her purpose was something else.

"You don't harm the Damhur because you think that you could work together again," Fes replied.

Jesla nodded. "There are some among my people who feel otherwise, but enough of us remain who would prefer caution to violence. If we could sway them, if we can convince them that we could once again work together, we have to believe that we could once more find peace."

The arguing continued to build around the table, voices all attempting to speak over another, and finally, it went silent.

All eyes turned to Chornan. It seemed as if a decision had been made, but from what Fes could tell, they waited on Chornan to share what that decision was.

"Is it time for a vote?" Chornan asked.

Everyone settled their hands on the table, placing them in front of them.

Fes watched, fascinated, but the same time concerned about how this might turn out. What might they decide? And if they decided one way or another, would it somehow mean that he would struggle?

"All who would offer our help to this Deshazl, signify your agreement," Chornan said.

Hands went up. There were a few, little more than a smattering of them, and Fes noticed that while Chornan was one of them, so too was Jesla, along with several of the others who had seemed impressed by the fact that he could travel with the dragon.

Still, it wasn't enough.

Chornan sat back, frustration evident on his face, and he nodded. "So it has been decided."

CHAPTER TWELVE

F es stood outside the domed building, looking up
at the night sky. The stars that twinkled were
bright, shimmering in the sky much the same way the
buildings seemed to shimmer around him. There was
something majestic about it, and he enjoyed the calm
night sky. It was quieter than what he was accustomed
to, and there was a certain tension in the air, though
he suspected that came from him more than anything
else.

Chornan stood next to him, having been silent ever
since they emerged from inside. Fes couldn't read him,
not well, but he sensed that there was great frustration
within the man.

Jesla had remained behind, speaking to the rest of the
people around the table.

"What does it mean?" Jayell asked, breaking the silence.

Chornan blinked, taking a deep breath and letting it out in a heavy sigh. "It means that you cannot stay here."

"That was the question?" Fes asked.

Chornan looked over at him, frowning slightly. "Is that not what you would have wanted?"

Fes shrugged. "I never wanted to request to stay here. I came looking for help."

"And if you were granted a place here, that help would have been yours," Chornan said.

Fes breathed out. He thought he understood. They had been trying to decide whether he could be allowed to stay so that he could then ask for their help. It actually surprised him that Chornan had presented him for that.

"What changed your mind?" Fes asked.

Chornan looked back at the building, staring at it for a moment. "You survived the Dragon's Eye."

"That's not the entire reason for you," Fes said. "If it were, you would have offered me help the moment that I was pulled from the water."

"That's not the entire reason," Chornan agreed. "The Dragon's Eye is a test, and it's not one that everyone is able to pass. You did. Not only did you pass, but you revealed something about yourself. You revealed the fact that you can connect to the same source of power as we do. And you have proven yourself with the dragon."

"Dragon, and not sky beast?"

"They call it that out of fear. They fear what it means that dragons have returned."

"It's not the only dragon that has returned," Fes said. "And they shouldn't fear a dragon that I share a connection with. They should fear the dragons the Damhur have Called."

"I understand," Chornan said.

"I'm not sure that you do. The Damhur control two dragons. They might be attacking the empire now, and they intend to raise more. If they can succeed in that, then your people, and the city, will no longer be safe. I came here looking for help, and I understand that you have no interest in helping, but at least help me know where I can go to get that help."

Chornan watched him, his frown remaining on his face. "I'm afraid that I can't offer you what you want. My people have refused. I'm unable to go against the wishes of the rest of the Hasazn."

"Is that them?" Fes asked.

"The Hasazn rules our people. We provide guidance, and it's one where everyone gets to offer their opinion. When a decision is made, one person cannot override the others. In that way, I cannot override the others, regardless of whether or not I agree with the decision made."

"You admit that you don't agree."

Chornan studied Fes for a moment. "It matters not at

all whether I agree or not. All that matters is that the Hasazn has decided. They have taken the information they had, and they have chosen their course."

Fes looked over at Jayell. "Then we need to go."

"Where would you go now?" Jayell asked.

"I don't know. We came south looking for help, thinking that we would find the Asharn, and maybe we still can."

"We don't know where to find them," she said.

"It doesn't change the fact that we need to search," Fes said. They would have to search throughout Javoor, and even in doing so, they might not be able to reach them, not easily. Anything they did now would take time, and it was time that they didn't necessarily have to spend, not with an attack being waged on the empire. They'd been gone a few days, hopefully not so long that the empire had fallen, but it was possible that they had been gone too long already and that the dragons had proved too much for the empire and the fire mages.

"I might be able to help with your search for the Asharn," Chornan said.

"You would help? After everything that you said about them?"

"I might not agree with their choice, but they serve a purpose."

"Where are they?"

"They hide within Javoor. They try to rescue as many

of the slaves as they can, and they oppose the Damhur."

"I've seen the Asharn. I understand what it is that they attempt to do."

Chornan shook his head. "You might have seen the Asharn, but I doubt that you have seen what they can do. They are ruthless. If that is what you want, then know that the ally you choose is a dangerous one."

"The enemy of my enemy—"

"Might still be your enemy," Chornan said.

Fes frowned. "Are they your enemy, too?"

Chornan looked down at the ground. "They should not be, but over time, much has changed. We once had hoped that we could help the Asharn, and we believed that we could rescue them from the violence that consumed them, but as I've told you, they don't want that rescue. Many of them refused to come here, and they refused to submit themselves to the Dragon's Eye."

"You can't be angry at them for failing to do what you want. They probably have a good reason for not wanting to submit themselves to the Dragon's Eye. Such as not wanting to die," Fes said.

"They will never be free if they don't," Chornan said.

"What if they don't want freedom?" Jayell asked. Fes looked over, but Jayell only shrugged. "What if it's not freedom they seek?"

"What would they want?" Fes asked.

"If they have suffered under the Damhur, maybe they

want nothing more than vengeance. Maybe that's all they're after."

"They should live for something else," Chornan said.

"You think they should live for something else, but they might believe otherwise."

The door to the building opened, and Jesla emerged. She glanced from Chornan to Fes and Jayell. "You may stay through the night, but the Hasazn has requested that you depart first thing in the morning."

Fes nodded. "We'll go. We will need the other with us. I don't know where she went."

"She has decided to explore the city," Jesla said.

"How do you know?"

"Because I can feel her."

"Feel her?"

Jesla smiled. "The Dragon's Eye grants many blessings, not the least of which is that it frees our people from the influence of the Damhur. There are some of us who are given even greater blessings. We come to understand our connection to our abilities and how that is connected to the Dragon's Eye, and through that, we know a certain type of power."

Fes nodded. When he had submerged in the Dragon's Eye, he had emerged with a greater connection to the dragon. Through that, he felt as if he were even more connected to his Deshazl abilities. Some of that might come from the fact that he was no longer influenced by the Damhur, but some of it might come from what he had experienced while in the Dragon's Eye.

"What did the Dragon's Eye grant you?"

"It granted me a connection to the people. That is how I serve."

"Not on the Hasazn?" Fes asked.

Jesla glanced at Chornan before shaking her head. "That is not my strength. I'm not here to guide the people, only to connect them."

"You're a priest," Fes said.

"If a priest means sharing a connection between your people, helping them understand their purpose, then perhaps that is what I am. I consider myself an advisor, little more than that."

"Can you bring me to her?" Fes asked.

Jesla nodded and started off, leading Fes away from the domed building. As they went, he glanced back at it and couldn't help but feel the power rising from its center. There was something more to the construction of these buildings, something that granted an innate ability, though what was it? It seemed to be more than the Deshazl magic within the buildings. It seemed almost as if whatever it was came from the structures themselves.

"How is it that you can follow her?" Fes asked.

"My blessing allows me to connect to those who have the right ability."

"Such as the Deshazl?" Jayell asked.

Jesla nodded. "The Deshazl ability is something innate, deep, and through that, there is a power that connects to the oldest of powers. Those of us who are sensitive to it understand just how deep that magic flows. We can reach it, and when we can, we can stretch beyond, using that ability and that magic to grasp for something greater than ourselves." She smiled, looking over at Fes. "You can feel it. Your ability to connect to the dragon allows that. I can sense that from you."

"I can't detect anything from others with the Deshazl ability," Fes said.

"Just because you can't detect it doesn't mean that it's not there. Most will never be aware of those deep connections. Most who can harness the Deshazl magic, that power that flows through us and through the dragon," she said, turning her gaze to the sky where the dragon still circled, "know it as little more than magic. And it is magic, but it is something more. It is a power that binds each of us, and to those who can feel that connection, they can become something greater."

They stopped in a small clearing, and Fes found Arudis sitting on a bench. She stared straight ahead, almost as if she were lost.

He approached her and took a seat on the bench next to her. The stone was cool, but not unpleasantly so. He looked out at the night, following the direction of her gaze, and saw that he could see the faint glowing coming from the Dragon's Eye. It was subtle, but it was clear, even from here.

"Arudis?"

"Fezarn. You don't have to come out here for me."

"I'm worried about you," he said.

"And you don't have to worry about me, either."

"What are you doing out here?"

Arudis took a deep breath. "Ever since I submerged within the Dragon's Eye, something shifted within me."

"Shifted?"

"I don't know what will explain any differently than that. It's as if the power I possess has been unlocked. It shifted."

"What power do you experience now?"

"I don't know how to explain it. I have always been connected to others, but now it feels as if I can detect them," she said, glancing over at Fes. "I suppose that doesn't make any sense to you."

He looked back at Jesla. She stood at the edge of the clearing, leaving Fes and Arudis alone. "It makes more sense than it would have a few moments ago."

She sighed. "I feel as if something has changed for me," she said. "It's almost as if my purpose has changed."

"What do you mean by that?"

"I came here with you, wanting to help you find Javoor and the Asharn, but after stepping in the Dragon's Eye, I can't help but feel as if there is something else for me, and it seems as if I need to understand it, but..." She sighed and shook her head. "It's almost as if I can't quite find it."

"You should stay here," Fes said.

Arudis blinked and her eyes cleared for a moment. "I can't remain here, Fezarn. The Deshazl need me."

"They do, but how much more will they benefit if you understand this new connection?"

"And what makes you think that there's anything for me to understand?"

Fes nodded to Jesla. "I have a sense that there are others here who understand exactly what you've gone through, and those others can help you understand what your abilities mean."

"Fezarn—"

"I need to go after the Asharn," he said. "I was hopeful that the people here would be able to help us, but the more that we're here, the more that I learn of them, the more I understand their fears. I can't force them to help us, and I don't know that they want to help. They are content with what they have, but it's more than that," he said.

"They have a different experience with the Damhur," she said.

"Long ago," Fes said nodding. "And I get the sense that there are some who hope that a time will come when the Damhur will return."

"I can't stay here," she said.

"Why not?" Fes asked.

"Our people need me."

"They do, but they need you to know your purpose so that you can help them find theirs. I can come back for you when this is all over," Fes said.

"Our people need me to help them survive this," she said.

"I don't know that there's anything that you can do to help our people survive this."

Arudis sat silently for a long time, staring off into the distance. Fes wondered what she was thinking about, but she said nothing. He shifted on the stone bench, trying to get comfortable, before looking up at the sky. The dragon continued to circle, though Fes didn't need to look up to know that he did. He was aware of the dragon, aware of his presence, and able to feel him even without seeing him. Would the dragon respond if Fes attempted to summon him?

They needed to determine whether the dragon would be protected from a Calling. If they experienced someone else who was as powerful as others on the Trivent, they needed to be ready.

"I fear for our people," she whispered.

"I fear for them, too," Fes said. "But more than that, I fear for all of the people within the empire. Many have a weakened form of Deshazl ability. We've seen that. How long will it be before the Damhur begin to use that influence on those who don't understand what that means? How long will it take before the Damhur begin to turn everyone into their slaves?"

"That's even more reason for me to return," she said.

Fes shook his head. "Even more reason for you to remain and understand yourself. Once you know your abilities, then you can begin to work with our people, and then you can be the leader they need."

"I never wanted to lead," Arudis said. "I did it because there was no one else."

Fes smiled as he looked back at Jesla. "Fine. Don't lead. You can advise them."

Arudis nodded. "That seems more appropriate."

He sat there with her for a little while longer, staring out into the distance. The faint glowing of the Dragon's Eye drew his attention, and with it, he could feel the power within it. It was almost as if he had connected to that as much as he had connected to the dragon.

Should he feel that connection? Was there a reason that he had connected to the Dragon's Eye? Fes stood, staring into the distance with more intensity. Maybe that was the key.

There *had* been power within the Dragon's Eye, that much he knew, and with that power, Fes couldn't help but feel as if he were connected to something else—something more.

It had bonded him and the dragon, tying them together, but it had done something else to the people here. It had ensured their strength and their safety.

Fes made his way over to Jesla, leaving Arudis on the bench. "She would stay here and learn from you if she could," he said.

Jesla looked past Fes. "She has a strong connection to others."

Fes nodded. "She does. She always has, and she's the reason that so many people within the empire are safe."

"How would she use those connections?"

"I imagine she would use them in the same way as you have," Fes said.

Jesla sighed. "If that's the case, I would be happy to have her remain here until she feels it's time for her to move on."

"She would be allowed?"

"It will be my request."

Fes had the sense that it made a difference coming from Jesla. The rest of the Hasazn wouldn't argue with their priest.

"Why would she stay?" Jayell asked.

Fes glanced over at Arudis. "The Dragon's Eye changed something within her, much as it did with me. For me, it feels as if it has connected me to the dragon with a greater intensity. For Arudis, it seems to have connected her to the people with a greater intensity."

"In time, she can come to know her connections, and she can use those to continue to help the people she wants to serve. There is much that she can learn, and much that I can try to teach her, though I can't guarantee that she will learn everything that she wants to know," Jesla said.

Fes studied Jesla. "Does stepping into the Dragon's Eye connect to it in some way?"

"The Dragon's Eye is a place of power," Jesla said.

"But is there any way to use that power?"

"The power comes from within. It comes from the Deshazl connections that you possess. There is no using the Dragon's Eye. You use that which is within you."

Fes looked out toward the Dragon's Eye, wondering how much of that was true. He felt as if he could feel something out there, could feel the connection to the Dragon's Eye, though maybe it was only that his own Deshazl connection had been unlocked.

"Chornan was going to tell me where to find the Asharn," Fes said.

"Chornan was going to do that?" Jesla asked.

Fes nodded. "He recognized that my finding the Asharn might be necessary to do what I need to help my people."

"Undoubtedly that is true," she said.

"And with your connections, I suspect you know how to find them."

"My connections are not meant to be used to track the Deshazl in such a way."

"I didn't ask you to track them for me to harm them. I asked you to track them so that I could look to them for help. I need their help. *We* need their help. And if they do this, it's possible that we might be able to help them."

Fes didn't know whether that was true or not, but if anything, it might convince Jesla to help.

"Many of them have committed to their purpose. Many of the Asharn have devoted themselves to lives that involve hunting down the Damhur, trying to free other Deshazl."

"And you disagree with that?"

"On the contrary, their willingness to help rescue others is noble. It's one that many here have failed to see. I can tell each time they rescue someone. I feel it."

Fes blinked. "Can you feel the Deshazl who remain Called?"

Jesla's eyes shut, and she nodded slowly. "I can feel them. I try not to, and I tried to push that out of my mind, but there is only so much that I can do. They are there within my mind, and that is my gift—and my curse —from the Dragon's Eye."

Fes couldn't imagine what it must be like for her to know the way the Deshazl were controlled, tormented by the Damhur. How awful must that be to live with that knowledge day after day, knowing that those people were out there, but also knowing that there was nothing that could be done to save them?

Even if she wanted to save them, there was nothing that she could do. They were trapped, controlled by the Damhur, and regardless of her connection, she could do nothing to save them.

"Let me help them," Fes said.

"I know that you want to help them, Fezarn, but there may not be anything for you to do."

"Just tell me where to find them. Let me see what I can do. If there's not, and if the only thing that I can offer them is the ability to hunt the Damhur, then that would be valuable to them, too. But if there is a chance that I can do more, that I can help them find a way to end their fighting, I would like to try."

It surprised him that he felt that way, yet as he said it, he realized that it was true. He *did* want to help the Asharn. He did want to ensure that they found some way to freedom, to end their fighting, and though he didn't know how to accomplish it, he felt it within him that he very much needed to find something.

Jesla studied Fes before nodding. "There is a place south of the valley. It's deep within the forest, much like this, though you will find the buildings elevated, off the ground, and in a place where the Damhur would struggle to find them."

"Elevated?" Jayell asked. "You mean in the trees?"

"In the trees. Above the trees. High enough that the Damhur would not find them, and high enough that any attempt to Call them, to enslave them, would be weakened by distance, even if they were walking right underneath them."

"And if they're in the trees, it's possible that now that the Damhur have controlled dragons, they have already discovered the Asharn," Fes said.

Jesla's eyes widened. "I had not considered that, but what you say is possible."

They needed to reach the Asharn. If they were in the trees, he understood why it had been difficult for others to find them. Thinking of the forest where they had wandered, trying to find Jayell, he hadn't been able to see all the way up into the canopy. If there was a forest similar to that, and if the Asharn had used the trees as a way to mask themselves, then the Damhur searching for them would never have succeeded.

"Where is this place?"

"As I said, it's beyond the valley."

"How far? How will I know how to find it?"

Jesla tapped him on the chest. As she did, power flooded into him, and Fes gasped. It came as a surge of Deshazl magic, and it filled him. At first, he feared that she was attacking him, but he knew that Jesla had no reason to attack him, and she seemed as if she honestly wanted to help him. Why would she attack him if that was her motivation?

The power settled into him, filling him, and with it came a certain understanding. It was almost as if a map formed in his head and he could see the entirety of this land within his mind. Dots of power were scattered all over, and it took a moment to realize that those were the Deshazl Jesla could detect. One such cluster was brighter than the rest, and he knew where it was that she wanted him to go.

She pulled her hand back and the image faded. Fes held onto it, straining to maintain that connection, to remember where she had wanted him to go, and hoped that it lingered long enough for him to find it.

"How were you able to do that?"

"That was my gift. And my curse."

Fes sighed. As he thought about all of the Deshazl that he had seen, it seemed impossible that there would be so many. Countless Deshazl had been on the other side of the valley, and countless Deshazl seemed as if they were still ensnared by the Damhur. How much must that torment her to see that when she closed her eyes?

He held her gaze. "I will find them. Somehow I will find them, and I will do my best to convince them to help."

"There is something that we might be able to offer to make that easier on you."

CHAPTER THIRTEEN

Fes sat atop the dragon, the wind whipping through his hair and pulling on the strange scaled cloak he had just been given. The fabric was unlike anything that he'd ever felt before, smooth and silky, and yet it was tough. He had played with the fabric, attempting to cut it with his dragonglass sword, and it had proven impenetrable. That alone surprised him, as nothing could withstand dragonglass.

The dragon stayed low to the ground, sweeping over the undulating hills, keeping close but far enough away that a straight arrow wouldn't be able to strike him. Fes didn't know whether arrows posed a danger to the dragon, but he didn't want to risk it, especially as other weapons might be problematic.

Jayell sat behind him, completely quiet as they flew

through the cool night air. The only sound was the flapping of the dragon's wings and the wind that whistled around them. Every so often, the dragon would erupt a mouthful of steam, and then they would feel a brief flutter of warmth as they flew through it. It rarely lasted long, but it was long enough to warm Fes.

"How much farther?" Jayell asked, yelling against the sound of the wind.

"It shouldn't be much farther," Fes said. He could still see the valley in his mind, and they had crossed that about half an hour ago. From there, they had to head across the forest until they found the Asharn in the midst of it. He looked down, twisting off the side of the dragon so that he could peer over it, wondering if there was any sign that he would be able to detect from here, but he saw nothing obvious.

Then again, they had just reached the outer edges of the trees. Fes could tell these were different trees that what had been in the forest near the Dragon's Eye, but they were still tall, and he felt a certain strength radiating from within the forest.

Maybe he detected Deshazl magic, though why would he detect it in such a way?

The dragon seemed to know where to go, and Fes wondered if it was tied to their new connection or whether Jesla had shared it with the dragon somehow. Either way, he didn't have to navigate for the dragon, and he could tell that they were heading in the right direction.

The dragon flapped his wings again and then shot up into the sky. He arced up over the forest, leaving Fes and Jayell clinging to his back.

"What are you doing?" Fes yelled.

"I am taking you where you need to go," the dragon said.

"Up?"

"Eventually," the dragon roared.

Fes squeezed onto the dragon's neck, holding on for fear of falling, but thankfully he did not. Neither did Jayell, though she pressed her entire body down upon the dragon, almost as if doing so would keep her in place.

The dragon changed direction again and flattened out, making it so that Fes and Jayell didn't struggle quite as much to hold on. Fes took a deep breath, feeling as if he had just run a long distance. The air up here was thin, making it harder to catch his breath. His ears popped and streaks of wispy clouds swirled around them, their mist making him even colder. What he wouldn't give for the dragon to breathe flames now.

As he thought it, the dragon let forth a burst of fire. The heat burned off the cloud nearest them, tearing free the mist, and left him a little more comfortable than he had been before.

"Thanks," Fes said. "How did you know?"

"Your discomfort is obvious."

"How is it that you can detect my discomfort?"

"How is it that you think to hide it?"

"I'm not trying to hide it," Fes said. "I just didn't realize that you would be able to pick up on it."

"The connection is there. All you have to do is reach through it."

"Reach through it?" Fes tried to pull on his Deshazl connection, straining to stretch between himself and the dragon, but he couldn't pick up on anything. If it was there, the connection was faint, almost too weak to pick up on. And yet, as he tried, he was aware of the dragon in a way that he hadn't been before. It was a sense of freedom that filled him, almost as if *he* were the one flying, not the dragon. He could feel the joy the dragon had in flying through the clouds, and he could feel the peace the dragon knew, heightened by the freedom that he felt.

"See?" the dragon rumbled.

"How is it that I can feel that?"

"There is a connection. You helped return the dragons to the world, and because of that, you share a connection to the dragons."

"I helped return you, not all of the dragons."

"Perhaps you only have the connection to me."

"I still don't know whether that connection will allow me to protect you from a Calling."

"No, we don't know whether that is the case."

"From what I experienced in the Dragon's Eye, it seems as if there should be some way to protect you, but..." He didn't know whether that would be his gift from the time in the Dragon's Eye or whether it was nothing more than a desire that would not come to fruition.

"We are linked," the dragon said.

"And I still don't know what that means."

"Neither do I, but what I can tell is your intention, much more so than I was able to determine before. I can tell your desire to keep the dragon safe. It flows through you, filling you, and because of it, you are to be trusted."

"I wasn't to be trusted before?"

"You are Deshazl, which means that you would be trusted, but you are not one of the dragons."

"You only trust the dragons?"

"The dragons have not betrayed us."

"Not intentionally," Fes said.

The dragon rumbled. "Not intentionally." With that, they started to dive, descending rapidly toward the ground. Wind whistled around him, making his eyes water, and Fes felt a moment of terror as they dropped, leaving him worried that he wouldn't be able to hang on. Even if he did, he feared how hard the landing might be.

When it happened, they nearly flipped off the dragon's back.

Surprisingly, Fes felt a surge of amusement come from the dragon.

He pushed forward his thoughts, the annoyance he felt, trying to make it clear so that the dragon knew that wasn't acceptable, but it only served to make the dragon even more amused.

They hovered.

They were just above the treetops, and as they hovered there, Fes looked down and saw the tops of the trees stretching toward them.

More than just the tops of the trees, he saw structures within them.

This was what Jesla had wanted them to see.

Fes tapped on Jayell's arm and pointed over the side of the dragon. "Look!"

She peered over, clinging tightly and much more cautiously than Fes had done. Her breath caught in a gasp. "That's the Asharn?"

Fes nodded. "From what Jesla said, this is where the Asharn have been hiding."

"When you said they used the trees, I hadn't expected this."

"What had you expected?"

"I don't know. I guess not this."

"It makes sense. They can stay hidden within the tree-tops, staying above the effect of the Calling. If some of them are not able to resist the Calling, they can use the distance to help." Fes looked over the side of the dragon. "We have to jump down, don't we?"

"If you want to reach these people, you do."

"And if we need to escape?"

"You know how to reach me," the dragon said. "If nothing else, the experience with the Dragon's Eye should have told you that there is something between us. Use that. Use your Deshazl connection. I will know."

Fes noticed a platform that they could jump to. It was quite a ways down, but the dragon angled, tipping off to the side as he adjusted his wings, staying in place. Fes could sense the strain within the dragon, the effort that it took for him to hold in such a position, and he motioned to Jayell.

"We have to head down," he said.

"We're just going to jump?"

"For now, but if this doesn't work—"

"If this doesn't work, then we will be facing the Asharn. You know what happened the last time we encountered them."

Fes nodded. "This will be different."

"Right. This will be different because this time, we will be invading their home. I saw how talented they were, and if this doesn't work, we might not be able to get free."

Fes took a deep breath and pulled on his Deshazl connection, letting it fill him. When it did, he jumped.

He pushed off the platform with his Deshazl magic, sending it out from him in a tight band of power, using that to slow his descent. When he landed on the platform, he did so with a soft thud, hopefully not so much that the Asharn would realize that they were here. It was unlikely that they would be able to arrive without any notice, especially considering they came by dragon, but the longer they could go without detection, the better off Fes thought they would be.

He looked up. Jayell clung to the side of the dragon for a long moment. Fes worried that she wouldn't jump, that she would remain clinging to the dragon's back and he would need to come face the Asharn alone.

Finally, Jayell jumped.

She shot toward him, and then a spell built. Fes felt it surge outward, and as she fell, the spell suddenly dissipated.

He swore under his breath and lunged forward, using his Deshazl connection to stabilize himself as he tried to catch her. She crashed into him, driving him down to the platform, where she collapsed upon him.

Fes helped her up and glanced at the dragon. He had already begun to ascend, getting higher and higher. There was a sense of amusement within him, as if the injury Fes had nearly sustained was enough to make him laugh.

He focused on annoyance, wanting the dragon to

realize how he felt, but the amusement within the dragon only intensified.

They would have to work on that.

"Are you okay?" Fes asked.

Jayell nodded. "My spell failed."

"I think that in this place, your spells might not be terribly effective."

"They weren't very effective in the last place we were, either."

"Just know that I am here and I will protect you as much as possible."

"How?"

"How? I will do everything that I can to defend you."

Jayell shook her head. "How would you do everything you can to protect me? The rest of the Asharn will have similar abilities. What makes you think that you have any greater abilities than them?"

"I have the dragon," he said.

"And they have more people, and probably more strength than you do. What if they treat you the same way as the last people treated us? What if they attack, holding us?"

"If they do, we have the dragon who will come and help."

"And what if the dragon can't reach us?"

"Then we have to convince them to work with us."

"And if they don't?"

"If they don't, then…"

Fes trailed off. There was the sound of movement below them, and he motioned to Jayell, trying to silence her.

They looked around the platform, but there wasn't any good place to hide. It was open, and while they weren't in any real danger, they weren't in an optimal spot for a first encounter with the Asharn.

Fes looked up at the dragon. He was now a dark smear across the sky, small enough that he thought the Asharn wouldn't recognize that a dragon flew overhead, but far enough away that if they were to need help, he wouldn't be able to get to them very easily.

"Where do we go?" she whispered.

Fes shook his head. "I don't know."

He looked around the platform. It was made from planks of wood that had been all fitted together, somehow elevated into the tree, making it so that it was difficult to see how it was anchored, though it was definitely anchored here somehow.

There was no railing, and there didn't seem to be any way down. They were trapped, though there had to be some connection to the ground. The platform was here for a purpose, but what was it?

He hurried around the edges, looking down as he went. A rope ladder led down, and he went over to it, motioning Jayell to join him.

"This will lead us down," he said.

"But down to where?" she asked.

"I don't know. Down from here."

She rested her hand on his arm. "Fezarn, I don't know that this makes a whole lot of sense, especially as we don't know what we'll find. We can call to the dragon. Let's head through the forest from the ground level, and then we can see what else we can figure out."

"I'm not sure that going at ground level makes that much sense," Fes said. "If we do that, it will take too long, and we are running low on time. I worry that the Damhur have already pushed back the fire mages. You know what we saw."

"If they have, then it might not even matter."

"It matters. We need help to oppose them. We need whatever help we can find to ensure that we stop them."

He glanced up at her, holding her gaze for a moment, and then he grabbed onto the rope ladder and quickly started down. The rope was stout, and it seemed covered with some sticky resin that kept him from falling. He was thankful for that resin, and he hurried down the ladder, looking through the trees as he went, searching for signs of someone following them, but saw nothing. There was no one around. There was no other platform along the way, either. How were they to find the Asharn? There had to be some other way from here, and there had to be some way to figure out where the Asharn might be hiding, but he saw nothing.

He glanced up. Jayell was descending, making her way down the rope above him. Fes paused until she reached him, and the two of them held onto the rope, looking around.

"What if this takes us back to the ground?" she asked.

Fes hadn't given it much thought. It was possible that the platform was separate from their living area. What if this was a place the Asharn used to look out, a way of ensuring that the rest of their territory was safe? Maybe they had chosen the wrong place to arrive.

"If it takes us back to the ground, then we will wander along the ground until we find some way of reaching the Asharn," he said.

"And if we don't find the Asharn?" Fes looked over at her, but she shook her head. "I'm just saying, Fes, that we have seen no sign of the Asharn other than this platform. What if there isn't any way to reach them?"

"Jesla showed me they were here. We will find them."

Fes continued to descend, making his way down the rope ladder with Jayell moving just above him. Every so often, he would pause and look up, mostly to ensure that she was still coming, but he was worried that there might be someone pursuing them from above. So far, he hadn't seen anyone coming at them from below.

They had heard the sounds of pursuit, Fes was sure of that, but where were they?

He hesitated, listening. As he did, he didn't detect anything, certainly not anything that would help him know whether there was anyone to fear nearby.

And he worried that they had made a mistake. Everything told him that they were taking the right path, that they weren't making a mistake, but he couldn't help but wonder if perhaps they had veered off in the wrong direction.

"I don't see anything," Fes said.

"We missed it," Jayell said.

"What if we didn't?" he asked. He looked around, and he thought that he could see the distant outline of the forest floor far below them, but maybe he was wrong. How high up could the trees be?

"What do you think it is?" Jayell asked.

"What if we didn't miss it at all? What if the platform is just like you said? What if it leads to nowhere other than the bottom of the forest?"

"Then the platform wasn't how we would get to the other parts of the Asharn," she said.

Fes let out a heavy sigh. That was it. They had missed it, somewhere. "We need to go back."

"Fes, I'm not sure that this is the right thing to do."

"If we don't go back, I won't be able to find out whether the Asharn are even here, and I know that they are." He had seen it in the vision that Jesla had helped him with. He was confident of what he'd seen, and while he didn't know exactly how she was able to show him, he was positive that what he had experienced, the vision that she'd shown him of the lights scattered throughout this land, represented people with shadow abilities. People like the Asharn.

They started back up the ladder, and now Jayell was above him, and Fes followed. She moved quickly, comfortably climbing the rope ladder, and Fes marveled at how well she adjusted to the strangeness.

Was he making a mistake? What did he really know about the Asharn? He had encountered them in Anuhr when they had attacked the palace, and he had very nearly not survived, but he had managed to escape. There would be more like that, possibly enough more that he should be concerned about it, but at the same time, he was sure that the Asharn had helped with the dragons.

That was the help he was after.

If he could find some way to get that help, if he could find the Asharn who had risked themselves to work with the empire, then maybe—just maybe—they would be able to get the help they needed.

When they reached the platform, Fes pulled himself up and realized they weren't alone. Jayell pressed her hand back, a warning to him.

"Two of you," a voice said.

Fes stepped alongside Jayell, wanting to protect her. He saw a man in a forest green jacket and pants, the colors practically designed to blend into the trees.

"We have come to ask the Asharn for help," Fes said.

"How did you find us?" the man asked.

Two others were standing on either side of him, both dressed in the same manner. One of them had a thick beard, and the other was a woman with short brown hair. She was lean and stood casually with a dangerous sort of grace. Something told him that he didn't want to fight either of these two.

"We had help," he said, motioning to the cloak he wore.

"You aren't with them. How did you get that cloak?"

"We are," Fes said.

The man took a step forward and glared at Fes. "I can feel the fire magic within this one. She uses it much like the Damhur, but if she were one of the Damhur, she would have attempted a Calling. As she has not, I can only assume that either she's incapable of it or she is attempting to mask her ability. As I said, where did you get that cloak?"

Fes pointed into the sky. "Do you see the dragon?"

All three of them looked up. It was almost as if they couldn't help themselves, and if Fes were going to attack, now would be the time to do so. He could dart forward and put a sword through them, but at the same time, he didn't come here to attack the Asharn. He came to look for help, and there was no way that he would be able to get that help if he harmed them.

Fes could feel the dragon circling and didn't need to look up to know that he was up there, flying, and every so often, he would breathe out fire. Fes realized that the dragon did it for his benefit, and for the benefit of those he was with.

Smiling to himself, he waited for the Asharn to turn their attention back to him.

"Do you control that?" the man asked, looking at Jayell.

Jayell crossed her arms over her chest. "I am not one of the Damhur."

"Then how do you command the dragon?"

"Because I'm Deshazl," Fes said.

The Asharn stared at him. "You? *You're* the one who controls the dragon?"

"It's dragon, not sky beast to you?"

The man laughed bitterly. "Those fools fear the dragons. They revere them, but at the same time, they are scared of them. They view them as something more than what they are."

"How do you know that they don't view them exactly as they are?" Fes asked.

"If you control the dragon, then you know that they are animals and nothing more."

The comment was almost enough to make Fes turn back. Anyone who would believe that the dragons were only animals was not the kind of person that Fes wanted to rely on.

Then again, maybe it was a test. Perhaps they felt the same way as him, and they were using statements like that to draw Fes out, to test and see exactly how he felt about the dragon.

It was Fes's turn to attempt a test.

"Animals who breathe fire. Animals who have long worked with the Deshazl," he said.

The man stared at him.

"And they are the same animals that others of the Asharn helped."

The man narrowed his brow. "How is it that you know this?"

"Because I was there."

"You were there?"

"I was there when the dragons were attacked by the Damhur and the Asharn helped. Without their assistance, the dragons would have been Called sooner."

"What do you mean, *sooner*?"

"The Damhur have Called the two dragons that were first raised within the empire. And now they have begun to attack."

"Fools. All of them."

The man turned away from Fes. At the edge of the platform, he jumped, disappearing into the leaves.

The other two followed, and when they were gone, Fes could do nothing other than stare after where they had gone.

"That was strange," Jayell said.

"Incredibly strange, and it makes me uncertain whether or not I should trust them."

"Why?"

"I don't know what to make of them. I'm not sure if the comments they have made are to test me or if that's actually how they feel about the dragons."

"Let's assume that a test. And let's assume that they didn't simply jump to the ground using their Deshazl magic. So what do you want to do now?"

Fes stared into the trees. "I think we have to follow."

"I was afraid you were going to say that. I'm not sure that I can follow."

"Why not?"

"If they have jumped off into the trees, and if they have used their Deshazl magic, I don't know that I will be able to do the same."

"I can help," Fes said.

"And what if you can't?" Jayell smiled at him. She rested her hand on his arm, as if to reassure him. "I can't use my fire magic here. They are too strong, or this place is too strong. Either way, it doesn't seem as if I'm able to do anything. I'm blocked, and my magic is blocked. If it comes down to it and I need to fight, I won't be able to. If it comes down to it and I need to use my magic to move through the trees, again, I won't be able to."

"I don't like the idea of going alone."

"I don't like it, either, but didn't you say that the dragon can sense your emotions?"

Fes nodded.

"I will stay with the dragon. If anything is wrong, he can tell me, and then we can come after you."

Fes didn't like it, but her idea made a certain sort of sense.

"If something happens to me, I want you to return to the empire. I want you to convince the dragon to help push back the Damhur."

"Nothing's going to happen to you, Fezarn," she said softly.

"But if it does—"

Jayell pulled him into an embrace. She looked up at him, grabbing either side of his face, and kissed him gently on the lips. "Nothing is going to happen to you. Come back to me."

Fes could only nod.

He sent a message through the connection to the dragon and waited. It didn't take long for the dragon to descend, dropping down to the platform and hovering.

"Jayell needs to stay with you. And you need to monitor to ensure my safety," Fes said.

"What if you are injured?" the dragon growled.

"Then I need you to tear through these trees to get me," Fes said.

"You don't worry about them Calling me?"

"I don't think that any of them can. They are Deshazl, so not able to Call, but that doesn't mean that they wouldn't try to manipulate you if it came down to it. You need to do what you think is best."

The dragon let out a throaty roar. "If anything happens, I will tear through these trees for you, Deshazl."

Jayell wrapped her arms around Fes once more, pulling him into a hug. He hugged her back, and when he released her, she climbed onto the back of the dragon. Together they soared, flying higher and higher until they became little more than a dark streak in the sky. It left Fes more comfortable knowing that Jayell would be safe.

He turned to the edge of the platform where the others had disappeared, looking through the leaves in the branches, trying to see where they had jumped but coming up with nothing.

He took a deep breath, pulling on his Deshazl magic, wrapping it around himself. He held it within him and pushed, jumping with everything that he could muster, until he stretched across the distance, disappearing through the branches.

He felt a burst of power as he parted through what must have been some sort of barrier, and once he was through, an entire city opened around him.

Fes went tumbling, landing on another platform, this one much larger than the last, and went rolling before he could spring to his feet. Three Asharn waited for him.

"Come with us, Deshazl," the lead Asharn said.

Fes glanced back. There was no way that Jayell would have been able to clear that barrier, and maybe that was the test.

He turned back to the Asharn and followed into their city.

CHAPTER FOURTEEN

The Asharn city spread out in front of him. Fes marveled at it. The entire city was elevated, raised into the trees, with most of it high above the treetops. Somehow, they had masked its presence from the platform, leaving the platform as the only evidence that there was anything here. Were it not for that, Fes and Jayell might never have known that there was anything within the trees, and had they not managed to encounter the Asharn, they might never have found the city.

Fes couldn't help but gape at his surroundings. He had never seen anything like it. Most of the structures were designed around the trees, and they circled the entirety of the upper canopy. They used the branches here and wove them together, creating rooftops. Bridges stretched between trees, most of them made of rope and wood slats, and people moved along the bridges.

Every so often, someone would pause and look over, and when they saw Fes, they hesitated. Was it his clothing? Did the cloak he'd taken from the other Deshazl name him as an outsider? The others had made it seem as if wearing that cloak would help him when it came time to getting integrated into the Asharn, but he wondered if perhaps it had the opposite effect and if it made him even more obviously an outsider.

The Asharn wore deep greens speckled with brown, clothing that camouflaged them as they moved through the trees. Most of their clothing seemed to ripple and shimmer, and Fes suspected that it didn't have the same resistance to dragonglass as his borrowed cloak. If nothing else, that resistance was valuable to him, and he would have kept the cloak for no other reason than that.

The lead Asharn guided him across one of the bridges, and as Fes stepped out onto it, it swayed beneath him. He grabbed the ropes, squeezing them and feeling unsettled, but considering how many people moved through here, he wondered if there was any reason to worry at all. Obviously it was safe enough for these people to move through here, and he needed to be less concerned.

The other two Asharn followed Fes, keeping right behind him. With each step, the bridge seemed to sway even more, and he wished they would give him more space rather than walking so close, but he couldn't necessarily tell them to back off. Instead, he hurried after the lead Asharn, trying to keep pace with him.

The leader stepped out near one of the buildings, and when he did, he glanced over at Fes. "Wait here," he said.

Fes looked around the Asharn city again. He tried to get a sense of how many lived here, but he couldn't tell. There had to be hundreds, probably thousands, but were they all Deshazl? Were they all people that the Asharn had rescued from the Damhur? If so, then how was it that they still struggled with the Damhur? They had numbers, certainly enough to resist the Damhur, even if it wasn't enough to overthrow them.

Unless they still feared a Calling.

That might be more the reason than anything else.

Another thought came to him. Could a place like this be where his parents had departed from? They had managed to escape the Damhur, and if that were the case, then maybe they had been here before. Perhaps he would find someone within this city who had known his parents. It seemed almost too much to hope for.

The Asharn man returned and nodded for Fes to follow him.

"What's your name?" Fes asked.

He looked back. "My name is Hodan Fehr."

"I'm Fezarn Varan."

The man stared at him for a moment before nodding.

They crossed another bridge, and it led them to another platform, and from there they crossed to another bridge, and then to another platform. On and on they went, bridge to platform to building, rarely giving Fes a chance to fully adjust. Each bridge was the same as the last, swaying under his weight and making him incredibly uncomfortable, fearing that perhaps he might fall over the edge of the rope railing and tumble to the ground below.

Once in a while, Fes glanced down, curious how far it would be if he were to fall, and each time he did, he regretted it. It was an impossibly far distance. If he were to fall, he would continue to fall, and he didn't know how long it would take until he hit the ground, but certainly there would be no surviving something like that. Even if he were to use his Deshazl connection, there would be no way to survive.

Someone pushed him from behind, and he glanced over at the Asharn woman who stayed with him. The other two had been silent as they made their way through the trees, and he wondered if they disagreed with the decision to bring him with them. Maybe it was going to be more like what he'd experienced with Chornan and Jesla, and he would reach a council who would refuse to work with him.

At one platform, he saw three Asharn, all of them armed with dragonglass and busy sparring. They moved quickly, every so often lashing out with a blast of Deshazl magic, enough that Fes could feel it within himself. They were powerful, skilled, and very clearly soldiers.

That was what Chornan had worried about. He disagreed with the way the Asharn had become soldiers, but without their willingness to serve, there would be no way to oppose the Damhur. Seeing Asharn fighting like this, seeing the way they were sparring, gave Fes hope. If they were willing to battle in such a way, and if they were willing to train like soldiers, he had to believe that they would be useful in a battle.

The woman shoved him again, and he staggered forward, nearly sprawling on the bridge. He caught himself and hung on for a moment before continuing forward.

At the next stop, they reached a massive building. The Asharn headed inside, leaving Fes to either go with them or wait outside. The woman gave him no choice and nudged him forward.

Fes stood at the doorway. It was an open door, with nothing more than a curtain blocking out the outside, and as he pushed through it, he smelled a floral fragrance that seemed to overwhelm everything else. He glanced up, noticing the way the branches were woven together, creating the roof overhead. Several windows had been worked into the walls, and curtains hung in front of them, too. Each of the curtains seemed to be made of the same cloth the Asharn wore, making it practically shimmer.

"Is this him?"

Fes turned to see an elderly woman sitting on a chair that looked to be made from the tree itself. She sat with her arms resting on two twisted armrests and stared at him. Deep gray hair hung down to her shoulders, spilling over her forest green jacket. She studied him with the same intensity that he'd once seen Arudis use.

Power radiated from her. Fes could feel it, and there was a potency to it that he couldn't deny. This was a powerful Asharn, regardless of how old she might be.

"This is him. He claims that he visited *them*." Hodan glanced over at Fes, watching him for a moment.

"Look at his cloak. You would question whether he does or not?"

"He came with another. She uses the dragon bones much like the Damhur."

"There are others who use those dragon bones in the same way," the woman said.

"Yes. He claims he comes from them," Hodan said.

The woman got up from her throne and made her way toward Fes. She circled around him slowly, staring at him. She was nearly his height, coming only a hand or so below him, and she only had to look up a little to meet his eyes. Hers were a steely gray, not anything like the deep blue eyes Fes had, and she studied him.

"You are from the empire?"

Fes nodded.

"And the report is that you traveled by dragon."

Fes glanced over at the others before nodding. "That is how I traveled."

"But you are not Damhur. You don't control the dragon."

Fes shook his head. "I'm not Damhur. I speak to the dragon, and we work together."

"You would have us believe that you are like the Deshazl of old."

Fes shrugged. "I'm not sure. If that's how the Deshazl of old were, then that's what I'm saying."

She glanced at the others a moment before pressing her hand out, pushing it onto Fes's chest.

A surge of Deshazl magic radiated from her hand, and Fes instinctively created a barrier around himself. Without meaning to, he drew upon the strength of the dragon, letting that add to what he was able to call upon, and the combined energies helped him suppress her ability to reach him with whatever it was she attempted to do.

She smiled. "Strong, too."

"What were you trying to do?"

"I was testing you."

"Then did I pass?"

She returned to her throne, settling down into it,

squeezing the arms of the chair. They seemed to be more like vines than branches, and the leaves blooming from them were a little different than those that were woven into the roof. While the leaves of the roof were broad and circular, those of the throne she sat upon were narrow and curled together.

"Tell me, Deshazl of the empire, why have you come here?"

Fes glanced at her before turning his attention to the others. Was she the ruler? Was she the one he needed to sway, to somehow convince to work with him? He couldn't tell. It certainly seemed as if the other Deshazl deferred to her, but that didn't mean that she was.

"I came for help."

"Help?"

Fes tipped his head in a nod. "The Damhur have come to the shores of the empire."

The woman flicked her gaze to Hodan before returning her attention to Fes. "If the Damhur have reached the empire, then we have no reason to help."

"You believe that their attention on the empire means that your people are safe?"

"You have insight. That's more than I was expecting out of you."

The woman might seem like she was motherly, but that wasn't it at all. There was a ruthless streak within her, and that's what Fes had to appeal to. That was how she managed to lead the Asharn.

"How long do you think it will take the Damhur to return their attention to the Asharn?"

"The Damhur don't pose any threat to us. And if they have turned their attention to the empire, then there is even less reason for us to be concerned."

"You believe that you are safe? You believe that you're protected within the trees?"

Fes took a step toward her, and the two Asharn who had escorted him hurried forward. Swords quickly slipped out of their sheaths, blocking his access to her.

He ignored them. Giving them any sort of attention was what they wanted, and by ignoring them, he would unsettle them.

"They have two dragons. They have Called them, and now they control them. How long do you think it will be before they turn their attention to the Asharn when they have more than two dragons?"

"It will take some time for them to conquer the empire, and by then—"

"How long do you think they will take to conquer the empire when they find more dragons to raise?" Fes asked.

The woman stared at him, falling silent. "What do you mean?" she finally asked.

"Only that there are other dragons they intend to raise, and if given enough time, they will succeed. When

260 | D.K. HOLMBERG

they do, your elevated city will no longer be safe. The dragon I traveled with was able to find it, and if he was able to find it, I doubt it will pose much of a challenge for the Damhur, people who have been searching for the Asharn for some time." Fes hoped that was true, and hoped that what Arudis had shared with him was accurate enough to make them concerned. If it was, then maybe he could get them worried enough to help.

"Raising a dragon is difficult," she said dismissively.

Fes shook his head. "I raised a dragon. It's not nearly so difficult as you would believe."

She leaned forward just a little, but enough that Fes knew that he had her attention. "*You* raised a dragon?"

He smiled. "Is that a secret that you would like me to reveal?"

"I take it that you won't reveal it without some incentive to do so," she said.

"I've told you what I came for."

"You told me that you came for help."

He nodded. "The Damhur and their dragons have begun their assault on the empire. The empire needs help, and they need people who know how to combat the Damhur."

"If they've already reached the empire, there's nothing that we will be able to do from here."

"Even with the dragon to transport?"

She smiled tightly. "Even if we were to trust your willingness to bring us to the empire, your dragon can only carry so many. I'm afraid that there is little that we can do to help." She leaned back, watching him. "You may stay with the Asharn. Your empire will fall, but we could use someone with your knowledge."

"If I stay, I intend to lead."

She smiled widely at him. "Is that right?"

"And if I lead, I intend to ensure the Asharn help."

"There are some among my people who would view that as a threat."

"There are some who might view your invitation as something other than an invitation."

She waved her hand, dismissing the idea. "It was a suggestion. It wasn't a statement that I would hold you here, certainly not against your will. You are free to leave, though it sounds as if there is nothing for you to return to."

"Are you afraid?" Fes asked.

The woman frowned, leaning back in her throne. "Afraid?"

Fes nodded. "There are those who say you fear the Dragon's Eye, and that's why you don't make the journey beyond this forest."

A flush worked up her cheeks, leaving them red and angry. "Fear? We continue to fight. We continue to release those who are controlled, unlike those who stay hidden in their homes, protected through the ancient magics, relying on the Dragon's Eye to conceal them. We fear nothing. We work to rescue those who need our help, and we will continue to do so."

He had gotten to her. He wasn't sure what it would have taken, but hearing that there were some among the Asharn who refused to go to the Dragon's Eye had been enough. Fes wasn't surprised that there would be some who would refuse to go. Had he known what he might encounter, he wasn't sure that he would even have gone.

"If you're not afraid, then why do you refuse to offer your help to those who need it?"

"Why should we offer our help?"

"Because there are Deshazl within the empire. Most know nothing about who they are, and I have traveled throughout the empire, trying to help ensure that those who have the Deshazl connection were not Called by the Damhur, but there was only so much that I was able to do."

She studied him for a long moment. "You did that?"

"They used wagons," Fes said. "They would Call those who were sensitive. They placed them into wagons, forcing them into the back as if they were no more than cattle. There were dozens the first time I encountered the Damhur, and when I escaped, I helped rescue the others, and I guided them away until we reached someone who was able to help. There are those within the empire who would fight the Damhur, but there is only so much they can do. None understand how to resist the Calling, and I very nearly didn't resist, but then again, it was one of the Trivent who had Called me."

The woman froze. "Which of the Trivent Called you?"

Fes closed his eyes for a moment. It was all too easy to think back and remember what it had been like when he had been under the influence of Elsanelle and Liza. He had lost himself, and there was a time when he wanted to serve them, and despite every intention to resist, he had struggled against it.

"Elsanelle. And her daughters, but she was the one who attempted it most of all."

"And where is she now?"

"Gone."

"Gone?"

Fes nodded. "Gone. Dead. Destroyed as she was trying to Call the dragon and failed." He flicked his gaze to the Asharn who were standing in front of him and then over to Hodan. Without Asharn helping, the dragon wouldn't have been able to resist the Calling, and he would have succumbed to Elsanelle.

"You were there when one of the Trivent, the worst of the Trivent, fell?"

Fes nodded slowly. He didn't care for Elsanelle, but he hadn't realized that she had been so awful to the Asharn. He should've known better, especially considering how she had been so willing to use the Deshazl within the empire, and he should have known that she would have done something similar here. How badly must she have treated these people?

"Tell me how she died."

"Does it matter?" Fes asked.

"It matters."

"She thought she had me Called, and the dragon gave me strength. Together we were able to overpower her." It wasn't quite like that, but it was near enough that it didn't matter. He had joined with the dragon, and together they had managed to overpower Elsanelle. It was much the same way that he worked with the dragon now.

Would she decide that he was telling the truth, or would she worry about him and decide to challenge his assertions about his experience with Elsanelle? If she did, Fes didn't know whether he would be able to convince her otherwise. He had shared everything that he could, and there was nothing more that he thought he would be able to tell her that might persuade her to trust him. Without anything more to share, it might be that any hope of convincing the Asharn to work with him was gone.

And as he stood before this woman, he wondered if she would even allow him to leave.

"She's gone," she said.

Fes nodded. "She's gone. I can guarantee that she is."

She leaned back in the throne, resting her head

against the wood. Fes couldn't see how it would be comfortable to rest on that and struggled to see how the throne she used would be relaxing, but she rested upon it as if it were as comfortable as any lounge chair could be.

"I am surprised that they sent her to your empire."

Fes wanted to argue and tell her that it wasn't his empire, but he was the one who had come looking for help from the Asharn. If it wasn't his empire, who else would claim it?

"They were after a dragon," Fes said.

"And your people couldn't prevent them from reaching them."

"We prevented them at first, but they were persistent. When they realized that they had succeeded in resurrecting a dragon, they continued to push, and began to Call throughout the empire, using their influence to reach for the dragon."

"They resurrected one dragon?"

Fes nodded.

"And yet, you claim they have two dragons."

"There was another. It was raised by those who came from here, though they didn't do so quite as effectively. The dragon they raised was weak and did not have nearly the same strength as the one raised by the Damhur."

"Then you will need to fear one dragon."

"The other dragon was healed."

Fes wasn't sure how much of the raising of the other

dragon was the result of the Asharn. Arudis was a part of that, but she was a part of it as someone who left Javoor, searching for safety, but did that mean that she was serving the Asharn at that time?

Fes didn't think so. If she served the Asharn, Arudis would have known more about them. No, Arudis went to the empire as a way to escape the Damhur, wanting to get away and establish a sense of safety.

"So that is how the Damhur have managed to acquire two dragons," the woman said.

"They knew about one, and when they chased that dragon, they discovered the other. We managed to fend them off a second time, but when they came a third time, we weren't prepared."

"And now?"

"And now they are at the shores of the empire, using the dragons to attack, and the fire mages—those who can defend the empire—are limited in how much they can oppose them. They try, but there is only so much that they can do, despite their best intentions."

The woman crossed her arms over her chest, studying Fes. "What is it that you would ask of us?"

"You have some way of protecting yourself from the Calling."

"Not as much as you would think."

"It has to be more than what most of our Deshazl are capable of doing. With protections like that, we would not need to fear the Damhur attacking, and we would be able to resist them."

The woman studied him. "It's not so much your fear for yourself that you are here for, is it?"

"I'm here to see if there's anything that we can do to help protect the dragons. I have a connection to one, but I'm not even sure if that connection is strong enough for me to protect him against the Damhur. And the other two need to be rescued, and we need to do so before the Damhur manage to claim additional dragons."

"You said that before. How is it that they would be able to find additional dragons?"

"What do you know of the history of the dragons?"

"More than you, I would imagine."

"Perhaps," Fes acknowledged. "But do you know the history of dragons and the empire?"

"Why don't you tell me what you know. I'll tell you if it's accurate."

"The Damhur came to the empire a thousand years ago. They had the ability to Call, and they used that ability upon the dragons. They controlled them, directing them and forcing them to attack. There were those within the empire at the time who resisted, and they fought as much as they could, but there were limits to their ability to resist. The dragons worked with the Deshazl, a people who shared with them a similar strength, but that wasn't enough, not against the might of the Damhur. They found others with a different ability, that which allowed them to use the remains of the dragons to generate great power. They called themselves fire mages, and they used the dragon bones to summon power. With that power, they were able to oppose the Damhur. The dragons willingly retreated, and as they disappeared, they did so to protect the people they cared about—the Deshazl. From what I can tell, the dragons always intended to return, but to do so, they had to wait, and they placed their memories—their essence—within a safeguard, in the hopes that one day they would be able to return to this world."

"And I imagine that you have found this safeguard?"

"Not intentionally. When I found the last dragon, it was accidental more than anything else. The key is finding the remains of a dragon, the bones to place the essence within. That is how the dragon is raised."

"Then we don't need to fear. If the Damhur have gone to your empire, there is little to worry about."

"Other than the fact that the empire has collected dragon remains for centuries. The fire mages have entire warehouses full of relics, and the Damhur have attacked that place first, and now they own many of those relics. All they need is the essence of dragons, and with that, they will be able to raise others."

She stared at him. He couldn't tell if she was trying to decide whether or not to help or if it was something else. It might be that she was angry at the fact that they allowed the Damhur to acquire the dragons, as Fes was angry with himself over that. If there were anything that he could have done differently, he would have. He wanted nothing more than to protect the dragons, to ensure that they were able to have the freedom that they longed for, to have them flying freely in the sky much as they once had, and much as they did in his visions, but that currently wasn't to be the dragons' fate.

To gain the trust of the Asharn, Fes would have to trust. These were Deshazl, at least they had been. They shared the same connection, and it meant that there had to be some among them who wanted nothing more than to protect the dragons. If he could find those of the Asharn who wanted to protect the dragons, those like the Asharn who had helped him when he had been in the forest, he thought that he would be able to find some who might view the dragons the same way that Fes did.

Trust.

It was difficult, especially with everything that he had been through with the people from this land. Not only the Damhur, but the Asharn had also attacked, leaving Fes wondering if he truly could trust. How much did he dare try?

And maybe this entire trip was a mistake, but it was a risk that he had been willing to take.

"The essence of the dragons were placed into sculptures," Fes said.

The woman stared at him. "Sculptures?"

"They were placed within sculptures of dragons. They are made of dragonglass, and some of them are larger than others, but I believe that all of them represent dragons who sacrificed themselves."

The woman glanced from Fes to the other Asharn with her. "How certain of this are you?"

Fes breathed out heavily. "Certain enough. They might not know what they are, but the sculpture that I found was definitely the dragon. There was a part of it that reverberated with me, connecting to me, and I was able to use it to help resurrect the dragon. Somehow I connected to that power even before the dragon returned, and when it did return, the dragon was even more connected to me."

The woman got off the throne and took a step toward Fes. "You are certain?"

"That's what I told you," Fes said, frowning.

"There is something the Damhur have. Most view it as a sign of their power, a signal of their wealth, but if what you say is true, then maybe it's something else, something that even they don't know. They have had them for years, long since the war ended and the Damhur returned to these lands."

Fes's heart began to pound within his chest. "What

is it?"

"They call it the gallery. It's a place within Javoor where they keep these sculptures. They are much like you describe, and they are incredibly detailed, something that the Damhur claim their greatest artisans created, and yet none have been able to replicate."

"Are they made out of dragonglass?"

"They are all dragonglass."

"Where is this?"

"In the heart of Javoor. Within the depths of the Damhur. It's a place that is unreachable."

How long would it take for the Damhur to realize that the sculptures contained the dragons? Now that they had Called the dragons, how long would it be before the dragons revealed that secret?

Fes had to think that it wouldn't be very long. There was only so much that the dragons could do to resist, and he had already seen how they struggled against the Damhur even though they wanted nothing more than to fight, to rip through the Damhur, to resist the way that the Damhur wanted to use them.

"We need to go to them," Fes said. If they were able to reach those sculptures, and if somehow he were able to resurrect dragons that he could control, that he could protect, then he wouldn't need to worry about the Damhur resurrecting them.

The woman shook her head. "What you say is impossible. These sculptures, and this gallery, are in a place within Javoor that we can't reach."

"Can't or won't?"

That attitude surprised him, especially because the Asharn seemed like warriors, like fighters, and he would have thought that they would be the most willing to take a journey like this and to risk themselves, but it seemed as if they remained afraid, and Fes understood that fear. It was a fear that he shared, but if they did nothing, they would never be able to stop the Damhur.

As much as the dragons had thought to retreat from the world to protect themselves, Fes believed that raising them, bringing them back into the world, was the key to saving them. It was possible that he was wrong. It was possible that his belief that resurrecting the dragons was mistaken, but he felt as if there was no choice. Finding those sculptures was one part of the way that he thought he could oppose the Damhur.

"It can't be done," the woman said. She turned away from him. "You may go."

"Go?"

She stood at one of the windows, looking out at the Asharn city. What did she see when she stood there? What was out there that drew her attention?

"Go," she said again. "I won't hold you here."

Fes wanted to argue, but what was there to say? He had come to these lands searching for allies, and instead he had found people who refused to fight, and then another people who were too frightened even though they wanted to give off appearances that they were not.

"If I fail, and if the Damhur come after you, they will have dragons. They will tear through your city. Your people will be destroyed."

"We will survive. We have done so over the last thousand years."

"That's how long you have been hiding in the trees?"

"Living, not hiding."

Fes looked around. "It seems to me that you're hiding. You want to seem as if you're not, but you are hiding."

She looked over at him and opened her mouth as if to say something, but snapped it closed and waved for him to leave.

Fes didn't have much choice in the matter, especially when the two Asharn with him pushed him out of the room, away from her, and back out into the Asharn city.

CHAPTER FIFTEEN

As they made their way across the platforms, traversing bridge to bridge, Fes couldn't help but look around the space. There were thousands of people living here. All of them under the protection of the woman and the rest of the Asharn. Not all of them would be fighters, and while he had seen some who were fighting, he had to believe that they were the exception rather than the rule. If that were the case, then why train?

He nodded at one of the platforms where two people sparred. "Why do they practice like that?" he asked Hodan.

Hodan paused and stood on the middle of the bridge they were crossing, looking out over the platforms. Where the two men sparred, the platform was open on all sides. A misstep would lead them to fall far into the forest below, a fall that would likely be fatal. All they needed were railings to make it safer, and Fes wondered why they didn't place them, unless doing so would destabilize the platform in some way.

"They practice so that we can be ready."

"Ready for what?"

"Ready for the possibility of the Damhur attacking."

"If you're ready for the Damhur attacking, then why would you not be willing to fight?"

"We prepare so that we can help rescue those who are still trapped. We do as much as we can to ensure the safety of our people, but there are limits."

"If you are willing to do that, then why won't you try to reach this gallery?"

"Reaching the gallery is suicide. It's at the heart of Javoor, within the city of Ranur, and a place where our people cannot reach, not easily."

"Is it because you fear getting Called?"

Hodan glanced over at him. "Many of us have learned to protect our minds. Those protections would keep us from a Calling unless it were particularly powerful. The Trivent might be strong enough to overwhelm the protections that we are able to place upon ourselves."

"If you can protect your minds, then why would you fear going there?"

"Some have tried," Hodan said, starting reluctantly. He glanced at the other two Asharn, but neither of them spoke. "When we have tried going after others, penetrating deeper into the Damhur lands, we always lose people. It's a price that we have been unwilling to pay, especially as there are so few of us and so many of the Damhur. It is safer to continue to work along the outskirts of Javoor, grabbing the Deshazl that we can, saving them and trying to free their minds. When we have the numbers, then we might be able to do something more, but until then..."

Fes looked around. "How long have you been here?"

"Hundreds of years."

He shook his head. Hundreds of years and they still had never brought the fight to the Damhur. He had been wrong about the Asharn. He had thought that they were willing to confront the Damhur, yet they lived in fear, despite their claims to the contrary. And they feared the Dragon's Eye, too.

"Why stay here? Why not travel beyond the valley, where you could find others who would help you? It would be a place where you are safe, and you wouldn't have to fear the Damhur."

Hodan stared at him. "We stay here because this is where we must be."

"Why must you be here if you aren't willing to resist the Damhur? What do you think that you need to do here?

"You wouldn't understand," he said.

"Help me understand. I came here to try to understand the Asharn."

"You came here looking for help."

"I did, and now that I see that I won't be getting any help, I would like to understand why that is. I would like to know what it is that is so important to the Asharn that they are willing to stay in a land that terrifies them." That might be a little harsh, but fear had worked on the woman, and maybe accusing Hodan of fear would be the same.

"You can't understand. You are an outsider."

"An outsider who is Deshazl. An outsider who has faced the Damhur and survived. An outsider who was willing to bring the fight to the Damhur. And I'm an outsider who recognizes the threat that they pose. If they continue to gain the strength of dragons, and if they continue to control them, Calling them, there will be no stopping them." Fes turned, ignoring the way the bridge swayed as he did, his stomach lurching up into his throat. "The Damhur were defeated a thousand years ago in my land because the dragons sacrificed themselves. They allowed themselves to be used in a way that would prevent the Damhur from controlling them, but I think that was a mistake. There has to be another way to defeat them, and I want to be there when that's done."

Hodan looked past Fes and the others. "Come with me," he said.

"Hodan," the woman said.

Hodan glanced back. "He's right. We stay here, hiding, but—"

"But we are safe," she said.

"For how much longer?" Hodan asked.

He guided Fes along the bridges, Fes moving carefully, running his hands along the rope railings so that he didn't fall, hating the way that the bridge swayed with each step. For his part, Hodan didn't seem to be bothered by it at all, and Fes tried to mimic the way that he moved, swaying with each step, but he didn't have the same comfort that Hodan did. It was a comfort that Hodan probably had from years crossing these bridges. They went from platform to platform, staying away from the buildings, and eventually stopped at a structure different than all the others. It was built entirely out of wood, a circular structure that was enclosed. Even the roof was different, not made up of branches woven together in the same way as the homes around here.

Hodan rested his hand on the side of the building. A small walkway circled the entire structure although Hodan stayed where he was.

"What's in here?" Fes asked.

"This is why we don't go anywhere," Hodan said.

"What is it?"

"This is incredibly valuable to the Asharn. This is the reason that we have stayed here."

"Hodan—" the woman said.

"No. There's no reason that we can't share this."

"Other than the fact that he is not from here," she said.

"And yet he is Deshazl, no different than the rest of us."

Fes stared at Hodan for a moment. He felt as if he were a different kind of Deshazl than Hodan, a different kind of Deshazl than most of the Asharn here. Then again, maybe the Deshazl in the north, those who had lived in the empire, had to be different.

Even if he hadn't been born there, he felt aligned with those Deshazl more so than he did with those he had discovered in these lands.

Hodan started around the building, and Fes followed, hugging closely to it. They reached a doorway that Hodan pressed his hand upon, pushing out with a surge of Deshazl magic. A barrier and it was one that was designed to keep out anyone who wasn't Deshazl. As he pressed his hand through it, the doorway opened. Hodan glanced over at Fes before stepping inside.

Fes stood at the doorway, curiosity raging through him. What might be in here?

Whatever it was had to be valuable, but was it something that would be valuable to the Damhur? Would it be something that they would be after, thinking to steal? And whatever it was would be high up in the tree, high enough that they had built this structure around it.

Fes stepped forward.

It took his eyes a moment to adjust. When they did, he looked around the inside of the room, looking to see what was in here. A faint, pale blue glow emanated from the center of the room. As Fes stepped toward it, he realized that the glow came from a hollow tube stretching deep into the ground.

It wasn't just a hollow tube. It was a tree, or it had been. Now it was nothing more than a husk, a hollowed-out emptiness that contained whatever it was that glowed.

"What is this?" Fes asked.

"This is the Asharn."

Fes frowned. "I thought that you were the Asharn."

"We are a people. We are descended from the Deshazl, the same as you, but this," he said, motioning to the hollowed remains of the tree, "this is the Asharn. This is why we are here. This is the reason that we cannot leave."

"What is it?"

"It's a connection to our people."

Fes stood at the edge of the husk of the tree, looking down at it. He had a hard time knowing what it was that he was supposed to be looking at. Whatever was down there glowed with the soft blue light, and there was something about that glowing light that called to Fes and seemed to fill him with a sense of familiarity. Why should that be?

"How is this the connection to your people?" he asked.

"This is the Asharn. We discovered it in the trees, and it fills this part of the forest. It's deep below the ground, a power that lives here, flowing through these trees. In this place, that power can bubble up, coming close to the surface, close enough for us to touch." Hodan dipped his hand into the liquid, stretching forward so that he could do so. When he was done, he leaned back, his hand dripping with the strangely glowing blue.

He nodded to Fes, who took a step closer, looking at the liquid.

"Is it safe to touch?"

"Only if you are Deshazl," he said.

Fes touched a finger to the liquid in Hodan's hand. He did so hesitantly, nervous to do anything more than touch his finger to it, but found that it was warm, and pleasantly so. Warmth spread through him, surging from his finger into his chest. His breath caught, and he gasped.

There was Deshazl magic within that, a connection to it that he had felt only one other time before. It was like the Dragon's Eye.

What did it mean that they had a place like that?

Could it be similar to Thoras?

"The place beyond the valley was founded by both the Deshazl and the Damhur," Fes said, holding his hand above the liquid.

Hodan frowned deeply. "Those who did not betray us made certain to protect this secret."

Fes stared at him a moment. "Your city was founded by both Deshazl and Damhur too?" He hadn't thought that likely, but it fit with what he'd seen in the city beyond the valley.

"They were not always Damhur," Hodan whispered, "and they once worked with us to reveal the Asharn."

When he said nothing more, Fes turned his attention back to the liquid. By its faint blue glowing, he knew that the power within it had to be different than the Dragon's Eye, which glowed orange. Why would that make a difference?

He closed his eyes, focusing on the dragon. *Can you feel this?*

He wasn't sure if trying to connect to the dragon would even be effective, but he had to know. If anyone understood what it was that he touched, it would be the dragon.

Deshazl.

The thought came from a distant part of his mind, drifting toward the forefront of his mind, and Fes breathed out in a sigh.

The Asharn was connected to the Deshazl magic, much like the Dragon's Eye.

"How did you find this?"

"Our people have always known this was here,"

Hodan said. "We have protected this section of the forest, and these trees, especially those where it comes forth."

That was why they were in the trees. It was more because of the Asharn than because of a fear of the Damhur reaching them.

"In how many places does it reveal itself like this?"

"There is this place, and a few others, but it only drips out in most places. This is the only place where it's concentrated in such a way. This is sacred to us, Fes."

He nodded. "You know what this is?"

"As I said, this is the Asharn."

Fes glanced at the three people with him before looking back down to the husk of the tree. "It's the same as the Dragon's Eye."

Someone gasped, and Fes looked back to see the woman staring at him. "This is the same?"

"If you've never seen the Dragon's Eye, you wouldn't know, but I've been within it. They're similar, perhaps not the same, but the power is the same. It connects you to the Deshazl?"

Hodan shook his head. "I don't know that they are the same. You must be mistaken."

Fes didn't think that he was. At least now he understood why the Asharn didn't want to leave the trees, much as he understood that they might be afraid of the Damhur, but they were afraid for a reason. They wanted to protect this, and they wanted to ensure the safety of the Asharn, to ensure that the power that flowed through these trees remained and that the Damhur weren't able to claim it.

Fes couldn't blame them for any of that. If the Damhur managed to acquire power like this, if they came to realize what exactly was here—or in the land beyond the valley—it was possible that they would abuse that power.

"I understand," he said. "I understand why you need to stay. I understand why you protect this place. And I understand why you haven't gone to the Dragon's Eye."

Those Deshazl believed that these people were afraid of the testing in the Dragon's Eye, but that wouldn't be it at all. And if the Dragon's Eye somehow cleansed the Deshazl from the Damhur connection, preventing their Calling, could this do the same?

"Does this protect you?"

"When we drink from it, those of us who have once fallen to the Damhur no longer suffer. We are able to resist the effect of their Calling."

"Not all of you do?"

"Some fear it," Hodan said.

"If it protects you from the Damhur, why would you fear it?"

"Because not all survive," Hodan said.

Fes looked at the others, and they stared at him.

Was it a test? Now that they had brought him here, did they want to know whether he was safe?

If he attempted to drink from this water, would it change him in any way? Stepping into the Dragon's Eye had; it had connected him differently to his Deshazl magic, but it also had connected him to the dragon.

Maybe by drinking from this water, he would prove himself to the Asharn. If he did that, it was possible that they would see him as one of them, and maybe he could convince them to help him.

More than anything, he thought that he needed to reach the gallery. If he could rescue the statues, steal them away from the Damhur and prevent them from being used, then he might succeed.

Even that might take too long. Already he'd been gone a long time, and he worried that it would be far too much for the empire to resist. How much destruction would they face?

How many people had already been lost? How many of the Deshazl within the empire had already been Called? That was his greatest fear. He wanted to protect them, wanted to ensure that they were safe, protected from the Damhur and their attempt to Call them, and there would be no way to do so until he did this.

Fes dipped his hands into the liquid. Warmth spread through him, racing up to his chest and then down into his belly, and then lower into his legs and toes.

He resisted the urge to cry out. It was not painful, but it was warmth, and it was different than what he had experienced while stepping into the Dragon's Eye.

He cupped the liquid to his mouth and took a drink.

He swallowed, letting the water run down his throat. It was warm, but the warmth spread through him, filling him. Power surged through him, and he was aware of the depths of the Deshazl magic. It seemed to come from everywhere, filling him and flowing through him. He had always known his connection to the Deshazl magic, though he had once believed that it was nothing more than his anger and rage. Now that he understood the magic better, he understood what it was and how it worked through him, but what he detected now was more than that. It was a connection to Deshazl everywhere.

Fes coughed, unable to hold down all of the liquid.

He looked around at the others with him, and as he did, it seemed as if he could see the Deshazl power glowing within them. He was aware of their connections, aware of them as something more, aware of himself as something more. They were Deshazl. He was Deshazl. All of them were together, connected.

"Is it like this for everyone?" he asked.

"Is it like what?" Hodan asked.

"I can see connections everywhere," he said.

Hodan glanced at the others before turning back to

Fes. "What connections can you see?"

"I can see the same glow within you as I see within this water."

"You see a glowing in the water?"

Fes nodded. "When we first came here, I saw the glowing immediately." He glanced from Hodan to the others. "Am I not supposed to have seen that?"

"Only a few have ever seen the Asharn glowing. It is considered a great honor, though it is rare."

"Why is it rare?"

"Because it is the Asharn revealing itself to the person, and it only truly reveals itself to those it deems worthy."

Fes thought that was attributing far too much to the pool than was necessary. It didn't seem to him that the Asharn would have any sort of intention. Maybe it was because he had been in the Dragon's Eye and it had changed something for him, allowing him to see the Asharn differently.

"Regardless of what I'm supposed to see, now that I've drank it, I see connections everywhere," Fes said.

And he couldn't help but continue to see them. He saw them within the Asharn, and he saw them flowing through the trees.

That had to be the residual Asharn and could be nothing else, but if that were the case, why would that same magic be flowing there?

"What else do you see?" Hodan asked.

Fes pointed to the tree. The same glowing flowed through it, lighting it up. It seemed to be everywhere. It made him think of Jesla and the connections she claimed that she saw. Was this what it was like for her? Did she see these sort of connections everywhere, or was this different?

Hodan guided him out of the building and motioned around the city. Fes looked around. As he had within the building, he saw the same glowing everywhere. It flowed through the trees, though faintly. It flowed through the people, equally faintly, though it was there. Everything had that strange glow.

"I see it everywhere," Fes whispered.

"He shouldn't have seen this," the woman said.

"But now that he has, he has proven himself," Hodan said.

"Proven myself how?"

Hodan shook his head. "Don't you see? He has come with the dragon, and he has drunk from the Asharn, and now he sees the connections. He is Deshazl."

"I told you that I was Deshazl," Fes said.

"This is different," Hodan said. "This is the kind of Deshazl that we have not often seen. There are only a few who have the ability that you do, and only a few who have the reaction from the Asharn that you do."

"And what reaction is that?"

"You can identify other Deshazl. It is a gift, and it's

one that is incredibly valuable. You can use that to help rescue those who have been enslaved by the Damhur."

"I don't want to rescue Deshazl throughout this land. I want to defeat the Damhur."

"If we rescue the Deshazl, we will defeat the Damhur."

Fes wondered if that were true. Would stopping the Damhur by taking Deshazl from them be enough, or was there something else that he needed to do? He didn't know. And he worried that even if this were what they were claiming, even if he did now see the Deshazl connections, it still wouldn't be enough. Seeing connections wasn't the same as protecting them, and that was what he sought. He wanted to protect those connections, to find a way to ensure the safety of the Deshazl, and if the Asharn weren't able to do that, if the magic that flowed through their trees was not able to accomplish that, then what did it matter?

"It's not just the Deshazl that I need to protect," Fes said.

Hodan stared at him.

"It's the dragons. The Deshazl and the dragons share a connection. We are filled with the same power, though we use it differently. We are connected in that way, and that is my purpose."

"No. You were given a gift by the Asharn. That gift is for you to see the connection between the Deshazl. That gift is for you to understand and reach the others. You can use that to help us identify which of the Deshazl we should rescue."

Fes frowned at him. "That's how you decide?"

"We draw those with the most potential," Hodan said.

"Just those with the most potential? Not all of the Deshazl?"

"We can't risk ourselves for those who are weakly connected to the Deshazl," Hodan said. "They would be unlikely to survive drinking from the Asharn, and if they can't survive that, then there will be nothing that we can do to protect them from the Damhur."

Fes glanced from Hodan to the others. They left behind those of the Deshazl who weren't that strong?

That horrified him.

"You have abandoned the Deshazl," he said.

"We haven't abandoned the Deshazl. We continue to protect them, doing everything that we can to ensure their safety, but if we didn't choose, we would lose too many. The entire purpose of the Asharn is to ensure the safety and perpetuation of our people."

Fes stared at Hodan for a long moment. "I think it's time for me to go."

"Go? You can't go. You have just drank from the Asharn. You have proven that you have the connection necessary to help our people. And you have—"

Fes shook his head. "It's time for me to go. I intend to go to the gallery, and from there I will take the sculp-

tures, rescuing them, and…" From there, he had a difficult journey. He would have to figure out if he could
resurrect the rest of the dragons. If he could, and if he
could find some way of protecting them, the dragons
might be able to be his ally.

It certainly wasn't the Asharn. They proved themselves too afraid, and even when they made an attempt to
fight, they made choices that Fes didn't agree with. He
would protect any Deshazl, even those weakly attached
to the Deshazl magic. Regardless of their connections,
they were still in danger from the Damhur, and if he did
nothing, and if those who had the power to do something
did nothing, then those people would suffer.

He started back across the bridge, heading toward one
of the platforms. He had no idea where he was going
within the Asharn city, but it was time to head back, find
the dragon, reach the platform, and disappear from here.

As he started across the bridge and reached the next
platform, Hodan caught him, grabbing his arm.

"I can't let you go."

Fes cocked his head to the side. "You can't?"

"You have an ability that the Asharn has proclaimed.
With that ability, we need you to stay here. You might not
see it now, but in time—"

Fes jerked his arm free. He pushed away from himself
with a surge of magic, but Hodan was equally skilled and
ignored it.

He shook his head sadly. "You will stay here until you understand. You will see. In time, you will come to see."

"I don't have time."

"Your empire is lost, but the Asharn does not have to be."

Fes took a deep breath and looked at the others, wondering if it would come to a fight. He didn't like his chances of getting free. They were powerful, and he suspected that the other two were trained fighters the same as those he had observed throughout the city. If they were, they would be incredibly skilled and might be more than he could manage.

"Don't do this," Fes said.

"I'm sorry. You drank from the Asharn, and you have proven yourself."

"If I've proven myself, then you need to allow me to go."

"You've proven yourself to be too valuable to allow to go," Hodan said.

"If that's the way you intend to do this, then I am sorry," Fes said.

Hodan frowned. "Sorry about what?"

"Sorry that you forced me into this."

Fes focused on the dragon, sending a surge of concern, and then he waited. It took only a moment before the dragon roared and Fes could feel him streaking downward.

CHAPTER SIXTEEN

When the dragon approached, he tore through the trees, ripping through them. Heat streamed from his mouth, burning away branches and leaves. Fes wished there was a different way, wishing that he didn't need for the dragon to be quite so destructive, but he hoped that by standing on the platform, not near any of the homes, he wouldn't destroy much of the Asharn city.

"This is your fault," Fes said, looking at Hodan.

"You would use the dragon against us?" Hodan asked.

"I would use the dragon to get myself free. You will not hold me here. I am not some pet, meant to be held by the Asharn, used the same way that the Damhur would use me. You will not hold me."

"We don't want to hold you. We want you to recognize that you could be useful," Hodan said. He took a step toward Fes, who reacted, pushing out with his Deshazl magic, drawing strength from the dragon and pushing out with even more power than he had used when he had tried to resist Hodan before. With the proximity to the dragon, he felt as if his connection were even greater. Strangely, it seemed almost as if he were drawing power from the Deshazl around him, almost as much as he pulled from the dragon. That power allowed him to send a blast that slammed into Hodan, sending him sliding across the platform.

He very nearly tumbled off the platform, and he screamed.

Fes darted forward and wrapped him in a bubble of Deshazl magic, lifting him back.

The dragon hovered in the air, his massive wings separating the treetops, splitting them apart, the wind coming off him sending bridges swaying. The people on the bridges scrambled, getting from the bridge to platforms, where they would be safe from the power of the dragon.

When Hodan was placed back onto the platform, he looked at Fes with his eyes wide. "How did you do that?"

"Do what?"

"Save me."

"That is my Deshazl magic. That's nothing more than that."

"Deshazl magic doesn't work in that way."

"Mine does."

He nodded to the dragon, which slowly settled down, coming to land on the platform. He propped himself up on his wing, his head darting around, steam bursting from his nostrils. Fes climbed onto his back and glanced at Jayell. She gave him a concerned look, but Fes shook his head.

"I'm fine."

"If you were fine, you wouldn't have summoned the dragon."

"Then I'm as well as I can be considering that I had to ask the dragon to come rescue me."

"What happened?"

"Oh, nothing more than another test."

"I take it you failed?"

"Unfortunately, it seems as if I passed, and because I passed, they thought that they would hold me here, regardless of what I told them was my intention."

"And what was your intention?"

"We need to go to a place called the gallery. It's somewhere in Javoor, in a city called Ranur."

"Do we have time for that?"

"It's where they have dragon sculptures."

"Dragonglass dragon sculptures?"

Fes nodded.

"Why do I get the sense that this will be a challenge?"

"Because it will. We won't have any help, and I had

hoped that by coming here, the Asharn would work with us, but they won't."

He turned his attention back to Hodan. Others had gathered on the platforms surrounding this one, and hundreds of Asharn looked out at Fes. He stared at them and, with a sudden inspiration, he stood on top of the dragon's back, looking around the Asharn city. As he did, he saw power connecting everyone, the glowing white from the trees connecting the people as well. That power, that connection to the Deshazl magic, flowed through everyone. It was amazing seeing it, and Fes couldn't help but feel as if his visit here had been worthwhile, even though he had failed to find allies.

Maybe in using this connection, he would be able to somehow help the dragons. If nothing else, that had to be worthwhile.

"The Deshazl and the dragons are connected," Fes said, letting his voice carry. "I came to the Asharn looking for help, wanting to find those who would be willing to resist the Damhur and their use of the dragons. They have already claimed two dragons, Calling them, and they will claim others."

The woman who led the Asharn came out of her small building and watched. Power radiated from her, surging toward him. He could *see* it. Never before had he been able to actually see that power coming off someone, but this time he was able to not only feel that power, but he could see it. It was amazing, and it reminded him of the glowing that he saw within each of the Asharn, but when it surged toward him, the colors changed. It took on a swirl of a different color.

When he had been attacked by someone using Deshazl magic in the past, Fes had resisted using his own Deshazl magic, and when faced with the Asharn, he had been initially overpowered, but this time, he saw the way that he could resist. It was different than what he had done before, and he took the connection coming off the woman and twisted it, diverting it.

It dissipated, drifting off into the trees.

He shook his head at her. He would not have her abuse him, and would not have her attacking him in such a way. He would resist.

It was because of her that the Asharn wouldn't help, and it was because of her that the Asharn refused to help others of the Deshazl who needed their help. Fes refused to allow himself to get caught up in that.

"And now your leader would attack me. I am Deshazl," Fes said, spreading his arms wide. "I am connected to the dragons. I am the reason that the dragons will be protected. And I refuse to allow the Damhur to Call and control the dragons. I have drunk from the Asharn. I can see connections all around me." As he said it, he glanced at the Asharn leader, and her eyes widened. "And that power is the same between all of us. But there are others who share that power, though they may not share it nearly as potently. And just because they do not have the same potency doesn't mean that they should be left to suffer under the Damhur. I will rescue them along with the others. But first I must protect the dragons. Even the dragons that have not yet returned." This was the part that Fes was least certain of. He looked around the Asharn, but what did it matter if they chose not to come with him? He would lose nothing by asking the question. "I look for help. I intend to go into the heart of Javoor, traveling to Ranur and to the gallery where there is power that must be rescued. That power is the key to the dragons' resurrection, and I will ensure their safety."

"Don't you think that's a bit much?" Jayell asked.

"Probably," Fes whispered.

"If anyone would come with me, I will ensure that you have an opportunity to face the Damhur. You will be fighting on behalf of the Deshazl—*all* of the Deshazl. You will be fighting on behalf of those who have not yet been saved and fighting on behalf of those who have not yet been enslaved but might still be. And you would be fighting on behalf of the dragons."

Fes took a seat. He waited, doubting that his words would persuade them. It seemed almost too much to believe that such a statement would make any difference to the Asharn, especially after what he'd seen so far, but what choice did he have?

"I will come," someone hollered.

Fes looked over and saw an older man with graying hair who nodded. He glowed with a bright light, a powerful Asharn, connected deeply to the Deshazl magic.

Did it matter? That was the question Fes needed to answer. Did it matter how connected to the Deshazl magic that any of these people were? Did it matter how powerful they could be?

No.

He knew that it did not. And even if it did, there was nothing that he would change. If someone wanted to come and help him rescue the dragons and wanted to help him oppose the Damhur, he would welcome them. He needed allies.

"I will come," another voice said.

Fes looked over and saw another older person, with equally gray hair, but she was slender. She glowed with a soft light, not quite as strongly connected to the Deshazl magic as the other man, but still with power.

"I will come."

"And I."

"And I."

One by one, Fes heard voices call out, and he couldn't believe how many. There had to be a dozen, maybe more.

"How many do you think you could carry?" he asked the dragon.

"I can carry quite a few a short distance, but if you had me carry them across the sea, I would be limited."

Fes welcomed the Asharn who joined him. One by one, they climbed up on top of the dragon and worked their way along his back. He saw faces that were mostly old, though a few younger people joined him. Surprisingly, the woman who had escorted him through the city was among them.

Hodan was not. And neither was the Asharn leader.

Fes jumped down from the back of the dragon and made his way over to Hodan. "You can still help. I sense within you your desire to help and know that you have been misguided. Others all deserve the same opportunity to be saved. If you fear their ability to survive drinking from the Asharn, then send them beyond the valley. Let the people there protect them. They would be safe there. They would be given an opportunity to be something more. But abandoning them…"

Hodan stared at him. "You could do so much here," he said.

"I can do so much outside of here. If I stay here, I would be useless. Anything that might change would be lost."

Fes flicked his gaze to the leader of the Asharn. She stared at him, but he couldn't read her expression. Was it anger in her eyes? He didn't think so. It seemed almost as if she were worried. Maybe she feared for the safety of her people going with him, and Fes wasn't sure that he could ensure their safety. How could he when he intended to go into the heart of Javoor, to travel to a place where he would put them in danger?

"If others wish to help, send them toward the empire. I know that you have some way of reaching the empire. I have encountered other Asharn there." Fes looked at Hodan. "The empire would welcome your assistance in battling the Damhur."

"The empire has never offered us the same assistance," Hodan said.

"Because the empire didn't realize there was a need," Fes said. He turned away, climbed back onto the dragon, and patted his side. "Let's go."

The dragon lifted off with a mighty beating of his wings, surging into the sky. He moved slowly. Fes could tell that the dragon was cautious, as if not wanting to disrupt the twenty people now sitting atop his back.

"Where would you have me go?" the dragon asked.

"We need to travel into the heart of Javoor, but we need to avoid people. As much as we can, we want to avoid detection before we make our move."

Fes glanced back at Jayell. "Can you ask how many of them know how to find the gallery?"

Jayell nodded. "This might take longer than we have."

"It might, but I don't know what other option we have. The Damhur have these dragonglass dragon sculptures, and the sculptures are what store the essence of the dragons. With enough protected dragons, we can push the Damhur away from the empire."

"There were once several dozen such sculptures," the dragon said with a rumble.

"Several dozen?" Fes asked. He had a hard time imagining what that must've been like. How was it that several dozen had been willing to sacrifice themselves?

"When the attacks came, the dragons recognized the dangers they posed. We willingly went to sleep, and as we did, we placed ourselves deep within the sculptures."

"How are there so many?"

"It was all the dragons who remained."

"How many were there before?" Fes asked.

"There was a time when there were dozens upon dozens. Dragons lived all over, but when the attacks came, we converged in the lands of your empire. It was safest that way. The people you know as the Damhur had proven their willingness to attack, and they had proven their ability to search and find the dragons, and their ability to Call had grown strong."

"They used the dragons to search, didn't they?"

The dragon snorted. "They did."

"And you converged in the empire because it was safest?"

"We converged in the empire because it was a place

where there were those willing to fight on behalf of the dragons."

Fes glanced over his shoulder at the Asharn. He thought of the Deshazl they had visited near the Dragon's Eye. Could none of them have been willing to fight on behalf of the dragons? Could that be the reason that the dragons had fallen?

It was terrible if it were true, and even if it were true, it had happened so long ago that it might not even matter. The people who were responsible at the time were gone. Anyone who had lived at that time, anyone who had failed to protect the dragons, had long since disappeared, leaving nothing more than the memory of the dragons.

"How did the Damhur manage to acquire all of the dragon sculptures?" Fes asked.

"When they attacked before, they invaded a great part of the empire. It required much strength to push back."

"You remember this?"

"I have vague memories of that time, not enough to recall with much detail," the dragon said.

"And the sculptures? Why would they have taken them here?"

"I do not know," the dragon said.

Fes remembered the look of the sculpture that he had rescued, and he remembered how it had felt, the smooth glass and a warmth within it. It was possible that the

Damhur had seen the sculptures as nothing more than decoration, and if that were the case, then they might have viewed them as valuable, or perhaps they sought them as a reminder of the dragons and they wanted to maintain that reminder, to hold onto it to ensure that if they had the opportunity, they would not miss out on the chance to control the dragons again.

Jayell tapped him on the shoulder. "I have discovered how to find the gallery."

"Why do I get the sense that it's not good?"

"Reaching the gallery will be difficult. Most of these people who decided to come with you were once enslaved by the Damhur. Several of them served in Ranur, and they know how to find the gallery, and they can help guide us to it."

Fes wasn't surprised that the people who had chosen to come with him had been Called by the Damhur. There had to have been some within the Asharn city who had been born free, but there were others who had been Called, controlled, and rescued by the Asharn, but those who were rescued would have been powerful.

Maybe it was best that they were the ones who had agreed to come with him.

"The gallery is in the heart of the city, in an area of artisans and artists, and surrounding that are people with much wealth."

"That doesn't sound all that bad," Fes said.

"You don't understand. People with wealth in Javoor are all those with a powerful ability to Call. They are the oldest families of the Damhur, and those oldest families have the greatest connection to their magic. Some of them, from what I can tell, are also fire mages. They don't call them that, but they would pose difficulty."

"It's more than just their ability to Call that we would need to be concerned about, isn't it?"

Jayell nodded. "It's more than their ability to Call. They would have dozens of Deshazl. And all of those Deshazl would be well armed and trained, and they would pose challenges to even you."

"To even me?"

Jayell smiled. "You have become quite powerful with your connection to your Deshazl magic, and now that you have this connection to the dragon, I can see how you can use that magic, how powerful that is, but I don't know that even you would be able to withstand an attack from several Damhur who were attempting to Call you while also withstanding an attack from dozens of Deshazl, especially as I know that you would be hesitant to attack those Deshazl, not wanting to harm them. I know you, Fezarn, and I know that you would want to rescue them."

She was right, which meant that they had to somehow sneak into the city and find a way of moving discreetly. If he were able to reach the gallery and get these sculptures and protect the dragons, they would finally have the advantage against the Damhur.

"There is something ahead of us," the dragon said.

Fes leaned over the side, looking out into the distance, staring down at the ground. There were rolling hills and the occasional tree that dotted the landscape, but in many ways, it reminded him of the empire. They had avoided cities, so he didn't even know what a city within Javoor would look like, other than the Asharn city, which was unique in how it was structured, suspended within the trees. The only other city that he'd seen had been the one beyond the valley, a city that was unlike anything else Fes had ever seen, and he suspected it would be unlike anything else found within the rest of Javoor.

"I don't see anything," Fes said.

"Not on the ground," the dragon said.

Fes pulled his gaze up and scanned the horizon, staring at the sky.

It took a moment to see what the dragon saw, but when he did, his breath caught. "That's too large to be a bird."

"It is."

"A dragon. There's a dragon coming toward us?" Fes asked.

"So it appears," the dragon said.

Fes glanced over at Jayell. "We have a complication."

"What is it?"

"There's a dragon coming toward us."

"Has the Damhur abandoned their attack on the empire?" Jayell asked.

If they had, maybe the fire mages had managed to push them back. If that was the case, then Fes had more time. It would give him an opportunity to rethink their plan to invade Ranur and go after the gallery. It would give them a chance to come up with a safe strategy, but first he would have to deal with this dragon. Even if they avoided it, the Damhur would know that he was here. That alone was dangerous.

"Fezarn," the dragon said.

It was unusual for the dragon to use his name, and Fes jerked his attention to him immediately. "What is it?"

"This is not one of the other two dragons."

As Fes stared, he realized that the coloring glinting within the sunlight was all wrong. This one had deep green scales, and they caught the sunlight in such a way that they practically would have blended in with the ground. It was beautiful and breathtaking... and terrifying at the same time.

"Then the Damhur have found a way to resurrect the dragons," Fes said.

"So it would seem," the dragon said.

Fes let out a heavy sigh. If that were the case, they were already too late.

"We need to land."

"Why?" the dragon asked.

"We can't maneuver with these Asharn on your back, and I suspect we are going to need to avoid attack quite soon."

The dragon dove toward the ground. Fes ignored the loud murmuring behind him, knowing that they needed speed, and when the dragon landed with a great fluttering of his wings, Fes turned and motioned to the Damhur.

"I need you to get off."

"What is it?" the woman who had accompanied him through the city asked.

Fes pointed up to the sky. "There is another dragon, and this one is different than the other two that I have seen."

"They have discovered how to raise them?" she asked.

"I think so."

"What will you do?"

Somehow he had to defend the Asharn, but at the same time, he wanted to protect the dragon. Was there any way to do that?

"I intend to save the dragon."

"Just you?"

Did it have to be just him? Wasn't that the reason he had come here? He had wanted allies, and he didn't need to do this by himself. "How many do you think you could carry and maneuver well?"

The dragon didn't hesitate to answer. "Three."

"Just three?"

"More than that and it will disrupt my balance. Perhaps in time I would be able to learn how to handle more than that, but right now is—"

Fes smiled and nodded at the dragon. "You don't have to explain." He turned to the Asharn. "I need the two most capable among you. We are going to try to rescue that dragon."

He could see the connections within them, and he could see the power glowing from them, but the connection to their Deshazl didn't necessarily mean that they were the most capable of the Asharn.

The woman stepped forward. Fes wasn't surprised. The power within her was tremendous, and he could see it flowing through her and knew that she would be formidable.

Surprisingly, an older woman stepped forward. She had long gray hair tied in a braid, and she looked at Fes. "I will accompany you."

Fes looked over at Jayell. "You will need to defend them if it comes to it. Do you have enough supplies?"

She reached into her pocket and pulled out a pair of dragon pearls, holding them out. "I have enough for now. We weren't well stocked when we started this journey."

"It probably doesn't matter. If we can rescue this dragon, then..."

Then what? Then they would have to find out if the Damhur had raised others. He looked up into the sky. The forest-green-scaled dragon was getting close. They would have to do something soon or else they would have to fend off an attack.

"Go," Jayell said.

Fes climbed onto the dragon's back and waited for the others to join him.

CHAPTER SEVENTEEN

They took to the air, the dragon beating his wings with a violent intensity. Power surged from him, and as he climbed, Fes's stomach dropped, and his ears popped. He marveled, as he often did, at just how powerful the dragon was. He clung to the dragon's back, twisting to look at the others with him.

"If we are going into battle, we should know each other's names."

The woman who had accompanied him through the Asharn city smiled. "I am Lena."

The older woman leaned forward. "I am Roshana."

"Both of you had once been Called by the Damhur?" Fes asked. He thought that they had been, and that was the reason they had been willing to accompany him but wasn't sure.

They nodded.

"Then you know what the dragon is going through. There will be a fight within the dragon, and we need to help rescue her." Fes wasn't sure how he knew the dragon was female, but something—probably something that came from his dragon—told him that she was.

They continued climbing, circling higher and higher, fire and steam bursting from the dragon's nose. As they rose, Fes searched for the green dragon. She was diving, trying to head to the ground, toward the Asharn.

He tapped the dragon on the side and pointed.

The dragon started to descend.

As he did, Fes took stock of the other dragon. Two people were sitting on top of her. Both wore deep blue cloaks, and their hoods were down, revealing long braids of blonde hair.

They reminded him of Liza and Elsanelle. Both of them were probably Calling.

And if that were the case, they had to work quickly. They would have to find a way to ensure that they were able to stop them, and when they did, they could figure out how to save the dragon. Fes wasn't sure what that would take, only that there had to be something that they could do.

He pushed out with a surge of his Deshazl magic and sent it streaming toward the back of the other dragon, aiming it toward one of the people riding on the dragon's back.

It struck her and then parted around her.

If nothing else, it drew their attention.

The dragon turned, peeling away from her attack on the ground. Grasses all around the Asharn were blackened, and Fes could see Jayell holding her hand up, a dragon pearl clutched tightly in it, and he could feel the spell she was using radiating around her.

She had protected them from the dragon blast, but how much power had she used to do so?

It might be that she had already tapped out the reserves of the dragon pearl. If that were the case, she would only have a little bit more power remaining.

He had to keep the dragon's attention on him.

Fes climbed forward, getting into a position on the top of the dragon's head so that he could see what the dragon saw and he didn't need to crane his neck off to the side.

"I hope this is okay," he said to the dragon.

"Only if you don't fall," the dragon said.

"I'll try not to grab your eyes or nose."

The dragon breathed out a streamer of fire.

They began to circle the other dragon. She was quick and sleek, whereas the dragon he rode upon was large and powerful but not nearly as fast. He and the others with him would need to help accommodate for that, which meant that they would have to attack quickly.

Fes glanced over his shoulder at Roshana and Lena. "Attack however you can. We need to disrupt the Calling."

"There are few ways of disrupting a Calling," Lena said.

"What's the best way?"

"Killing the person responsible," she said.

"I'm not opposed to that, but I blasted them with my most powerful Deshazl attack, and it still wasn't enough."

"Maybe the distance was too much," Lena suggested.

Fes wondered if that were the case. "Can you get closer?" he asked the dragon.

"Are you sure that's what you want to do?"

"Not really, but getting closer might allow me to attack more effectively. All I need is to knock one of them free, and it should disrupt the Calling enough for us to reach the dragon."

"When she is free of the Calling, she will be disoriented," the dragon said.

"Are you sure?"

"I have some experience with the Calling."

"When?" This dragon had not been Called in the time since Fes had raised him, which meant... "You were Called before you went to sleep."

"I was. I understand exactly what we face. She will be

disoriented when their Calling fails, and it will take a steady hand and someone who is able to reach her."

Fes understood.

Lena gasped.

Fes glanced back, looking over at her. "What is it?"

"The rider."

"What about the rider?"

"I recognize her. The one on the left is Ursal Forass."

"Am I supposed recognize that name?"

"Would you recognize it if I told you that she is the sister of Elsanelle?"

Fes blinked. "That I would recognize," he said.

If she were related to Elsanelle, he had to imagine that she shared some of the same power, and if that were the case, then he needed to be even more proactive with this. He had faced her sister and had plenty of experience with just how powerful she was and knew that she could Call even him. If he wasn't careful, she might extend her influence to him, and then would he be able to withstand it?

He didn't know.

Fes wrapped his mind in Deshazl magic, using the tricks that he had learned when facing Elsanelle, and hoped that it would be enough. He pulled on the connection to the dragon, using even that power to protect his mind.

That wasn't all he needed to do, though. He didn't

need to only protect himself, but he also needed to protect the dragon. Fes shifted the focus of his connection, wrapping it around both his mind and the dragon's. As he did, he found that he bound the two of them even more tightly together.

More than before, he was aware of the dragon. It was an awareness of a motion, and not quite the same awareness of thought, though he suspected if he were to try, he might be able to reach and connect to the dragon and could use that to help.

Within the dragon, Fes sensed fear. The dragon worried about what would happen if they were to fail. The dragon feared the Calling, feared suffering from that fate again, and Fes knew that he needed to do everything in his power to protect the dragon. More than that, he sent his intention through to the dragon, letting him know that was his plan. He didn't want the dragon to worry that he would abandon him, and he didn't want the dragon to worry that he had to fear the Calling or had to fear suffering from that fate again.

I will protect you.

Fes pushed that thought out with everything within himself, sending it to the dragon so that he would recognize Fes's intention.

As he did, he sensed a relaxation within the dragon.

Let's attack.

The dragon roared, and they streaked toward the

oncoming dragon. As they did, Fes pulled upon his Deshazl connection, drawing from deep within the dragon and extending that connection, drawing from the Asharn down on the ground. He borrowed from the connections that he could detect, drawing from those connections so that he could reach even more power and use it, wrapping it around himself, and then he sent it out in a blast, surging toward them.

He struck one of the Damhur, but not Ursal.

Fes watched as the attack split around the Damhur, parting around them.

He hadn't seen his attack fail quite so spectacularly before, and seeing how it parted around the Damhur like this, he felt helpless. Even with an enhanced ability to reach his Deshazl magic, would he be able to overpower them?

The green dragon swooped toward them and let out a massive streamer of flame that burst toward him.

Fes raised his hands and pushed out with his Deshazl connection, creating a barrier around them. The heat from the dragon's breath split around them, but thankfully his Deshazl magic held, and he pushed back, holding off the power from the attack.

"We need to try something different," Lena said.

"I'm open to suggestions," Fes said.

There didn't seem to be any way to redirect the attack, and as much as he wanted to use his Deshazl magic to overpower them, they both had ways of ignoring it.

Likely they were fire mages as well as capable at Calling.

Was there anything different that he could do?

Nothing came to mind that would be effective.

The dragon banked, rolling off to the side, and Fes took the opportunity to push out with his Deshazl connection, sending a blast of magic at the dragon this time, focusing everything that he could upon the dragon, thinking that if he could find a way to use his magic, he might be able to disrupt the Calling.

It struck the dragon, but nothing changed.

He could feel Lena and Roshana working with their connection to Deshazl magic. It flowed from them, leaping from them to attack the Damhur, but much like when Fes had attempted it, nothing changed.

It was possible that these other two were just too powerful.

If they were, if there were nothing that he could do to overpower them, he would need to direct the dragon to escape if it were still possible.

It might already be too late. Fes didn't know if they had spent too much time here, but he worried that remaining here placed them in danger and the longer that they stayed, the longer that their attack was ineffective, the more likely it was that they would be overpowered by the Damhur and their ability to Call.

"I think—"

Roshana didn't get a chance to finish. A blast of dragon's breath came at them, and she ducked, slamming up a barrier of Deshazl magic around herself, but doing so somehow forced her back, and she started to tumble.

She rolled off the side of the dragon.

"No!" Fes lunged for her, but he wasn't fast enough. He grabbed for her, wrapping her in his Deshazl connection in the same way he had with Hodan, and he tried to pull her back up onto the dragon. For a moment, she remained suspended in air, streaking above the ground, practically dragged by the dragon, but the longer that she was there, the more difficult it was for Fes to hold on to her.

"Swing around!"

The dragon tried turning but wasn't fast enough. The female dragon swooped in, and power erupted from her as she burst forward with a blast of speed that was even more than Fes's dragon could match.

With a rapid lunge, the female dragon snapped Roshana in her jaws.

The Deshazl connection was severed.

Fes jerked back, gasping.

Lena sat stiffly on the back of the dragon next to him. He turned to her. "We need to continue to fight."

"I'm not sure that I can do anything," she said.

"You can do more than you realize. We need to resist."

"How? Roshana was the strongest of us," she said.

Fes focused on the Damhur on the back of the dragon. They were to blame, not the dragon, for what had happened. Somehow he needed to help Lena see that, and he needed to get through to her so that she would recognize that it wasn't the dragon who was responsible for what had happened. The dragon had no interest in attacking those with Deshazl bloodlines, not without the influence of the Damhur.

"It's not her fault," he said.

"The dragon just attacked. She just—"

"It's not her fault," he said again. "What happened to her is the Damhur, not the dragon."

"The dragon simply *devoured* her. How can it not be the dragon's fault?"

Fes turned his attention to the dragon they rode upon. "Can you help her understand?"

The dragon rumbled, circling higher into the air. They needed to get higher, to gain altitude, and from there, Fes could see how they might be able to turn their attack once more upon the Damhur. Somehow, he needed to remove them from the dragon, but he didn't know how to do that. Every attack that he had attempted had been thwarted, diverted by their ability to disrupt his

Deshazl magic. How was he supposed to defeat them if they could overpower his magic?

"We must change our approach," the dragon said.

Fes looked down and realized that the female dragon was streaking toward them, rising higher and higher into the air, moving with much more speed than his dragon could manage.

How was she that much faster?

"Can she hurt you?" Fes asked.

The dragon rumbled. "It's unlikely that she could hurt me, but it is possible that she could do damage to you and the other."

"I'm well aware that she might harm us," Fes said. Would he be able to protect himself using his Deshazl magic if it came down to it? Could he somehow prevent the dragon from chomping through his magic?

There had to be a different way. If his Deshazl magic didn't work, and if there was some way for the Damhur to avoid his magic, was there something else that he could do?

He looked down at the two Damhur on the dragon's back. Every time that he attempted to throw his Deshazl magic at them, nothing changed. Attempting to use it on the dragon failed, and regardless of how much Deshazl magic he could summon, it didn't seem to make a difference.

Find another way.

Could he change his approach? It might involve separating himself from this dragon, but the reward could be enough that it would make doing so worthwhile.

"Is it possible that I can work with the other?"

"The only way that I know to disrupt the Calling is to remove the person responsible for it," the dragon said.

That had been Fes's concern, and if the dragon believed that was the only way to do it, then Fes suspected it to be true. How else would he get to them? His attempt to use the Deshazl magic failed, and there was no other way to reach the two Damhur.

The dragon banked, twisting and diving toward the ground, narrowly avoiding a burst of flame.

There were only so many times that they could avoid this speedier dragon. Eventually, the smaller dragon would get close enough to attack Fes and Lena, and the moment that she did was the moment Fes would have to make a decision about what they were to do.

The dragon changed angles, skimming above the surface of the ground. At least they had put some distance between them and the other Deshazl, but was it enough?

Fes looked up. The green dragon dove toward them.

They started to climb again, twisting and spiraling outward, and as they went, Fes continued to pull on his connection to the Deshazl magic, drawing through the dragon and through the Asharn on the ground, and as he did, he sent out the attack, sending it slamming into the Damhur on the back of the green-scaled dragon, but the attack made little difference.

As before, his Deshazl magic parted around them.

Were they using fire magic to deflect his? And how were they able to do so, especially with as much Deshazl magic as he was drawing?

The dragon.

That had to be what they were using. He hadn't considered the possibility that the dragon was somehow summoning Deshazl magic from within herself and pushing out with that, creating the barrier that would make it nearly impossible for Fes to attack.

As they passed the dragon, a blast of fire mage magic streaked toward them, and Fes quickly unsheathed his sword, sliding it through the spell, letting it part around him. They continued to climb, leaving the dragon and the Damhur to turn and try to catch them.

Fes looked over at Lena.

"I don't want to be Called again," she said in a whisper. "I thought that my time with the Asharn would have protected me, but the Trivent is too powerful. We won't be able to stop her, will we?"

Fes wanted to tell her that everything would be okay, and he wanted to tell her that they would be able to defeat the Damhur, but deep within himself, he knew that not to be true. There might not be any way to defeat

324 | D.K. HOLMBERG

the Damhur. There might not be any way to get through this. Magic had failed them.

He looked down at his sword. Magic had failed them, but that wasn't the only way that he had to fight.

"I need you to get me overtop the other dragon," Fes said.

The dragon rumbled. "Overtop?"

"Do this, and I will finish this." One way or another, Fes would end this fight. They couldn't withstand an ongoing battle with the dragon and with two Damhur who were far more powerful than him, using both of their abilities and that of the dragon to overpower him. They couldn't withstand that, not for much longer.

But there was something that he *could* do.

"What are you doing?" Lena asked.

"Stay on the dragon. Hold onto your connection to the Deshazl magic and protect yourself—and the dragon."

The dragon twisted and Fes looked down and saw the green-scaled dragon directly below him. Squeezing the hilt of the dragonglass sword, he jumped.

"Fes!"

He ignored Lena. Wind whistled around him, and he streaked toward the dragon, shooting toward her. Part of him worried that his angle was off, and as he came close, he pushed off with his Deshazl magic, wrapping it around him and pulling the dragon toward him using that connection.

He landed on the back of the dragon with a crash. He managed to buffer his landing only a little, enough that he didn't jar the sword free.

Fes lunged forward, catching one Damhur in the back.

She gasped and slumped over to the side. He shook his sword free, and the woman fell to the ground below.

That was one of the Damhur, but he knew the one he'd killed wasn't the one he had to worry about. It was Ursal.

She turned toward him, a dark smile twisting her mouth. "Interesting, but foolish."

A powerful fire magic spell built from her and Fes sliced through it with his sword, darting forward on the back of the dragon, but as he did, the dragon turned, twisting, and he went staggering off to the side, tumbling onto one of the great beast's wings. He clung to it, afraid that if he let go, he would be thrown to the ground. Even with his connection to the Deshazl magic and his ability to use it in ways that he had never considered before visiting the Asharn, he wasn't certain that he would be able to survive a fall like that.

The dragon twisted, turning into a tight spiral as she streaked into the air. Her wings had a rhythmic speed to them, and as she went, he could feel the heat radiating from her and realized why and how she moved so quickly.

Ursal used some spell to augment her speed.

If he could disrupt that, he could at least slow her, but first, he had to return to the dragon's back.

Fes scrambled forward, reaching the dragon, holding tightly, wrapping himself with his Deshazl magic to bind him to the dragon. It diverted his strength, and he didn't know how long he would be able to hold onto his magic in this way, but if he weren't careful, he would end up thrown from the dragon.

Ursal turned toward him. "You have already lost, but you don't yet know it. Once you're gone, the other will be mine."

"The dragons will never be yours. They are meant to be free."

She smiled at him. A wave of a Calling struck him.

It was intense, and it filled him, flowing through him, a demand that he respond and do exactly as she wanted. There was a threat of pain and a promise of pleasure mixed within the Calling, and he wanted nothing more than to obey, but at the same time, there was something different.

He knew that he could resist.

Was it because of his time in the dragonlands? Or was it something else? Was it because he had drunk from the Asharn? Either way, Fes was able to resist the Calling, and he pushed out with his own Deshazl magic, slamming it into Ursal.

It had less of an effect than he wanted, but it still threw her back, disrupting her Calling if only for a moment. If he could disrupt the spell...

"I knew your sister," Fes said, glaring at her as he clutched the dragon's back, clinging to the scales. A few spikes protruded along the dragon's back, and he grabbed onto those, hoping for a better grip.

Ursal glared at him. "You would not have known my sister."

"She came to the empire. She chased dragons. Then she died because of it." He smiled at her, holding his sword out, waiting for her response.

He expected rage, and he expected her to attempt another Calling, but he didn't plan on her using the dragon to suddenly thrash, twisting wildly as it balked, sending Fes flipping over so that he landed on his back, one hand squeezing onto the dragon's scales, barely managing to hang on. He used every bit of power in him to bind himself to the dragon, holding on with his Deshazl magic so that he wouldn't fall.

The dragon continued to twist, and Fes maneuvered himself so that he could see Ursal again. She faced him, and power flowed from her, fire magic that she slammed toward him. It was everything that he could do to hold up a Deshazl magic barrier to prevent her from striking him with the brunt of her magic.

He crawled toward her, squeezing the dragon's back.

As he did, he shifted his Deshazl magic. It was just a little, but enough that he sent it probing toward the dragon.

"You can fight this. I can help."

Ursal grinned at him. "You are too late, Deshazl," she spat. "We have become linked."

Fes blinked. Could they have linked? It was what he felt that he and the other dragon had done, but he wouldn't have expected Ursal to have managed the same with this dragon, certainly not without having any Deshazl magic of her own. Was it possible that she used the Calling and combined that with the inherent magic of the dragon to link them?

He didn't think that was possible. More likely it was that she used only her Calling, and the nature of that magic was what she use to hold the dragon, forcing her to serve.

Fes would fight for the dragon.

"If you fight, I can continue to fight on your behalf," he said to the dragon.

He wasn't sure whether she even knew, and he couldn't tell how much she was aware of, but it seemed to him that her fighting seemed to change and the thrashing eased if only a little. If that were the case, was there some way to use that?

Ursal surprised him again. She withdrew a sword from a sheath and crawled toward him. Heat radiated from the blade, and while it wasn't dragonglass, it seemed as if it were made of something of power. He stared at the blade, struggling to understand why it would flow with power, and he realized with a start that it was dragon bone.

The bone had been blackened, but the heat radiated from it. She pulled through the sword itself, creating her spell.

The fact that she had a sword like that troubled him. Dragonglass was nearly indestructible, but what would happen if he fought her with a bone blade that she pulled fire magic through?

Fes had to end the fight quickly. He didn't know how much longer he could hold on. Every so often, the dragon would twist, and as she did, he strained to cling to her back, but it seemed as if the thrashing lessened, becoming much less aggressive, letting Fes hold on more easily.

"I will end this," he said to the dragon, pushing out with his Deshazl connection, hoping that she would understand.

He lunged toward Ursal.

As he slashed at her blade, his dragonglass sword crashed against the blackened bone. Neither shattered.

Fes had fought others with his dragonglass sword, and it had cut through steel. The bone was not only blackened but hardened by her magic.

He cut again, carving toward her, and she blocked.

She was skilled.

She smiled at him, and she shifted so that she could get up on her knees. Fes didn't dare do that, uncertain when—and if—the dragon would change directions, something Ursal didn't have to worry about. She knew when the dragon would change positions, and she could use that knowledge to hold on to the dragon's back more easily, allowing her to cling to the dragon in a way that Fes couldn't. It took away his ability to use that magic to attack Ursal. From the way she looked at him, she knew it.

Fes glared at her and stabbed forward, attempting to reach her with the sword, but she was skilled enough that she blocked. The dragon twisted and he rolled off to the side, barely managing to catch himself in time to block her next thrust.

Fes spun his sword, and she blocked, and a powerful fire mage spell built from her. His sword was twisted down, and he wouldn't be able to cut through it. He reached for his other sword, unsheathing it and carving through the spell before it struck him.

Heat washed over him, but he managed to stop it just in time.

"I imagine you gave my sister some difficulty," Ursal said.

Another attempt at a Calling struck him, washing over him, and if anything, it was even more powerful than the last. Was she directing her focus from the dragon to attempt to Call him?

If she was, it gave him an opportunity with the dragon.

Fight this.

He sent it through his Deshazl connection, hoping that the dragon could somehow hear him, not certain whether she could, but thinking that if nothing else, he would try to communicate with her, letting her know that he would help.

Ursal lunged toward him, and Fes brought his sword around, crashing down on hers. He ignored the effect of the Calling, able to fight it, recognizing what she was trying to get him to do. Within the Calling was a demand that he set down his sword, that he serve, and that he abandon the Deshazl.

He could—and would—do none of those. He smiled at her.

"You've already lost," Fes said.

"And you fail to see your mistake," she said.

"What mistake?"

"Do you think this was the only dragon we have raised?"

His breath caught, and he looked up, barely in time to see a small black-scaled dragon diving toward him.

CHAPTER EIGHTEEN

F lames burst from the dragon's nostril, and Fes rolled off to the side, barely avoiding the flames as they struck the green-scaled dragon's back.

There were two.

How many more dragons had they freed?

He laid on the dragon's back for a moment, collecting his thoughts. Wind whistled around him, and everything seemed to hurt. This shouldn't be the way that he would go out. They shouldn't be able to overpower him like this, and they shouldn't be able to overpower the dragons like this, but it seemed as if anything and everything that he tried was defeated by Ursal.

How was it that her sister had been on the Trivent and not her? Ursal seemed much more powerful than Elsanelle, and while he had felt the effects of Elsanelle's Calling, he had never seen her with a sword. Then again, maybe she had not thought that she needed one. Maybe she had believed that fighting with a sword was somehow beneath her.

He could hear the dragon roaring. It had a higher-pitched rumble than both the green-scaled dragon as well as the blue-scaled one that Fes had been working with. Was this an adolescent?

What if they hadn't raised a second dragon at all? It was possible they had hatched it. Either way, it didn't matter. They had a second dragon, which meant that there were others that he had to worry about, others who could Call, and he still hadn't managed to disrupt the Calling that Ursal held on this dragon.

He rolled back onto his stomach, wrapping his Deshazl magic around him, trying to bind himself to the dragon. Had his last comment to the dragon made any difference?

He couldn't tell. It was possible that Ursal's brief Calling to Fes had disrupted the effect of what she was using on the dragon long enough for him to reach her, but he didn't think so. Not the way the dragon was twisting. She was still trying to throw him off her back, and every so often, Fes would catch glimpses of the ground below, enough glimpses that he still didn't know whether the Asharn had been harmed.

Hopefully, Jayell had managed to protect them if the other dragon had attacked.

Maybe with an adolescent dragon, she would've had an easier time defending them, but there were limits to how much power she could draw, and there were only so many dragon relics that she had with her. Eventually, her power would run out. And then she would not be able to defend the Asharn. They were all powerful, and they had enough of a connection to their Deshazl magic that Fes didn't think they were in too much danger, but against the dragon?

He had already seen how a skilled Damhur could use the dragon's magic to prevent the Deshazl from using their magic on them. Even an adolescent dragon would likely have enough power to make it difficult for the Asharn to overpower it, but then there were more Asharn on the ground than he had in the air.

Fes had to hope that they managed to attack the dragon, disrupting it from reaching them, but it was possible that they could not.

It was time to end this battle.

It might mean sacrificing himself to a certain extent, but wasn't he willing to do that? For the dragon, shouldn't he be willing to do that?

He gathered his power, focusing on the Deshazl connection within him, the same connection that bound him to the dragon, along with all of the Asharn that were here with him. He could use those powers and that connection, and with them together, he would be able to at least try something.

Fes pushed off the dragon's back with a burst of Deshazl magic.

He flew toward Ursal, driving his sword at her.

The dragon twisted and his sword missed. Ursal brought her sword around, blocking him. Fes scrambled, pulling on the dragon with his Deshazl magic, wrapping it around the dragon's neck, pulling him to it, at the same time he jabbed with his other hand, slamming his other sword into Ursal's side.

She gasped.

Fes sliced up, cutting through her, the dragonglass meeting very little resistance much as it often did, and her blood streamed over his hand, hot and unpleasant.

"The dragons are not to be Called," he said.

"You. Have. Already. Lost." With each word, blood burbled from her mouth, and Fes twisted his sword and pulled it out of her, wiping it on her clothing before throwing her from the dragon's back.

Now that she was gone, he had to somehow disrupt the effect of the Calling that she placed on the dragon.

"I'm here to help," he said.

The dragon roared, streaking toward the ground. Flames shot from her mouth, and she twisted. The effect of the sudden movement forced Fes to grab onto her back, clinging to her, and he worried that he might be thrown free. If she continued to fight in this way, there would be no way he could avoid such a fate.

"Let me help you," he said again.

The dragon continued to thrash, and while he didn't think there was still a Calling pressing upon the dragon, he didn't know how long the residual effect would linger.

Fes directed his Deshazl connection toward the dragon. As he did, he drew from the other dragon, trying to bridge them. It seemed to be the only way, and all he wanted was to help release her mind from the effect of Ursal's Calling, but he didn't know whether he could.

The dragon continued to fight, to twist. She streaked right above the ground and wind whistled around him, and then she reached a forest, twisting through the trees. Branches slapped at Fes, and it took everything within his power to push out a barrier to protect himself from those branches, to avoid getting slapped by them, and still he almost didn't have enough.

She broke free from the forest, climbing into the sky. In the distance, he could see the blue-scaled dragon and the black-scaled dragon twisting in battle. Occasionally, flames would erupt from the black-scaled dragon, but his dragon ignored them, continuing to climb. Hopefully, Lena was safe on the dragon's back, but for how long? Much like with the green-scaled dragon, the black-scaled dragon seemed to have a boost of speed, and from what he could tell, it came from fire magic, used in much the same way that Ursal had used it to help speed the green-scaled dragon during her attack.

He didn't have time to think about that. He had to focus on getting free and had to figure out some way to stabilize this dragon. There had to be something that he could do, but what was it?

He should have asked the other dragon what it had taken when he had been freed from the Calling, trying to get a sense of what he could do to help. There had to be something, some way to reach this one.

And he didn't think she wanted to harm him, not really, which meant that whatever she was experiencing, this frenzied attack that she was using, was not of her own choosing.

Fes pushed through her, using his Deshazl connection and trying to wrap her mind with it. This time, he attempted to reach through the dragon, drawing from what he could detect of her. In doing so, he felt a strangeness within that connection.

Fes funneled all of the Deshazl power that he could summon into her, trying to smooth out the strangeness that he detected, wanting to use that to offset the power and to ensure that she could find a measure of relaxation.

There had to be some way to do that.

He continued to push his Deshazl magic into her, drawing more and more, and he found himself pulling from the blue-scaled dragon, and even from the Asharn on the ground.

The dragon roared, and Fes pushed again.

Suddenly there came a shifting.

The strangeness within her changed, the unsettled sensation within her improved, and he was able to use that and draw upon it until he felt her relax. With the sudden change in her, he knew that he had finally managed to reach her.

Her flight settled, and she leveled off, making wide circles over the clearing.

"Are you better?" Fes asked.

"Thank you," the dragon said.

"Is the Calling still influencing you?" He didn't think so, not with the way that she had suddenly leveled off and the thrashing had stopped, but he couldn't be entirely certain without asking.

"It doesn't seem to be," she said.

Fes let out a sigh. He relaxed his grip on her back and pushed on his Deshazl magic, trying to connect to her, wrapping it around her mind, probing for the possibility of an ongoing attack, but there was nothing there.

"Are you convinced?" she asked.

"It seems as if you are better. I didn't realize that the effect of a Calling could linger after the Damhur was gone."

"She was trying to change something within me."

"What was she trying to change?"

The dragon breathed out flames. "I don't know. I could feel it changing me, twisting me, altering me, but you seem to have stopped it."

"Only stopped it?" He wanted to have done more than that, to have restored her, but he couldn't tell whether he had been successful.

"It seems to have been stopped. I can't tell yet whether it had been restored," she said.

That would have to be enough.

"We need to help the other."

"I'm not sure how," she said.

"Get me close. I will take care of the rest."

"They will only raise more."

"Are they using the sculptures?"

"You know of this?"

"That's how I helped the other dragon," Fes said. "He said he was sleeping and we woke him. Was it the same for you?"

"My last memory of this world was a millennia ago. Much has changed in that time, but much is still the same."

Fes hated that the dragons had gone to sleep, trying to hide from the effect of the Damhur, only to be awoken by the same threat. It was time for that threat to end and, if it were up to him, he would ensure that the Damhur no longer harmed the dragons again. Ever again.

The dragon rumbled.

Fes frowned to himself. He *felt* her satisfaction with what he wanted. How was it that he was able to detect that about her? They didn't have any sort of bond, not the way he and the blue-scaled dragon did.

Had his attempt to heal her changed that? Had they connected because of it?

It didn't matter. All that mattered was that he would find a way of reaching the others.

They started to climb, and as they did, they streaked toward the black-scaled dragon. They angled upward, heading toward the other dragon, rising higher and higher, and then she twisted, diving to the ground, much in the same way the blue-scaled dragon had done.

From this angle, Fes could see that there were two Damhur on the back of the black dragon.

He pushed out with his Deshazl connection, hoping to startle them, but they seemed to be prepared for that, and his magic parted around them, much the same way as it had happened with this dragon.

"They use our connection," she said.

"That's what I was afraid of," Fes said.

"They force us to fight. We know that we should not, and we know that the Deshazl work with the dragons, but there is nothing that we can do to resist, not when the effect of their influence is there."

"It's not your fault," Fes said.

"I am aware of what I'm doing when they influence us. Even though I'm aware, there's nothing that I can do to stop it."

There was anger from the dragon. Fes could feel it from her and could feel her rage at the Damhur. He would have to help calm that somehow. He didn't want the dragon to be violently attacked to avoid becoming the creatures the Damhur believed them to be.

"Let me be the violence," Fes said.

She rumbled, but he felt a stirring of her agreement and thought that if nothing else, she wouldn't attack without the need.

As they twisted around, Fes jumped.

He angled, streaking through the air, holding onto his sword. This time, he managed to maneuver, pushing against the air with his Deshazl magic, using it to help him navigate until he reached the black dragon.

He slammed his sword through one of the Damhur as he landed on the back of the dragon, and he threw the person free.

The other turned to him, seemingly startled that he would suddenly appear. She attempted a Calling, but hers was not nearly as strong as Ursal's had been.

"You may live if you stop," he said.

"You would offer me a bargain?" she asked.

"I don't need to kill you. I will if you continue to attack me and the dragon."

Fes could feel the influence of her Calling, but it wasn't so much that he would struggle against it. She was strong, but nothing like Ursal. There had to be good within some of the Damhur, and as much as he hated the idea of giving them the opportunity, he felt as if he couldn't slaughter all of them. Some of them had to be salvageable, didn't they? He thought of Indra and the fact that she wouldn't have wanted to attack the empire, but she was forced to by her father.

Maybe the Damhur were treated much the same way. Maybe there were those within the Damhur who forced those who didn't want to fight.

If there were, they would be the ones that Fes would save. They would be the ones that he would have to unite, because after he managed to stop the attack on the empire, there would have to be something different, some change, that would allow the dragons to live in peace and not have to fear for their safety.

She lunged toward him, using a belt knife and not a sword.

Fes batted the knife away. She got too close, and he slammed his fist into the side of her head. She collapsed, and he prevented her from falling to the ground.

This time, he was ready for the sudden change of the Calling, and he immediately began to push his Deshazl magic into the dragon, soothing the creature. He was ready for the possibility that he would need to be stronger than the dragon, prepared for the chance that if he wasn't, the dragon would continue to thrash and eventually throw him off.

Using that connection, Fes was able to smooth out the influence that the Calling had placed upon the dragon, and he was able to press that down, and the dragon calmed. Could the adolescent dragon be easier to calm? If so, Fes was thankful that he didn't have to fight nearly as much as he did with the green dragon.

"Take me down, if you would," Fes said.

The dragon puffed out fire.

As he did with the green dragon, he sensed the dragon's emotions. There was relief, but it was tinged with fear. The dragon was terrified that another attack would come, and if it did, would he be ready?

"I can't promise you that you can stay protected, but there are those who will do their best to defend you."

"There is no defense against that."

"That's where you're wrong. I can fight the effect of the Calling, and if I can, that means that you and others can."

And maybe there was something more that could be done.

Would it matter if the dragons drank from the Asharn?

It seemed to have some way of offering protection from the Calling, but then again, so did the Dragon's Eye.

Maybe the combination of the two would help protect the dragons to ensure that they weren't subject to the effect of the Calling.

It was almost too much to hope for.

Fes glided down to the ground with the dragon, and when they landed, he jumped free. He looked up to see the blue dragon coming down. Lena scrambled down, looking at Fes with a wide-eyed expression. Eventually, even the green dragon came to land. The dragons looked at each other, and there was a sense of suspicion within them, but within that was a measure of respect.

How could he feel that?

It was unmistakable. Fes could feel that measure of respect from the dragons, even if he didn't know why he could. There had to be some way, some reason, for him to be so attuned to it. Maybe it was merely the Deshazl connection, the shared bond that he had with the dragons, and if that were the case, then Fes would embrace it. How could he not?

He made his way over to the green dragon, standing in the middle of the three. He looked up at her. "How many others have they raised?"

"Only the two of us."

"He was raised?" he asked her, motioning to the black dragon.

If he was raised, that created a different set of problems, those that he had not necessarily anticipated. Fes thought there was a limit to how many dragon relics the Damhur possessed, but maybe that had been wrong. If they had enough relics to raise two dragons, would they have enough to raise even more?

But then, he remembered how infrequently he saw them using the dragon relics. What if their hesitance to use them wasn't so much out of a concern for the number of relics they possessed, but more out of a concern for using up the power within them, sacrificing what they wanted to have to raise more dragons?

"He was raised. He was very young when he first went to sleep," the blue dragon said.

Fes looked over at him. There was something about the way he spoke that told Fes there was some connection between them. While he knew the blue dragon was an elder dragon, he didn't exactly know what that meant, and he didn't exactly know what that meant for the other dragons.

"Did you know him?"

"There weren't so many dragons in that time. There never have been."

"So you knew him?"

The blue dragon glanced over at Fes, regarding him with his dark golden eyes. "We knew him."

"I need to find the other sculptures," he said, looking at the green dragon and the black dragon. "If they have them, then they can raise others. If they raise others, then they will suffer the same fate you nearly did. The sculptures have been held in a place called the gallery. That's where we were heading, wanting to free the sculptures from the Damhur, so that we could protect them."

"They have moved them," the green dragon said.

"Where did they move them?"

"Away," she said.

Fes frowned. "Away?" That wasn't specific enough, certainly not specific enough to know where to go to look for them, and if they didn't know where to look for the dragon sculptures, there would be no way to rescue the dragons.

And did they even need to at this point? Now that he knew the key to fighting off the Damhur and rescuing the dragons that they Called, could they do that, or did they need to go after the other dragons first?

Either way, he felt as if he were letting someone down. If he abandoned the other dragons, he would be letting them down, but if he went after the dragons and the empire continued to suffer, then he would be abandoning the empire.

Now that there were three dragons, three *freed* dragons, it seemed as if they would be better prepared to take on the threat of the Damhur, and if they were able to do that, they should be able to defeat them.

"They were moving them, and they intended to use our remains to raise them once again."

"Why are the dragon remains required?"

It was something that he didn't fully understand. It would make sense if the remains were tied to a specific dragon, but that didn't seem to be the case. Or maybe it was. Maybe a dragon resurrection would fail if it didn't use the correct remains, but then again, how would they know? There was no way of telling which dragon remains belonged to which of the sculptures.

"It's not so much the remains as it is the power that flows through them," the blue dragon said. "You have felt this. You are aware of how that power flows through the dragons, even when we are gone. We absorb that power as we return, reborn from it."

Which meant that using the dragon remains did waste energy that the dragons needed for their return.

It was something that the dragon priests in the empire had feared, and Fes had always brushed it off, but if that were the case, if the use of dragon relics to power the fire mage spells did use up their magic, it would prevent dragons from returning.

He glanced over at Jayell, who stood in the distance. So far, the Asharn hadn't come any closer, and it seemed almost as if they were afraid to approach the three dragons. Fes couldn't blame them, as they might not know that the other two had been rescued, restored, but he hoped that Lena would go and share with them that they were no longer a threat.

Lena approached, and Fes glanced over at her. She had been listening, but from a distance, and now she came toward him, watching the dragons, but her gaze lingered on the black dragon. "If they use up the power within the dragon remains, they won't be able to resurrect them?"

"If the energy stored within our remains is gone, we won't be able to reawaken," he said.

Lena stared at the dragons for a moment before turning to Fes. "That's the key."

"No," Fes said.

"We need to ensure that they can't hurt any others, and if the key is using up the power within the remains..." She glanced over at Jayell and the others, but Fes knew immediately what she was thinking about.

The empire had already used great power from the dragons, and they had already sacrificed the possibility of returning many dragons to the world, so Fes had no interest in continuing that.

"This is not the dragons' fault. This is the fault of the Damhur," he said.

"Blaming doesn't change anything," Lena said. "If there's anything that we can do to prevent them from doing anything to get stronger, it must be done," she said and looked over at the dragons, sadness lingering in her eyes. "I'm sorry, but they are a threat, and the Damhur have already proven that they are all too willing to use any resource they have available, and with that, they have proven that they will destroy. What happens if they raise a dozen dragons? Two dozen dragons?"

Fes shook his head. He couldn't handle that suggestion. The idea of not helping the dragons was not something that he could even fathom, especially with what they had been through to stop the Damhur in the first place.

"I intend to reach the dragon sculptures. We can save them and prevent the Damhur from using the power within them to continue to attack," he said.

"And if you're too late?"

"If I'm too late, we've already seen that there are ways for us to protect the dragons, and we can use that. We can fight if it comes to it, and we can stop them."

"What if it fails?" she asked.

"If it fails, then we have tried." He looked up at the dragons, feeling as if they had to do something, anything, and abandoning the dragons to hide from a potential threat was not anything that he was willing to do.

Lena watched Fes, and he worried that she would resist. If she did, he didn't know what he might be able to do to convince the other Asharn. He suspected that if Lena resisted, the others might as well.

"Are you sure that you can do this?" she asked.

Fes looked over at the dragons before turning back to her and shaking his head. "No. But I am sure that we need to try. The dragons were lost during the last war because people were afraid. The dragons were afraid. The Damhur were able to control them, but we know how to resist. The Asharn have learned to fight the Damhur. And I have shown that we can protect the dragons. We have to do this."

Lena stared at him for a moment and finally nodded. "I will stay with you."

Fes breathed out a sigh. He didn't know what he would've done had she decided otherwise. "Good. Because now we have to go and find the sculptures and stop the Damhur before they bring any more dragons back. And then we will go to the empire and end this."

CHAPTER NINETEEN

With the trees around him, Fes felt as if he were almost back in the forest in the empire, close enough that he felt a sense of comfort, almost as if it were embracing him. There was something about these trees that reminded him very much of that forest, and he almost imagined that the dragon's breath would rise up from the forest floor, masking the presence of the dragons.

He looked between the trees. Deeper into the forest, he could see the Asharn. They stood in a circle, and they all held hands, singing as they looked up at the sky. Roshana's body lay in the middle of the circle, covered with a cloak, concealing her. The Asharn had wanted to come into the trees, wanting to have an opportunity to allow Roshana a final resting point in a place they considered home.

Their song was beautiful and mournful, and it tugged at something deep within Fes. He felt something like an outsider and wondered if he really should be listening to their song, but curiosity kept him close.

She had died bravely. She had been willing to go and fight and had lost her life fighting the Damhur. He feared that she wouldn't be the last.

If only others of the Asharn were willing to fight, maybe they would have a better chance against them, but their numbers were limited.

And now they had to wait.

Perhaps it was best that they did, waiting for the return of the dragons, giving the Asharn a chance to mourn. A part of Fes knew that they needed to be moving quickly and that they couldn't be resting for long, but there was a necessity to giving the Asharn this chance to grieve.

Every so often, he would glance over at the black dragon, still uncertain how he might react. Everything seemed off still, and while he had been rescued from the Calling, Fes couldn't help but feel as if there was some remaining connection. Each time he attempted to push through the Deshazl magic, trying to reach through with his connection, he felt nothing that would make him concerned, but he couldn't shake a worrisome sense about this dragon.

"You keep watching him like that," Jayell said.

Fes glanced over at her. She cupped a dragon pearl, the last one they had. Now she had a dragon bone sword sheathed at her side, the blade reclaimed from Ursal's remains. If nothing else, they would use that to help strengthen them. Ursal had several other dragon relics on her body, and they had claimed all of them, thinking that they could use them to help fight off the threat coming from the Damhur.

"I'm not certain that he is completely recovered," he said.

"I thought you restored him," she said.

"I think I did, but there is something within him that's troubled. It bothers him that he was Called."

"It bothers you that you were Called."

Maybe that was it. Perhaps it was a matter of the frustration that the dragon felt about having been controlled in the way that he had been. It was something that Fes certainly would understand, as he had experienced much the same.

"How much longer do you think we need to wait?" Jayell asked.

"Not much longer."

The blue dragon had guided the other across the valley, giving her a chance to dive into the Dragon's Eye.

Fes wasn't sure whether it was worth the distraction, but he thought that they needed to take the time and the opportunity to restore the dragons entirely. Reaching the Dragon's Eye was easiest, and while he wasn't sure if they would be able to reach the Asharn, especially as it was hidden within the Asharn city, Fes thought that the Dragon's Eye would serve well.

"Do you think that you can find the sculptures?" she asked.

"I don't know. If they are connected to the Deshazl, then I should be able to. Especially with this new ability that I have, it seems as if everything connected to the Deshazl illuminates for me." He looked around. The black dragon glowed with the same soft Deshazl light as all of the Deshazl did. With that, he was able to determine just how much power was within the dragon, and Fes could feel that there was significant power within this youngster. It was much the same with the green dragon. He could feel that she was incredibly powerful, and maybe that was tied to something else, something beyond the Dragon's Eye.

"We've been gone too long," Jayell said.

"I know," he whispered.

"You think the fire mages will have been able to withstand the attack?"

"With Azithan directing them, I think that they have a chance, but I don't know how long they will be able to

DRAGON RIDER | 355

hold out." And that was all it would be. It would be holding out, not attempting to overthrow the attack, especially as there might not be a way to overthrow the Damhur. The fire mages would fight, but some limits were tied not only to the fire mages themselves but to the power that they drew through the relics.

And he wondered if perhaps the Damhur were attempting the same strategy Lena had suggested, wanting to draw out all of the power from the empire's dragon remains, wasting that power and leaving the empire defenseless.

If that were the case, they needed to hurry.

"He's coming," Fes said.

"Just him?"

He closed his eyes, focusing on what he could detect of the Deshazl. In the sky above him, he could feel not only the blue dragon but also the green dragon. Something had changed within her, and she seemed better connected than she had been before. There was a certain relief within her, a sense of relaxation and freedom.

"They both come." Fes looked over at the black dragon. "It's your turn now."

"Does it hurt?" the dragon asked.

Fes shook his head. "It is an unusual sense, but pain isn't a part of it."

He could feel the dragon reaching through him, reaching through the Deshazl connection they shared and felt a sense of relief coming from the dragon. He trusted Fes. He needed that trust, and he needed that help.

The other two dropped below the trees, diving, and landing on the ground near them.

"He needs to go," Fes said.

"We saw movement as we were returning," the blue dragon said.

"What kind of movement?"

"The kind that you would be interested in," he said.

Damhur. And if the Damhur were moving, did that mean that they had spotted the sculptures?

"Can you show me?"

"You would rather do that than allow him the chance to cleanse himself?"

Fes squeezed his eyes shut. He didn't want to do that —he needed the black dragon to have relief and the opportunity to be safe no differently than the green dragon had—but he couldn't risk the relics getting away from them and the Damhur taking them beyond his reach.

Was there a different way?

He looked over at the green dragon. "Can you guide him?"

She let out a breath of steam and stared at Fes for a moment. "I can bring him, if that's what you think needs to happen."

Fes nodded. "I think that we need to. I will go and see what we can find from the Damhur, and you go with him, giving him a chance to be cleansed." It was an interesting phrase, but it seemed fitting.

He turned to look at the black dragon. "She will guide you. You will be given the opportunity you need, and when you're done, you can decide what you're willing to do."

He had a sense that the dragons weren't entirely sure how much they were able—and willing—to help. The green dragon wanted to help, and he sensed within her even greater desire than she had before leaving for the Dragon's Eye, but he could sense uncertainty within the black dragon. Fes couldn't blame him. It was the same uncertainty that he had seen from the Deshazl when they had been in the empire. After they had been Called, many didn't want to risk exposing themselves to the Damhur again, and why should they want to? Doing so placed them in a position of danger and risked them losing control of themselves, losing a sense of themselves. Fes didn't want to be responsible for that, but at the same time, he thought they needed all of the dragons to help. If they were to stop the Damhur—and prevent them from furthering their attack on the empire—it would need to be more than just the Asharn and Fes. It would need to be the power and strength coming from the dragons. Maybe two dragons would be enough, but having greater numbers than the Damhur possessed might be required.

Fes turned to the blue dragon. "Show me what you saw."

As he scrambled onto the dragon's back, Jayell joined him.

"Let them have their time of mourning," she said, nodding to the Asharn still circled and singing.

They hadn't paid any mind to the return of the dragons, and Fes wasn't surprised by that. Every so often, he would detect a surge of Deshazl magic from them, and when he looked over, he could see their magic flowing from person to person. He wondered whether it was something they did intentionally or if it came from the nature of the song they created.

"I don't intend this to be a fight," he said.

"You often don't intend for there to be a fight, but that doesn't change what happens," Jayell said, smiling at him. She slipped her arms around him as she sank down on the dragon's back and Fes grinned, enjoying their proximity. The dragon took to the air, quickly circling, and as he did, the other two lurched into the sky behind them, headed toward the valley in the distance.

"Do you think he will be okay?" he asked the dragon.

"He has questions," the dragon said.

"And they are questions without answers, aren't they?"

"When it comes to the Damhur and the Calling, there are many questions without answers," he said.

They turned northward, streaking low to the ground, and he wondered how the dragon had seen anything. They would've come from the other side of the valley, and there shouldn't have been any reason for them to have traveled this way.

When he said something to the dragon, he was greeted with a blast of fire.

"When she was released from the Dragon's Eye, she wanted to circle," he said.

"Circle?"

The dragon started to ascend, and Fes thought he understood. She wanted to be higher, and from an altitude, they would have been able to see many things.

He kept his focus on the ground, looking for signs of Damhur. It took a while until he saw something, but what he observed was not what he expected. Flashes of pale white light.

Deshazl.

Fes continued to stare out over the side of the dragon, watching the connections between the Deshazl that he saw down below. They glowed with a soft light, many of them nearly as strong as the Asharn who had traveled with him, but there was something else down there that glowed differently.

Jayell pulled on his sleeve, and he sat up, looking over at her.

"You were about ready to fall off," she said.

Fes pointed over the edge of the dragon. "There are Deshazl down there."

"If there are Deshazl, that means there are Damhur," she said.

Fes nodded. "Damhur, and I see something else that makes me a little concerned."

"What is it?"

"It's possible that it's only more Deshazl, but…"

"But what?"

"But it's also possible that it's the sculptures that we've been looking for."

"Why would they be here?" she asked.

"The green dragon said they were moving them, so what if they were moving them to raise the dragons? They wouldn't do that in the city." At least, he didn't think that they would. Why risk others seeing them? More than that, why would they risk others being injured by them?

Unless they weren't concerned.

The Deshazl present here made him wonder about the intention behind the Damhur. All of this was Javoor, and all of this was their land, so there was no reason that they couldn't be here, but there was something that he needed to understand.

They circled, staying high enough above the ground that they would hopefully be nothing more than a shadow. Fes leaned forward, close enough that he didn't have to yell as he tried to get dragon's attention, and said, "Do you see any signs of other dragons?"

The dragon's eyesight would be better than his, and if anything, the dragon would be able to recognize whether they were attempting to raise more. It was late enough in the evening that darkness had begun to fall, and it seemed an unusual time to attempt to raise a dragon, especially if there was any confusion within the creature after it awoke. Fes remembered the confusion within this dragon, though it had resolved fairly quickly. What would've happened had the dragon awoken in the middle of Anuhr?

Probably nothing, but it was possible that the dragon would have struggled with coming around, and he had to worry that perhaps the confusion of the sudden awakening would have been disruptive and destructive.

"There is nothing," the dragon said.

Nothing, which meant that either there were no sculptures or they simply weren't attempting it.

"How many do you see?"

"Close to one hundred," the dragon said.

One hundred would be more than they would be able to manage even with the Asharn. If there were one hundred, and even if a majority of them were Deshazl, they would be too difficult to overpower.

And if the majority were Deshazl, it meant that there were enough of the Damhur present who would be able to Call them and control them. There was a possibility that it put the dragon in danger.

"We must find out," the dragon said.

Fes shook his head. It seemed as if the dragon understood what he was thinking and understood his concern, but he couldn't risk them, not like that. "We don't know whether it will work on you."

"It didn't work on you, and I sensed that she attempted great power with you."

"Did she attempt to Call you?" Fes hadn't paid enough attention to what Ursal had been doing during the attack, but what if she had been trying to Call the dragon? She had failed with Fes, and he didn't know if that was tied to his time in the Dragon's Eye or because he drank from the Asharn or whether it was his experience that had changed him, preventing him from succumbing to the effect of a Calling, but if she were to have used it on the dragon, she would have been able to throw him off, and she had not succeeded in that.

But then, she had only truly tried to Call him when he had jumped down to the green dragon and gotten closer to her.

"I did not feel the effects."

"I know that you fear the possibility of another Calling."

"If they have the others, we must rescue them."

"What do you propose?"

There were too many for him to handle alone. Not entirely alone, he realized, glancing over at Jayell. She had the dragon sword, and with that, there was quite a bit of power that she could summon, but how long would that last? Would it be enough to resist the Damhur? The Deshazl would be able to cut through her spells, and with the Damhur controlling them, it would put Jayell into a precarious position.

"There is only so much that they can do to me," the dragon rumbled, turning his head to the side so that one eye managed to look over at Fes. Heat wafted off him, swirling around him like a mist.

It might involve them having to harm the Deshazl who were there.

Everything that Fes had done had been about protecting Deshazl, and had been about saving those he could, but in this, he would have to make a choice. Would he try to protect Deshazl or would he try to protect the dragons?

He doubted that he would be able to do both, and if he didn't, it meant that either he would lose the dragon sculptures—if they were there—or he would be forced to attack and harm Deshazl. He'd killed the Damhur Deshazl before, but only when there hadn't been another option. If he could rescue them, break them free from the effect of the Calling, maybe they would be able to be saved. They could be brought to the Dragon's Eye, or brought to the Asharn and given a chance to be saved there. Anything that would allow them to be freed from the influence of the Damhur.

"Fes," Jayell said softly, touching his arm.

He squeezed his eyes together, shaking his head. What choice was this?

It wasn't one, certainly not one that he wanted to make. It was an impossible choice, the kind that he had tried to avoid, but coming to face the Damhur took away that choice.

"We have to do this," he said softly.

The dragon huffed out a streamer of fire and smoke and then dove to the ground, skidding to a stop in the midst of the Damhur. As soon as they landed, the power of a dozen Callings struck him and the dragon.

At first, Fes feared for their ability to withstand it, but he realized that neither of them suffered from it. He could feel the lack of effect through his connection to the dragon, and it was much the same for Fes. He was aware of the Calling, but his awareness didn't mean that he felt compelled by it.

Jayell pushed out a barrier of her fire magic.

That barrier created a buffer around them.

It did nothing to stop the Damhur and their Calling, but it was enough that he was able to avoid the effect of fire magic thrown in their direction. The dragon roared and sat propped up on his wings, sending streamers of flame out.

The combined magic from the Damhur and the Deshazl created a shielding that protected them.

"I'm not sure that this was the best idea," Fes muttered.

Jayell glanced over at him.

He jumped off the dragon and quickly surveyed the clearing. They were in the middle of a campsite, which the dragon's landing had disrupted, sending the once-orderly tents into a scattered mess. Several people had been crushed by the dragon, and they lay broken and not moving beneath his feet. The others had reacted in time, backing away from the threat of the dragon, getting far enough away that they didn't have to succumb to the attack.

It was easy enough to make out the Damhur. They were dressed in the typical deep blue jackets and pants, not armored in the way that the Deshazl were. The women had long hair, tightly woven into a single braid, whereas the men all had close-cropped hair. Three of the Damhur carried swords much like the one Jayell now used.

Those were the fire mages, and he suspected they would be the most powerful of them.

Where were the sculptures?

"Keep attacking," he said to the dragon.

The dragon continued to roar, sending flames streaming out. The barrier held, but Fes could feel it shimmering. They would only be able to withstand the force from a dragon for so long.

Unless they came in and attacked.

The connection to his Deshazl magic showed him where he needed to go. The Deshazl were there, and if he could disrupt them…

No. They weren't the ones he had to finish off first. That had to be the Damhur.

"Focus on the Damhur," he said to the dragon.

Fes started forward, drawing the shield with his Deshazl magic around him, creating a massive barrier that he drew through the dragon, pulling away from the Deshazl, taking from their magic as he attacked. The barrier was power that he continued to summon, pulling more and more from them, and with each draw, he weakened them.

Throughout all of it, he could still feel Jayell holding her shielding. As he did, he realized what she was doing. The shielding wasn't so much for her. It was for the dragon, and she was using it in a way to protect him.

He smiled to himself. Could the ancient people of the

empire have used the dragon magic in such a way? Would they have fought with the dragons, sitting atop them, holding a barrier with magic drawn from dragon relics?

Fes had to think that they did not.

Two Deshazl jumped forward, and Fes slammed his Deshazl magic into them, setting them flying backward. Another approached, and Fes did the same, diverting magic from the dragon and pushing it into the Deshazl, slamming him back.

He kept his focus on the Damhur. The dragon continued his attack, shooting flames, focusing his fire on the Damhur. They were able to hold them back, withstanding the force of the attack.

He continued forward, pushing out with his Deshazl magic, and he approached the nearest of the Damhur. He was an older man with deep brown hair and deep brown eyes, and he held a bone sword. He glared at Fes.

"You are the one they have spoken about," he said with derision dripping from his voice.

Fes chuckled. "If they've been speaking about me, it means that you're afraid." He pushed on his Deshazl magic, trying to force it through him, but the Damhur resisted. It surprised him how skilled they were at resisting the force of his fight, but as they managed to do so, he continued to push forward.

The Damhur tried to push a Calling upon him, but Fes only shook his head.

"Your Calling won't work on me."

"Then you are not Deshazl."

Fes smiled at him. "I'm Deshazl, but I have also learned how to ignore the influence that you would press upon us."

The man glared at Fes. Waves of Calling pushed on him, and they were almost enough to influence him, but Fes held onto his connection to his Deshazl magic, holding it wrapped around his mind, and used his Deshazl barrier to push on the man.

It sent him back a step.

It disrupted the Calling just enough that Fes was able to step toward him again.

Again he tried to Call, and Fes sliced toward him with his sword. The man reacted, bringing his dragon bone sword around, blocking Fes, but Fes was prepared for it, and he carved through the bone, crashing at it. Infused with his Deshazl magic, his sword sliced through the bone, shattering it.

The man's eyes went wide.

Fes slammed his sword into the man's belly.

He turned to the two women. If they carried the bone swords, they would be powerful, and he needed to bring them down much like he had the other man. He lunged, swinging his sword around, but they pushed him back.

The force of it surprised him. It was fire magic, but it was blended with something else.

Deshazl magic.

How was that possible?

Fes looked over to see that two Deshazl stood behind each of these two women, flanking them. His connection to the Deshazl magic showed him that they were powerful, and in the growing night, they practically glowed with the intensity of their magic, and with that, they were able to merge their magic with that of the Damhur.

It was enough to push him back.

"You don't have to do this," he said to them. "I am here to release you."

One of the Damhur laughed. "Release them? They serve us willingly."

Fes stared at her. "They serve you because you force them with your Calling."

"They have been trained, much like you should have been trained. You have caused challenges, but not for much longer."

"You're wrong. You've already failed, but you just don't know it."

"We have not failed. You have made a mistake."

There came a surge of fire magic. It was enormous, the kind of burst that he had felt only a few times before, but through his Deshazl connection, Fes was fully aware of what it was and where it came from.

The fact that he felt it and the fact that they were able to draw upon it told him that he *had* made a mistake.

These might be powerful Damhur, and the Deshazl with them might be strong, but they weren't the focus of this at all.

He took a step back, hurrying backward, holding onto his barrier until he reached the dragon. He looked up at Jayell.

"What is it?"

"We're too late," he said.

"What do you mean?"

"They have already raised more of the dragons."

As he said it, the thunderous roar of dragon voices erupted in the night.

CHAPTER TWENTY

Fes jumped onto the dragon's back, his heart in the pit of his stomach, quickly scanning the clearing. There had to be some sign of the other dragons, but where were they? How many had they managed to raise?

"Do you see them?" he asked the dragon.

The dragon roared, leaping into the air, sending a streamer of flame circling around the clearing. It was a powerful burst, more so than any of the others that he had drawn, and it exploded through the barriers that the Damhur and the Deshazl were able to hold, burning dozens of people.

Fes didn't have an opportunity to feel remorse at their passing, and all he was able to feel was the fear that he, his dragons, and the Asharn would soon face many more

Called dragons. Facing two had been hard enough, and more than that would be too many to withstand.

Was there something else that they could do?

If they were recently raised, maybe they weren't fully controlled yet.

The blue-scaled dragon roared into the air, circling, climbing higher and higher, and Fes looked over his side. As he did, he saw what he had feared, and his heart dropped.

Five dragons.

It should be reason to celebrate. The raising of five more dragons should be reason to be excited, an opportunity to see what he had only seen in his dreams, but these five dragons were already influenced by the Damhur.

He looked down at the ground. There was no sign of the Deshazl that they had seen when coming here. Could they all have been killed by the dragon as he had taken to the air? If they had, it would've been a high price to pay for failure.

"How many do you see?" Jayell asked.

"I see five dragons," Fes said.

"How many do you think that you can help?"

"I don't know that I can help five. There are too many for me to take on one at a time. Even when we faced two dragons that were Called, it had almost been too much. If they work together"—and Fes had no reason to think that the Damhur wouldn't be prepared for the possibility that they would need to work together—"then they would be able to get past us."

"Is there anything that you can do?"

There might be, but he had to be willing to risk the Deshazl beyond the valley. For the dragons, he had to be, wouldn't he?

He leaned over the side of the dragon. "Do you think it will work?"

He didn't have to question whether the dragon knew, as he could feel through their shared connection that he was aware of what Fes thought.

"It's possible," the dragon said.

"If it works, we can free them. We can protect them. The challenge will be if the Damhur realize what we are after."

"What are you talking about?" Jayell asked.

He looked over at her. She still held the bone sword, gripping it tightly. "There might be something that we can do to help the dragons, but it is risky, and I'm not sure that it will even work, and even if it does, it puts others at risk."

"You intend to take them to the Dragon's Eye?"

"I intend to try to lead them to the Dragon's Eye," he said.

"How?"

That was going to be the real challenge. In order to

succeed, they had to stay ahead of the other dragons, and if his experience with the other two had taught him nothing else, it was that by using the Damhur and their fire magic, they were able to fly faster than the blue dragon.

"That's where you will need to help," he said.

She looked down at the dragon bone sword. "I don't know how long this will be effective," she said. "There might only be a limited power store remaining within it. She had used it already on us, and I think she was using this to do some other spell."

"It's the same spell I'm hoping that you can use," Fes said.

Jayell nodded. "What about the other two?"

"Leave that to me."

Fes pulled on his Deshazl connection, drawing through it as he tried to reach the two dragons. He didn't even know if they were finished with what they had done, and if they weren't, it might not even matter.

Faintly, distantly, he began to detect them. As he continued to pull on his Deshazl connection, he felt that connection grow.

There was a part of him that was concerned that the black dragon would remain scared, afraid of getting involved in anything that might have to do with the Damhur, fearing the possibility of getting Called and controlled once again.

In order to convince him to help, Fes needed him to know that he would be protected by the connection that he had joined by going to the Dragon's Eye. The blue dragon had remained safe, and if he had remained safe, there was no reason that the other dragon wouldn't, too.

Fes pushed that thought through the connection and pushed through an image of the five dragons trailing behind them. That was the reason for their urgency. They needed to help these dragons, to ensure that they were offered the same chance at freedom.

It was the same reason that he struggled with the fact that he might have to harm the Deshazl who had been captured. They weren't acting on their own. They were acting based on the Calling, the controlling that the Damhur used upon them. And if he did nothing, if he were not able to help them, they would remain Called, no differently than the dragons once had been.

There had been a sacrifice the last time, and it had come from the dragons, but did it mean that this time, during this war, the sacrifice had to come from the Deshazl? That was more of a price to pay than Fes really wanted.

His uncertainty came through the connection to the dragons, and he tried to withdraw it, tried to conceal it, but it was too late. He had already shown too much concern.

Surprisingly, the black dragon responded to that uncertainty.

The same concern flowed back to Fes. Within it, he felt the concern from all three dragons. All of them had experienced a Calling, and now that all of them had survived and been restored, none of them wanted to return to that, but they also were willing to risk it on behalf of the other dragons. They recognized the need.

There was willingness within them to fight.

Fes pushed on his Deshazl connection. *We need to gather the Asharn.*

He didn't know whether that would be clear enough, but he hoped that they would recognize what he wanted from them. He needed the Asharn, needed to ensure that it wasn't just the dragons fighting this time. It was all of them. The dragons needed to be a part of it, but so too did the Asharn, if only so that they could understand what it was that had been placed in danger. And having the Asharn—and their connection to the Deshazl magic —might be the key to ensuring that they were able to withstand the Damhur attack.

He leaned back, letting out a heavy sigh.

Jayell glanced over at him. "Did it work?"

"I don't know," he said.

"I could see that you were doing... something. I'm not sure exactly what it was, but I could feel the nature of what you were attempting."

Fes nodded. "There's a connection between the dragons and me. It seemed to have formed after I helped free them from the Damhur Calling. With that, I can speak to them."

She arched a brow at him. "You can speak to them even from a distance?"

"I don't know how to explain it any better than that, but I can reach them, and when I do, I can convey emotion."

"Do they agree with what you ask of them?"

"I think so," he said.

"What now?"

"Now you take us back toward the Asharn, using the fire magic that you can summon from that dragon blade, and we will try to meet with the others, and once we do, we need to head beyond the valley."

Fes looked over to see the other dragons still following. They were getting closer, chasing, streaking toward them much more rapidly than they would be able to do on their own. It was sort of the same way that the fire mages of the Damhur used the Deshazl to work together, augmenting their barriers.

Strangely, he thought also of Thoras and the way that the Damhur and the Deshazl had once worked together, creating their magic, binding together in such a way that they were able to create a city that was unlike anything else.

Was that the key?

The Damhur and the Deshazl had once lived together. They had once worked together, and then something had changed, and the Damhur had begun to try to overpower the Deshazl, but perhaps the Damhur who had lived at that time had placed the key to it all there.

And maybe there had always been Damhur who had opposed what they were doing.

He thought of the Asharn city. Hadn't that been cofounded, as well?

It wasn't about defeating the Damhur. It couldn't be. Together, they were something more. Something greater. If he destroyed the Damhur, then all of that potential would be lost. Everything that the Damhur and the Deshazl could be together would be sacrificed.

He looked down to see the black and the green dragon bursting from the trees. Both were heavily laden with the Asharn who had come with Fes, and the black dragon, in particular, would struggle.

"Focus on helping him," Fes said, motioning for Jayell to look over at the black dragon. "He's going to need the most help."

"I don't know if I'd be strong enough to help all three of these dragons stay ahead of them," she said.

"They don't have to stay ahead for very long. We have to get beyond the valley and to the Dragon's Eye, nothing more than that."

Once they succeeded in that, then the real work would begin. That would be something that Jayell would be unable to help with, and he wondered if they would even be strong enough.

Fes looked ahead of him, watching as the dragon streaked through the air, making his way toward the valley. Jayell's spell pushed on them, guiding them faster and faster, but still they weren't fast enough. He looked back and saw that the five dragons still chased, and every once in a while, Fes could feel the effect of a Calling washing over them, trying to reach them, but it failed.

And then two of the dragons began to break off.

This wouldn't work if they didn't have all of the dragons with them.

"Catch up to the others," Fes said to the dragon.

With a surge of speed, the dragon reached the others.

Fes looked over at Jayell. "You're going to need to join them."

"*What?*"

"Help them reach the Dragon's Eye. Go, and I will reach you."

"Fes, the blue dragon isn't fast enough, not without having a fire shaping. These other two might be able to stay ahead of the others, and they can lead them."

The black dragon was struggling. It was his size and his age, nothing more than that, but because of that, he couldn't keep up while holding the others on his back.

"They need you more than we do," Fes said.

"What happens if you don't make it?"

"You need to force the three dragons into the Dragon's Eye."

"*Force* them?"

"The dragons will have to do it, but it might require the Asharn to help."

Jayell looked at him. "That was your plan?"

"That's the only thing that will help free them."

"You could do it. You did it before."

"I did, but that was with one at a time, and even with three..."

With three, he thought that he might be able, but would he be able to do that in time? Not with the other two dragons flying away. And he didn't even know where they were heading, but they had veered east, and that alone troubled him.

The forest was to the east. The rest of the Asharn were to the east.

"Go," he said.

Jayell stared at him a moment before finally nodding. "How do you propose to get me down there?"

"You'll have to trust me."

"I do."

"Good."

He grabbed her and lifted her, then threw her off the side of the dragon.

Jayell screamed, but Fes had sent a connection through the green dragon, and she scooped up and caught Jayell on her back.

Thank you.

Power from Jayell's spell burst from her, and the other two dragons lurched forward, speeding off.

"We need to go after the others," Fes said to the dragon.

He roared, shooting a streamer of flame, and veered off, heading toward the other two dragons. They were distant specks, and much too far ahead to be easily reached. Could he use his Deshazl connection in the same way as the fire magic?

He hadn't tried it before, but maybe he could add that to the dragon, at least enough to give them a boost. He pushed on it, drawing the Deshazl magic through him and sending it behind him in blasts, but it wasn't enough.

There was nothing that he could do. He didn't have enough power. Deshazl magic didn't add to that of the dragons, not the same way that fire magic did.

If only he had something that would help him draw fire magic.

But then, he did.

He had forgotten about the gift Azithan had given him before leaving. He pulled it out of his pocket and looked at it. It reminded him of the dragon pearl, but the shape was slightly off, and there were no streaks of color within it the same way as there were within dragon pearls. Fes focused on it, pushing his Deshazl connection into the totem, and as he did, there was a strange burst of heat.

They lurched forward.

He cried out in excitement.

If he could use it, could the dragon?

"This helps connect to the same source of power she has access to," Fes said. "Is there anything within it that you can use?"

The dragon let out a rumble. "If it is one of the dragon remains, I'm not sure that we can."

"'This was fabricated by a fire mage. This isn't from dragon remains."

"I can try."

Fes set the totem on the dragon's back. It was a strange thing, and he didn't think that Azithan had intended for it to be used in such a way, but he could feel the trembling of energy coming from the totem, and the surge as the dragon reached for that power, drawing it out. As he did, they burst forward with even more speed.

Fes clung to the dragon, holding tightly. They streaked toward the distant shape of the other dragons. Soon the dragons loomed closer, but so too did the sight of the Asharn city.

It was a platform. That was it, but it was enough for

Fes to see that they were heading directly toward the Asharn.

If the dragons reached the Asharn city, and if they were still influenced by the Damhur, they would tear through the Asharn city with nothing—and no one—to stop them.

They had to get to the dragons first.

"Can you reach one of them?" Fes asked.

The blue dragon roared, and Fes could feel the way that he pushed through the strange totem Azithan had made so that they shot forward, like an arrow from a bow. And then he was near enough to attempt to reach one of the dragons.

It was risky, but then again, he had no choice but to try it. Fes stood and pushed off with his Deshazl magic, shooting toward the nearest dragon.

His aim was off.

He pulled on Deshazl magic, forcing it through himself, drawing more than he had tried to draw before, connecting to the dragon, but even that wasn't enough.

Out of desperation, Fes pulled on the power he felt deep within the city. It was the connections from the Asharn and their connections to the Deshazl magic.

With all of that power, Fes managed to lurch forward, and he landed on the back of the dragon.

There was only a single Damhur.

He turned toward Fes, seemingly shocked at Fes's

sudden appearance, and he unsheathed a bone sword. A fire spell came at him, but Fes cleaved through it with his sword and lunged, slamming the hilt of his sword through the man before he had a chance to attempt anything else.

The dragon was freed from the Calling.

Fes forced the connection to the Deshazl magic through the dragon, trying to help heal him. He managed to connect to the dragon, and he soothed out the disruption that had been caused by the Calling. He didn't dare take any more time than that, and he knew that it was a hasty attempt, but if he managed to succeed in this, there would be time for more later.

"I need you to take me closer to the other," he said to the dragon.

The dragon responded by circling, flying upward, and Fes dove.

Now that he had done it once, he knew that he could draw upon the connections throughout the Asharn city, and he used them to guide him as he streaked toward the other dragon. When he landed, the Damhur sitting astride the dragon was ready for him.

A blast of Calling mixed with fire magic surged. The connection slammed into him, but it was more than that. It seemed to be augmented in a way that Fes was not prepared for.

He was frozen in place.

It was more than just a Calling. It was the effect of the combined magic that did it.

The Damhur smiled. "Impressive. Once you are controlled, we will have to learn how you have managed to be quite as effective as you are."

Fes ignored him. The hold on him wasn't a Calling. If it was a Calling, he would've felt pain from his resistance to it. This was something else.

It was a combination of barriers.

It was the same thing that had been used when he and the dragon had encountered the others, and that combination of barriers was more than he could overcome on his own.

He would be trapped.

More than that, he would be overpowered.

And now that this Damhur knew the trick of it, others would know.

He still had his connection to the Deshazl magic. Through it, Fes pushed out a plea, a cry for help, and he hoped that it was effective, but he no longer knew whether it was or not. He sent out a request, a cry that was simple, but hopefully enough that one of the two freed dragons would understand.

Help.

Even in his call, he didn't feel as if he sent out nearly as much strength as he needed. The request was limited, as if the barrier that held him somehow confined his cry, limiting his reach through the Deshazl connection.

Fes tried to move, but he couldn't. His body didn't react. Nothing seemed to react.

He needed to move. He needed to get free.

The Damhur continued to watch him and seemed content with the fact that Fes couldn't move. "What was your plan?"

Did he think that Fes was Called? Did he think that was the reason that he couldn't move?

If that were the case, maybe he had more time. All he needed was a chance to break free. He had to believe that his connections to the Deshazl magic would be enough. He had to believe that continuing to draw on that power would help him, but could he overpower the combined effects of the fire magic and the Deshazl magic? So far, he had not been able to do so.

He tried to draw through the dragon, through the Asharn down in the city below him, but even as he did that, Fes knew that he wasn't quite able to reach it.

It was there, but it met resistance.

"What is your plan?" the man demanded.

Fes stared at him, refusing to answer.

And in his refusal, the Damhur realized that he was not Called.

He slid forward on the back of the dragon. They were circling, spiraling above the Asharn city. If the man reached him and the dragon suddenly dove, the Asharn would be under attack from the dragon. It would be more than they would be able to withstand, especially with the Damhur using his fire mage magic.

As he neared, Fes sent another request, begging for assistance. *Help.*

The distant sound of a dragon roar caught his attention, but would they be fast enough? A stirring fluttered within him.

That wasn't quite right. It wasn't within him; it was the stirring that he felt around him. It came from Deshazl magic, of that he was sure, and Fes could feel it as it struck him.

It wasn't so much that it struck him, but it struck the dragon. It struck the Damhur.

It was incredible. That power washed over Fes, seemingly avoiding him, and crashed into both the dragon and the Damhur. It was more than a single Asharn or Deshazl attack. It was dozens of them. Hundreds. All of them were focusing their attack on the Damhur. They were focusing their attack on the dragon. The Deshazl magic they used wouldn't harm the dragon, and it didn't actually harm the Damhur, but it was enough to distract.

Fes found himself freed.

He lunged forward, slicing with his sword through the fire mage spell the Damhur attempted to push back on him, and carved into the man, slamming the hilt of his sword deep into him.

The Damhur stared at him, a question in his eyes as his life departed.

"You made a mistake," Fes whispered.

He drew upon the Deshazl magic that he felt all around him, pulling upon it and using that to smooth out the effect of the Calling that had affected the dragon.

As he did, he looked down at the platform now visible in the Asharn city. There he saw Hodan among the others. The old lady, the Asharn leader, stood there as well. How had they known?

It was him. It was his cry for assistance. *He* was the reason that they had known.

And now he was the reason that they had assisted.

"Can you take me down there?" he asked the dragon.

The dragon drifted down, streaking toward the platform. He hovered, and Fes jumped, landing on the platform.

He looked at Hodan. "Thank you."

"You did this?"

"The Damhur raised these, and there are three more that need our help."

Hodan nodded. "We will help if you would still have us."

CHAPTER TWENTY-ONE

The three dragons made their way beyond the valley. Fes didn't know if they would be in time, and he worried that they might not be. And if they weren't, would the other two dragons, the green and the black, and the Asharn with Jayell have been injured?

He had to believe that they had time.

He saw them in the distance.

As he did, the faint glowing from the Dragon's Eye became visible as well.

He pointed, and Hodan's eyes widened. A dozen Asharn sat upon the blue dragon, and the same number sat on each of the other two dragons as they streaked toward the valley. The dragons had drunk from the Asharn, freeing them completely. Much like with the green and black dragons, Fes's willingness to help them and the use of the Deshazl magic to separate them from the effect of the Calling had connected him to them. Much like with the others, he could feel their emotions. There was a mixture of fear and excitement and desire for vengeance.

That last was what he worried about most of all.

If Fes was right, it wasn't vengeance that they needed.

They reached the other three dragons as they circled over the green and the black ones.

"We need to force them down," he said to the blue dragon.

The massive dragon had size on the others, and that size was what he needed now. There was no benefit to speed, not as there was when they were chasing the dragons.

He heard a shout, and the Damhur on the three remaining Called dragons seemed to realize that they were outnumbered.

Two of them tried to veer off, and Fes jumped, pushing off with his Deshazl magic, drawing from Asharn and Deshazl and the dragons as he shot toward one of the dragons.

He threw his sword, striking the Damhur sitting astride the dragon before they had a chance to react and try to push a Calling upon him, or worse—use the combined fire magic and Deshazl to hold him in place. Fes soothed the dragon, using his connection to the Deshazl magic to do so.

"If you would like to be protected, dive into the Dragon's Eye," he said to the dragon.

The dragon started down, and Fes grabbed his sword and jumped, this time pushing upward. He looked around as he did, flying through the air, using his Deshazl magic to soar, feeling for a moment like one of the dragons. He saw the other dragon that was trying to get away, and he angled toward it. When he reached the dragon, the Damhur sitting astride the dragon tried to attack, but Fes grabbed him and threw him off. While the man was falling, the connection to the dragon faded and Fes pulled on his Deshazl connection, trying to soothe the dragon.

"Reach the Dragon's Eye," he said.

The dragon thrashed, the Calling resisting him, but Fes continued to push on the connection to the dragon, drawing through it and sending a reassuring sense. He smoothed out the effect of the Calling, reassuring the dragon that he could be protected from the effect of it.

"The Dragon's Eye," he said.

The dragon's thrashing continued, but he began to gradually head toward the ground, making his way toward the Dragon's Eye.

A shadow crossed overhead, and the blue dragon's

massive talons grabbed onto the dragon Fes was on, helping to guide him into the Dragon's Eye. As they struck the water, Fes grabbed onto the blue dragon, scrambling around and onto his back.

Hodan looked at him with a wide-eyed expression. "What did you do?"

"I helped those two dragons."

"You were flying!"

"I was using my Deshazl connection. Nothing else."

Hodan shook his head. "That's more than Deshazl magic. I have Deshazl magic, and I don't know that I could do that."

"Maybe you could if you tried."

He looked around. There was one dragon remaining that had to be freed from the Damhur connection.

"Where is she?" he asked.

The blue dragon continued to circle, heading higher and higher. As he did, Fes caught sight of a deep-maroon-scaled dragon. She was beautiful and easily the same size as the dragon Fes rode. Her green-hued eyes seemed to catch him, locking onto him. Power emanated from her.

"She's an elder dragon, isn't she?" Fes asked.

The blue dragon rumbled. "An elder. One of the greatest."

"We have to help her."

"She's too powerful for us," the blue dragon said.

"How is she too powerful for you?"

"She holds us off."

It was more than that, but Fes wasn't going to argue. It was more than that she was too powerful. He suspected that it was because she was an elder dragon, much like his blue one, and because of that, there was a hesitance to attack, to risk harming her. It was an emotion he understood, but one that would lead to danger.

He looked over at Hodan. "I need you and the rest of the Asharn who are here to pull on her."

"*Pull* on her?"

Fes nodded, looking up at the sky. "Wrap your Deshazl magic around her. Create a barrier."

"She's a dragon. She'll fight through that."

"Maybe, but it should give us time."

They swooped for the ground, hanging on for just a moment so that the Asharn could jump off the back of the blue dragon, leaving Fes alone. They took to the sky, spiraling up and up, the dragon drawing through the totem Azithan had given Fes, granting him more speed so that they could move even faster.

They reached the same level as the elder dragon.

Two Damhur sat on the back.

This would be difficult.

They would know he was coming, and more than

that, he wondered if they had some way of knowing that the combined magic of the dragon with the fire magic would be enough to hold him.

He felt the fire magic building.

"Blast them," he said to the dragon.

"It will do nothing to her."

"I don't care about hitting her, but hit the Damhur."

The blue dragon belched flames that struck the Damhur, forcing the Damhur to redirect their effort and use a barrier to protect themselves rather than attempting to attack.

Fes had to wait, needing to make time. If nothing else, he needed to give the Asharn a chance to get into position, ready with whatever it was that they could do.

A Calling came toward him.

It was striking, but not so powerful that he couldn't resist it.

Then again, the Calling wasn't focused on him.

It struck the blue dragon.

It was a powerful Calling, and Fes worried for a moment that the dragon would succumb to the effects of it, but he need not have feared.

Much like Fes, the dragon had drunk from the Asharn, and he had been in the Dragon's Eye. The dragon was safe from the effect of the Calling, immune to it.

That didn't mean the dragon wouldn't be angry at the attempt.

He roared.

He lurched forward and wrapped his talons around the maroon dragon, and as he did, he dropped, the two dragons twisting, spiraling through the air as they plunged toward the earth.

Fes held on, clutching the dragon's back, but realized that wasn't necessary.

He pushed off, using his Deshazl magic, and grabbed the two Damhur as he did, pulling them free. They hung in the air, hovering above the two dragons as they spiraled down toward the Dragon's Eye. Deshazl magic wrapped around them. Fes could feel it, and he marveled at the strength. It came from not just the Asharn, but it came from other Deshazl within the city, too.

They were helping.

Then Fes began to fall.

The Damhur cried out, and Fes let them go. He pushed off with his Deshazl connection, using it to float for a moment, and then he dropped. His strength faded, and he plunged into the Dragon's Eye for a second time, but not before seeing that the blue dragon and the other elder dragon went in first.

For a moment, Fes feared that it would try to hold him the same way it had before. Without the dragon to rescue him, he wasn't sure that he would be able to get free. But rather than sinking, he floated.

He pushed up with his Deshazl magic and used that to

396 | D.K. HOLMBERG

reach the shore. When he stepped free, not only did he see Hodan and the other Asharn, but Jesla was leading a line of Deshazl. They stood eyeing the dragons, all of them.

"How is this possible?" she asked.

"The Damhur discovered a way to raise the dragons."

"How would they have learned?"

"From the dragons themselves," Fes said.

Her eyes widened. "What now?"

Fes looked over at the Dragon's Eye. The blue dragon reappeared. Then the maroon elder dragon came free. Fes watched as they soared into the sky, spiraling around, and the other dragons took to the air, following them, circling over the Dragon's Eye.

Fes smiled.

"What is it?" Jesla asked.

"It's like what I had seen in a vision."

"That must have been some vision."

He turned toward her, hating to look away. "The Damhur and the Deshazl created this place together."

"They did," Jesla said.

"I think they prepared for this, but it was forgotten when the Damhur began their attacks. You have used it for testing, and you have used it to protect the Deshazl from the effects of the Damhur, but it was meant for the dragons just as much. They are free."

"What if the Damhur attempt to Call them again?"

Fes shook his head. "I was on the blue dragon when they attempted to do that. It failed."

"What now?"

Fes breathed out a sigh. Now was almost easy considering what he had been through to get here. "Now I will bring these dragons across the sea, we will push back the Damhur, and we will rescue those dragons from what they have done."

"And that's it?"

Fes smiled. "That's not it. Much more must take place. The Damhur must be saved."

Hodan looked over at him, his brow furrowed. "You would save them?"

Fes motioned to the Dragon's Eye. "Look at this. Look at what the Damhur and the Deshazl can make together. Go into the city and see what they were able to do. We were meant to work together. And if we can, there is much more that can be done."

They were silent for a while, and Fes stared up at the sky, watching as the dragons began to return. They sensed his need and what he intended. He was connected to the Deshazl, but he was connected to the dragons, and maybe that was the key to saving them.

Now all he had to do was find a way to connect to the Damhur.

He wasn't sure whether that was even possible, but if

he could, if he could reach them, then greatness could return.

"Do you still want help?" Jesla asked.

Fes glanced over to Jayell. They would end this together. "I would always welcome the help from Deshazl."

Crossing the sea had been easy, especially once they paused to reclaim the remaining dragon sculptures. There were nearly twenty, and now Fes had them safely secured on the backs of the dragons. It was early morning as they made the crossing and the sun began to crest above the sky, reflecting off the ocean, making it glow with a soft orange light that reminded him of the Dragon's Eye. He smiled to himself as the wind whipped around him.

Jayell held his hand as they flew. She clutched the bone sword, holding tightly to it, and held on to a fire mage spell, using that to speed all of the dragons as they soared across the sea.

"Are you afraid of what we might find?"

Fes glanced over at her. He shook his head. "I was

afraid when we first started this. I worried that we were taking too long and that even when we found allies, it still might not be enough, but..." He shook his head again. "I'm not worried like I was. I'm not afraid of the Damhur, not anymore." And that might be the greatest accomplishment of all. No longer fearing the effect of Calling gave him a chance to feel at peace. He no longer worried that he would somehow have to protect the dragons. Though he was willing to do so and willing to fight to ensure their safety, Fes didn't know if he even needed to.

All he had to do was stop the Damhur who were Calling them. From there, he could rescue them and end the fighting.

"Aren't you afraid of what you might find in the empire?"

Fes took a deep breath. "I am, but there is nothing that I can do about it. We've found help," he said, looking out at the seven other dragons making their way across the ocean with them. Each dragon carried a dozen, sometimes more, Asharn and Deshazl. They would be enough. Combined with the fire mages, Fes knew they would be enough. Their magic would be able to overpower the Damhur.

"I'm worried more about what might have happened in our absence, but there isn't anything that we could do about that now. We come to save them, and that's all that we can do."

Jayell smiled at him. "I hope so."

The outer shores of the empire came into view. As they did, Fes's stomach sank. Everything was blackened, and entire swaths of land had been charred and destroyed. How much of that was from the dragons and how much of that was from the fire mages? Maybe it didn't matter. Either way, there had been destruction because of the fighting.

Was this what had happened a thousand years ago? Would this land take millennia or longer to recover in the same way the dragon plains had?

Maybe it never would recover.

None of that mattered.

What mattered was ending this.

They continued to sweep inland, following the destruction that pushed in, a path leading them deeper into the empire. Every so often, Fes caught sight of the charred remains of bodies.

How many of those were from the empire, and how many were Deshazl, and how many were Damhur? He pushed the thought out of mind. He had the solution. They would be able to end this.

And then he saw one of the dragons.

They headed toward it, moving quickly, augmented by Jayell's fire mage spell. The eight dragons made a ring around the other and Fes jumped, landing on the back of the dragon. There were three Damhur.

"It's over," he said.

One of them attempted a Calling and Fes slammed through him with his sword, forcing him off the dragon to drop to the ground below. He turned to the other two.

"It's over. We have a way of protecting the Deshazl and the dragons from your Calling. And we have seen what the Damhur and the Deshazl can do when working together. There is no need to attempt to force that rapport."

One of the two remaining Damhur, a woman with a dark braid and deep blue eyes, grabbed for a bone sword and Fes stabbed her with his sword, hating that it was necessary. Would he have to cut through all of the Damhur to end this?

And maybe he would. Most of the Damhur believed that they had a right to control the Deshazl, and they believed that they had a right to Call the dragons.

It left only one of the Damhur.

He was younger, barely twenty if Fes were to guess, and had golden hair and deep blue eyes. Surprisingly, he didn't attempt to Call Fes. He didn't carry a bone sword, and Fes felt no fire magic coming from him.

"We can work together," Fes said.

The man blinked, looking around at the dragon,

seeming to realize that Asharn and Deshazl sat upon them.

"I don't want to die," he said, his voice catching.

"Then work with us. It will be hard, but there's no reason for us to be enemies."

The boy—Fes couldn't think of him as anything other than a boy—nodded.

Fes closed his eyes and pushed out, wrapping the dragon with his Deshazl connection, freeing him from the effect of the Calling. As it happened, the dragon roared.

The boy shook, looking at Fes with wide eyes, and Fes smiled. "The dragon is freed." He looked down at it. "The others will guide you to a place where you can go to ensure that it never happens again."

The dragon roared again.

Fes jumped, rejoining Jayell on the blue dragon, and they continued north. When they came across the other dragon, the maroon dragon, they restored her quickly. Beyond the maroon dragon, the battle took place.

The dragons landed in between the two warring sides. Empire on one side and Damhur with Called Deshazl on the other. The sudden appearance of all the dragons startled the fighting. Fire magic bloomed from the empire side, and a combination of fire magic and Deshazl magic came from the other.

All of the Asharn and all of the Deshazl sitting atop

the dragons built a barrier that the dragons added to, enough strength that they forced the fighting to stop.

Fes jumped down.

A figure in a maroon and gold cloak approached, and Fes smiled at Azithan.

"What is this?" Azithan asked.

"A long story, but all you need to know is that they are allies."

"You brought dragons here that would be Called? Are you insane?"

"They won't be Called. Never again."

"How?"

"A long story," Fes said.

He turned to the Damhur. He started forward, pushing out with Deshazl magic that he drew from the dragons and the Asharn, and even pulling from the Deshazl with the Damhur. Jayell joined him. She mingled her fire magic with his, and they pushed back, forcing the Damhur away.

"It's over," he said.

One of the Damhur started forward. He was an older man with gray hair and flat gray eyes, and he unsheathed a bone sword, bringing it as if to attack Fes, but Fes flung his dragonglass sword without giving him a chance to fight. The man fell.

He looked at the other Damhur, turning his gaze to the Deshazl. "It's over. The Damhur and the Deshazl are meant to work together. If you refuse, the dragons will ensure that you don't do anything else. You will not leave this land if you intend to harm others."

Two of the Damhur and two Deshazl stepped forward, and power built from them. Fes shook his head, but they pushed out with a combined spell.

Fes sent his magic, joined with Jayell's, and he lunged forward, slamming the hilt of his dragonglass sword into the nearest Damhur, then he turned to the other, holding it up, hesitating a moment. "It's done."

The fire magic and the Deshazl magic coming from the Damhur hesitated, but then it died out.

Fes looked around. There were hundreds of Damhur, and with them were a greater number of their Deshazl, enough that he didn't want to have to slaughter them all. He waited for the next attack, but it didn't come.

"It's over," he said again.

Fes stood atop the fire mage temple, the sculptures arranged around him. There were dozens of them. He had no idea how many of them were able to be resurrected, but it was possible that there would be dozens of dragons that would return. Every so often, he would catch sight of a shadow streaking overhead, and a smile would come to his face.

"I can't get over seeing them," Azithan said.

Fes looked over at the fire mage and shrugged. "Everything has changed."

"I fear for this change," Azithan said.

"Why?"

"Because we have used the dragon relics for centuries to power our spells. What will happen now?"

"There are still dragon relics," Fes said.

"It feels… wrong."

"I think the dragons mean for you to use them."

Azithan looked out into the distance, his gaze staring northward. "I wonder what will come next."

Fes looked down at the dragon sculptures. They were all made of dragonglass and all impressive for various different reasons. For now, fifteen dragons had been resurrected, and he would continue to try to raise more.

"Javoor remains, and the Damhur there still have Deshazl enslaved. This isn't over. Not without going there and confronting them."

"You would push the fight across the sea?"

"I would rescue the Deshazl."

"You intend something more, Fezarn."

Fes smiled, thinking of Thoras. It seemed too much to believe that they could find a way to bring back that time again, but maybe there would be a way. "You know me too well, Azithan."

"You have never been the easiest to work with," Azithan said.

"Is that a compliment?"

"I'm proud of you," he said.

Fes snorted and glanced over at the fire mage. "You're *proud* of me?"

"You have become so much more than the man you were when we first met. You were angry, searching for wealth, but you had something within you that I recognized. I don't know that I ever would have known that you would become this person, but it suits you."

"I came from Javoor, but I suspect you knew that."

"I suspected that you came from elsewhere. You were too powerful, even when we first met."

"I wasn't powerful."

"You had a different kind of power about you, Fezarn, and you had potential. Perhaps it's only fitting that someone from Javoor, orphaned in the empire, will be the one to bridge our peoples."

It would be difficult, and it meant more fighting, and it meant that others might suffer, but Fes no longer felt as if it were hopeless. There was a way to protect himself— and others—from the effects of the Damhur. And perhaps most surprisingly, it was the Damhur and the Deshazl together who had created that way. More than anything else, he thought that appropriate.

"How many more of these dragons do you think you can raise?" Azithan asked.

"I'm still trying to understand all that's involved in that. And with each one we raise, they have to reach the Dragon's Eye to ensure that they can't be Called, and once that's done, then I suppose we will work on the next step and determine if there is any way that we can save as many Damhur and Deshazl as possible."

Azithan joined him at the edge of the tower, looking out at the sky. In the distance, dragons circled high overhead. "They really are majestic."

"They really are. And they belong in this world."

"It's good that you returned them," Azithan said.

Fes smiled. After everything that had happened, he felt as if it were worthwhile. It really was good that the dragons had returned.

The Dragonwalker series concludes with Dragon Sight.

A centuries old war must end.

After saving the dragons, Fes knows what must come next, but the empire has other plans. Rather than saving the Deshazl from slavery, the emperor bargains for peace. Can real peace happen when his people remain enslaved?

When a summons draws him south, Fes discovers an ancient threat to the dragons that he might not be able to stop. Worse, the Damhur might finally have what they want—a way to control or destroy the remaining dragons.

Survival means going to the heart of Javoor for answers, but not only must he be strong enough, he needs to find answers before the dragons are destroyed... this time forever.

ALSO BY D.K. HOLMBERG

The Dragonwalker

Dragon Bones

Dragon Blessed

Dragon Rise

Dragon Bond

Dragon Storm

Dragon Rider

Dragon Sight

The Teralin Sword

Soldier Son

Soldier Sword

Soldier Sworn

Soldier Saved

Soldier Scarred

The Lost Prophecy

The Threat of Madness

The Warrior Mage

Tower of the Gods

Twist of the Fibers

The Lost City

The Last Conclave

The Gift of Madness

The Great Betrayal

The Cloud Warrior Saga

Chased by Fire

Bound by Fire

Changed by Fire

Fortress of Fire

Forged in Fire

Serpent of Fire

Servant of Fire

Born of Fire

Broken of Fire

Light of Fire

Cycle of Fire

The Endless War

Journey of Fire and Night

Darkness Rising

Endless Night

Summoner's Bond

Seal of Light

The Book of Maladies

Wasting

Broken

Poisoned

Tormina

Comatose

Amnesia

Exsanguinated

The Shadow Accords

Shadow Blessed

Shadow Cursed

Shadow Born

Shadow Lost

Shadow Cross

Shadow Found

The Collector Chronicles

Shadow Hunted

Shadow Games

Shadow Trapped

The Dark Ability

The Dark Ability

The Heartstone Blade

The Tower of Venass

Blood of the Watcher

The Shadowsteel Forge

The Guild Secret

Rise of the Elder

The Sighted Assassin

The Binders Game

The Forgotten

Assassin's End